HELLFIRE!

Out of his throat come the single word that ignited the everburning fire he'd called from Hell itself. This fire was not red and gold, but blue and white and in it danced devils and demons. From it rose a smoke that was black and ectoplasmic and which formed itself into giant vipers, four of them, that rose like dancing spirals, swaying to the music, from all four compass points of the bier.

And these vipers of smoke, he was sure before the flames grew too hot and the smoke too thick and people started screaming instead of singing and the whole crowd surged backward, dragging him with it—these four hideous vipers of smoke seemed to close themselves around each god's statue.

The vipers wound about the statues and the statues moved. Their arms of granite came to life and wrestled with the ectoplasmic pythons threatening to crush the ████████ their throats of sto ████████████ sand.

Before the ████████████████ smen pushed him ████████████████ saw one single, gia ████████ red and gleaming eye arch itself over the city, its trunk wound around the king's tower, hissing with a forked tongue as long as a man.

And he thought he saw Enlil—or Nikodemus, or a phantom of white smoke in the shape of a god or a man—rise up and plant its feet firmly upon the battlements, smoky sword in hand, to do battle with the viper from beyond the grave.

...with the ectoplasmic python
...to crush them, to coil around that
...one and crumble that stone to sand
...as the gates were closed and guarding
up to his knees, he thought he
...ant viper with a red and yellow

JANET AND CHRIS MORRIS

CITY AT THE EDGE OF TIME

CITY AT THE EDGE OF TIME

Copyright © 1988 by Paradise Productions

A Baen Books Original

Baen Publishing Enterprises
260 Fifth Avenue
New York, N.Y. 10001

First printing, November 1988

ISBN: 0-671-69787-0

Cover art by Gary Ruddell

Printed in the United States of America

Distributed by
SIMON & SCHUSTER
1230 Avenue of the Americas
New York, N.Y. 10020

PROLOGUE

The city crouched like a thirsty lion on the rock-strewn coast of Memory, as if it had always been there. All the beasts of the field slunk away from her sudden walls, into the forest beyond, growling and lashing their tails, herding their young out of harm's way.

For there were men in the city, heroes and hunters of legendary prowess, princes and warlords and priests and warlocks, all in service to a king who loved life so much that he could not leave it. Thus the city had a ruler and its ruler had a passion and that passion seemed eternal, like the ruler and the city itself—a passion for being that not even the laws of nature had been able to override.

Because of this passion, the city of the king had survived natural and human disasters of every kind, and even the ravages of time. But there had been a price. To overcome the tests of time, the city had found a way to become an ephemeral place. To withstand the storms of fate, the city had become fated, intertwined with the very laws of universal process.

1

Among the lost cities of men's minds, it had acquired many names. It had founded many legends. It had overlooked many seas and nestled in many mountain valleys. It was thought by some to be a sanctuary, and by others to be a hell, and by others to be a myth pure and simple. Men looked for its ruins beneath the seas and beneath the rocks and beneath the desert sands, but never found them.

Nor would they ever: the city of legend could never fall into ruin, never become splintered plinths and shattered columns and bits of pottery for later men to find. It had made its bargain with all the gods of all the times and its fate was then, now, and forever sealed: as long as man lived, the city would live as well.

It had its own life. It had its own heart. It had its own myths and its own spirit and its own gift to give to the men who inhabited it and gave it life thereby: those who dwelled within its lofty walls could do so free from misery, so long as their hearts allowed.

It had been called by many names in many lands, and all of them were true, though most of them were lost. It had raised its walls on more coasts than this world had, for it was not bound in place by its foundations. It was bound by legend and by need. And since all men make legends and all men know need, it came to all the coasts of all the worlds of men eventually, wherever time and the sea met the moment of need of a certain kind of man in a certain kind of time.

This time, on this forbidding coast, the city rested uneasy. As it woke, while its inhabitants knuckled their eyes and looked out their windows to see the restless ocean of time itself beyond their walls, people began wondering about their own legend—about their own mortality, their own fate, their own foretold story.

Change comes to all things; life is a broad and

varied category. The city had given for thousands of years and no one doubted that it would keep on giving. But in the household of the king, seers began casting dice and reading omens when the odd dawn broke full of clouds over a sea with no end.

For even the universe was finite, and the roaming city had come to the edge of time itself. All the omens confirmed it. The priests and the seers and the wise wizards in the palace looked at one another and shook their heads. The king must be told. The prophesies unveiled. The gates locked. The city must be made fast against invaders, lest the soulless one of legend come and suck the very heart from the city so that it became trapped in the mundane world—so that, at the edge of time itself, it would begin to die.

"All things run down," said the premier seer to the king on his throne.

"Entropy," offered a handsome warlock through blue and clumsy lips, "is the fate of all the universe."

"Unless," put in the young priest of the Storm God, "we can reverse the effect through sacrifice, prayer, and the proper precautions."

"The proper precautions?" demanded the long-nosed king, whose name was Genos. "I thought you said this was fated—the secret and hidden end of everything, which you and your brothers had kept from me to save me grief." Grief was there in the king's broad and weathered face, in his knotted shoulders and his clenched fists, true. But there was another emotion too and the force of it made the great chalcedony audience hall seem close and confining, like a grave or a prison cell: fury was in the king, and it made the very walls of the city tremble and the earth beneath it quake.

Because the king was the heart of the city, all his advisers spoke at once to calm him. They placated and they temporized. Fearing for their lives, they went further: they fabricated, they qualified, they restated and reinterpreted. They told King Genos that no awful fate was certain, that man and especially king had free will, that the omens might have been . . . well . . . overstated.

"It's been so very long, Sire, since there's been anything wrong at all in the City," soothed the fair and sturdy seer, "that we became, ah, agitated at the visions of danger on the horizon—a danger which is avoidable."

The warlock, being a man of flexible morality and expedientist nature, saw his chance and elaborated: "Surely my colleagues will agree that our combined forces of wisdom, foresight, prayer and magic can bring us safely through this crisis."

After all, the warlock told himself, if the city died, then the king died too—but the warlock might survive, though the king did not. Sorcery was not time-dependent, as was human flesh. Thus the smile that curled the warlock's lips was reassuringly truthful. "Tell King Genos, friend priest, that I speak the truth. And say what the gods will take to set the city free."

The priest was the youngest of the men in the chalcedony hall, and the least powerful. The day to day running of the city had offered little opportunity for the man who interpreted the will of the gods to ingratiate himself with the king: until now, the gods' favor had been taken for granted, the right of the king which had been conferred upon him long before—before the city had been built, before the priest had been born, before the gods had lost their power in the eyes of the citydwellers.

When the priest had been ordained by an ancient who had tired of the city and wished to walk in the worlds of men, the old priest had told the youth: "Gods have blessed this place and this king, but not all gods. The time will come when you are tested. The time will come when the faith and the quality of the citydwellers is tested. On that day, do not despair. It will be your finest moment. The shadows of peace and war will fall across your path and you must fight through them to the light beyond. All things come into being out of strife, and that moment of transition will be yours to husband." The ancient had clapped him on the shoulder with a hand as smooth as his own and said, "In those moments, be unyielding. The Storm God will show you the way. War will be in the hearts of men. And death will fly over the city as She has not done in millennia. Pluck a heart from a stranger, if the king loses his, and give it to the god if it is not his already."

Remembering this, the priest said to the king, "To free the city, we must pluck the heart from a stranger and give it to the Storm God—any heart he chooses."

All eyes turned to the priest, young in city terms, half the age of the warlock and the king and the seer, each of whom had been with the city since its beginnings. In the eyes of the seer were horror and disgust at the thought of human sacrifice in this place where death was a banished entity. In the eyes of the king lurked suspicion and caution, as if the priest's remedy was a veiled threat aimed at Genos himself. But the stare of the warlock held the worst omen of all: triumph was there, and amusement, and a dark lust that made the priest clutch his robe to his throat.

Eventually, but far too long a time after the priest had had his say, King Genos intoned, "So be it; let it be written; let it be done. All strangers will be tested by omen, by magic, and by the gods, so that the heart we need can be found."

This euphemistic pronouncement was not enough for the warlock, who said, "And when such a heart is found?"

"It will be plucked and given to the god," said the king uneasily. There had been no death in the city for time untold, no violence, no strife. "Outside the city walls, if possible."

"And if that is not possible?" pressed the warlock. "How can we bring death to the city, where it has never been?"

"That's your problem, Seth," snapped the king, which was exactly what the warlock wanted to hear. "I will decree that all strangers must be brought to you, and you will use your talents to make sure that the will of the Storm God is done and that prognostications are satisfied," added the king, which was exactly what the warlock wanted the seer and the priest to hear.

Thus black sorcery was given free reign in the city which had come to rest at the edge of time, and the people found more to worry them than the endless sea beyond their walls.

CHAPTER 1: RAIN OF FISH AND MAN

The red cloud rising out of the east was borne seaward on a hungry wind that howled like a devil. It was a hot cloud, a wet cloud full of the promise of rain, and yet it shed no drop on the forest below. It spread across the wilderness without end, a cloud like a funnel, a cloud like a waterspout turned on its side.

It crossed the scorched earth between the forest and the city on the coast, low to the ground and howling. Then it arched up like a striking snake, a hissing serpent that ate the sky and reared high over the city's walls.

By then there was no one on the streets. Everywhere the city's folk had fled indoors, even from the courtyards of the king. No peltast stirred on the battlements; no sentry held his ground. From within the walls of the palace, men peered out through slits at the unnatural red storm.

Women held each other in their boudoirs, and

children were made fast under mothers' skirts. The noise was everywhere, carried on a wet and flailing wind that made hairs stand up on arms and necks and dogs scramble under sturdy beds to whine.

Macon was in his father's stables with his sister Tabet when the storm started, and there he stayed, working with the grooms to calm the horses, lest one break a leg rearing and kicking. Among horses, like men, hysteria travels fast.

He'd lost track of his sister until he heard her scream above the whinnying and the kicking and the cursing of the grooms.

Macon ran to the stable door just in time to see the end of the deluge in the stableyard—and nowhere else.

Water was coming down as if the Storm God Enlil had emptied his bucket there. And more: In the sluice of water that made a sea of mud in the stableyard were fish. A hundred fish at first, then a thousand. Big fish. White-bellied carp as long as your arm. A rain of fish that continued even when the water stopped.

Macon saw his sister, drenched and knocked to the mud by the water, raise her arms to fend off the fish pelting her. He should have gone to help but he was rooted to the spot. His eyes were fixed on the red sky, so opaque and full of raining fish.

Then something even larger cast its shadow over the courtyard and once again a torrent descended from the sky. And in that torrent, turning and rolling and falling among the carp, was a man.

Falling man and fish and water all hit the mud and fish and water in the courtyard with a thud and a splash and Tabet screamed again.

This second scream released Macon from his trance—or perhaps the sky did, for suddenly it was no longer red and low and raining fish, but clear and blue with puffy clouds skewered by a double rainbow that arced over all the city, it seemed.

Tabet was trying to get to her feet among the mud and the fish by the time he reached her. It was slippery going, and treacherous. The stableyard's walls sloshed with muddy water as if their father had decided to turn the king's stable into a fish-filled pool.

Some of the fish were attempting to swim; some were flopping on piles of their fellows; some floated dead with gaping jaws on the water slowly draining. Macon had to get his sister out of there, he knew.

When he reached her, she was sitting calmly, up to her hips in water, knees bent and skirts revealingly high, staring at the man who had fallen with the fish from the sky.

His head and shoulders were out of the water, free of fish, only spattered with mud. He was beginning to stir.

"Get up," Macon whispered to his sister. "Close your legs. Let me help you. Get in the stable—"

Tabet laughed too loudly, pretending that it was an everyday occurrence to be covered with mud and fish that rained from the sky and brought a man with them in a deluge. "Get up? Walk in this? On a carpet of fish and mud? You sit down, brother, and wait for the yard to drain." She pulled at his belt. Overbalanced and surprised, he fell and landed, rump first, on a pile of carp that gave way with a sickening squish.

A grunt that wasn't hers stopped Macon's hand as it was raised to swat his sister, all dishevelled and muddy and grinning crookedly as she pushed carp away from her.

The stranger was stirring.

He got his elbows under him and raised his head, looked Macon straight in the eye, and then let that head fall back. Macon, the eldest prince of the city, had seen many men and many strangers, but never a man with a look like that upon his face. The eyes of the stranger had wanted to know only if harm was imminent. They had asked the question as clearly as words could, before the eyes closed and the head fell back.

It was Tabet, not Macon, who said, "I think he's half drowned," and started to crawl to the aid of the man who'd fallen from the sky.

It wasn't easy to make headway through the treacherous carpet of carp. By now grooms were out of the stables, elbowing each other and whispering, unsure of anything but that it would be best not to laugh at the prince and princess. Mirth-choked voices began tentatively to ask after Macon's health.

He called for help to get the newcomer inside. "And get Matilla, to tend to a man half drowned—have her bring her herbs and tea and whatever else she needs. For us, too. Let's get this man into the stableboy's quarters. Now!"

Thus the prince himself forgot to consult the palace warlock in the matter of this stranger; by then, Tabet already had the stranger's head in her lap and her lips to his.

"Sister!" The prince scrambled toward her, slipping as he went, muddy arms held high like a dancer's to balance himself.

"Matilla taught me how to save a drowning soul!" said Tabet huffily. "Here, help me." She took the man's unresisting arms and showed Macon what to do.

A cough came from the stranger's chest, then another. He seemed to want to roll over and they helped him. Macon kept his face out of the mud as he coughed up water and it wasn't until then that Macon became uncomfortably aware that the man who'd fallen from the sky was naked as a newborn.

When the stableboys, slipping and sliding through the mud and the flopping fish, came to help, they had nothing to cover the man with any more than Macon did.

So the princess Tabet was treated to the sight of a mature, naked man's muddy front and backside as the stableboys carried him out of the courtyard and up the stairs.

She herself would accept no helping hand. "What do you mean, not go up there? I found him, didn't I? He fell to earth nearly by my side. Of course I'm going, Macon. And you should come too. This is a fine and wondrous omen, I'm sure." She rubbed at the mud on her face with the back of her hand and smeared her pale skin even more. Her honeyed eyes were bright with excitement. "Come on, before we miss our chance. He's ours—we found him. Lose this chance, and Seth and the rest will have him off where they can keep him to themselves. We haven't met anybody from Outside, not to talk to . . ." Her voice was breathless with excitement, and pleading.

And there was something else there that Macon didn't want to think about, something that made her words thick and husky and . . . unsisterly.

He said, "Yes, I suppose. We did find him. Anyway, the stableyard's my responsibility . . ."

Princess Tabet was already making her way across the yard and her dress was sticking to her revealingly.

"And you all get back to work," Macon called to the help still loitering and staring unabashedly. "Get these fish out of here. Get this yard dried out if you have to use all the shavings we have on hand. And make sure those horses are bedded first—dry and bedded."

There was no way to traverse that fish-strewn ground in a princely fashion. But then, he was too muddy and too excited to care, really. For the first time in far too long, something had happened to lighten the dour and pregnant and infinitely boring pall that had come down over the city since Father had turned over the running of things to the warlocks, seers, and priests, and sequestered himself in the high tower.

Possibly, this wondrous event would bring King Genos out of his rooms, where Macon could talk to him about the way the stewards were running the city. Perhaps the prince might even find out why, if Father had truly decided to retire, his eldest son had been neither consulted nor drafted into the service for which he'd trained so long.

CHAPTER 2: WORLD'S END

The cyclone was full of red dust and it howled like a banshee as it cut a swathe through the forest, hurling tall pines as if they were javelins. Swaying like a harlot of destruction, it switched its hips and sang its awful song and everywhere it went, chaos rode before it and devastation followed close behind.

It keened through the peasant lands and through the rich towns of the blue-water coast, and back again into the hinterlands. There it seemed to spend its fury on every poor hovel and hamlet, as if people and their doings drew it like a lodestone.

When finally it came over the hill into the deserted village of Scant, all the people had fled but a single houseful. And this was as poor a houseful as Scant had to offer in as sad a house as ever there was. The woman who lived in the house was a tenant farmer's widow, a lonely lady too old to care for the baby she was bearing while the cyclone bore down on the town.

Squatting there and screaming at the top of her

lungs with only a deaf and half-blind midwife for
company, she hardly heard the coming of the cyclone: she'd been in labor for more than a day, and
the midwife had been with her all that time. No one
in the town had thought to warn them but the baby's
father, who owned the land that the widow farmed,
and he had thought better of it: if the woman and her
child died in the cyclone, it would be a boon to him.
His wife was of violently jealous temperament and
he had three strong sons already. He couldn't expect
their equal from a slut who should have been too old
to bear a child at all.

So the woman, whose name was Fiah, yelled and
pushed and cried, squatting on her makeshift child-
bearing chair, while the midwife boiled water by
touch and rote, and neither of them cared a fig for
the great red funnel bearing down on the scatter of
hovels that was the town of Scant.

The red, towering, hip-switching cloud sounded
like an engine of destruction, a not-too-distant land-
slide, or a copper mine caving in on those below, but
the two women paid no heed—not even to the chug-
ging, whistling thunder of the tornado's approach as
it leveled the landlord's fortress and came on toward
the hovels of the tenants which had sprung up outside the rich man's walls.

They were busy having a baby, which, when it
arrived, was as red as the sky above, as ugly as the
passion that had seeded it, and (worst of all after a
day and night and another day of labor) female.

The crease-faced mother slumped back, exhausted,
while dirty sweat ran down her hairy lip, a lip that
trembled in disappointment and curled in wrath.
And from those lips came a curse, upon the girlchild
she had borne, upon the father who'd invaded her
wizening loins with its burden, and upon the world
of men in general. "Take them all to hell," she
screamed to heaven, "all the men and all their seed,

and scourge them from the earth! Let no more mothers bear girl children to expose upon the hillsides! Let mine be the last!"

Perhaps because of the funnel of the storm, her words were sucked out the paneless windows of the hovel and up to heaven, and into the ears of the gods, who nodded, having confirmation from a human that the time was right to end the suffering of the people of Scant and such people everywhere, as they had long suspected.

The words of Fiah, the unwilling mother, drew the cyclone unerringly toward her hut. But when it reached there, only the deaf and aged midwife was still inside. Thus the funnel missed the mother and lifted only the midwife and every stick and blade of thatch and hearthstone of the hut up toward heaven.

Confused, the red and festooned cyclone hovered, halted, danced in place. In it and on it could be seen lightning jumping, and crushed bodies whirling, and chairs and chickens and children and chests of wealth, all spinning round and round like a festival top or a prayer wheel.

But the mother named Fiah paid attention to none of that. She was already out on the hilltop, exposing her ugly red girlchild to the elements. Her eyes were blinded by tears and her ears heeded nothing but the squalling of her helpless, luckless brat, who was a victim of custom and furiously railing against its fate. Her tiny red fists were balled; her sightless eyes glared heavenward; her toothless mouth was open to indict a universe too cruel to commute her sentence.

The mother stood up from the baby whom she'd laid naked on the hilltop, and only then did Fiah notice the maelstrom behind. Covered with blood and water and sweat and dirt, barefoot and clothed in filthy garments, she put her hands on her hips and stared straight at the swaying funnel which hovered where her house had been, at the path of destruction in its wake, and at the tumbled foundations of her baby's father's fortress. And she laughed.

"Bring my revenge to earth, did ye, Lords?" she cackled into the wild wind coming closer as the storm saw her and approached. "I'm ready for ye." She held out her hands as if to a lover as the cyclone came up the hill and enfolded her in its shrieking majesty, snapping her neck in one neat swat as it grabbed her up to heaven.

When the body had arisen, and the baby too was swept up and gone skyward, the cyclone seemed to lose its fury. It wobbled. Its great mouth began to quaver. Its lofty top, no longer lost in the sky, began to droop. It slowed. And as it lost its speed, it lost its height, and came slowly toward the ground, dropping bits and pieces as it did.

It dropped splintered trees and featherbeds. It gave up its hold on cows and troughs and wagon wheels. It let haystacks and plowshares fall back to earth. Even losing its bounty, it did not lose it shape, but sank to earth as if it were a snake no longer roused to strike.

And when it lay entirely upon the ground, its mouth wide yet and spitting stuff, a horse and rider and another could be seen within it. Not a dead horse, or a shattered rider, as were all the corpses that the cyclone dropped like litter in its wake—but a live horse, picking its way through rufous cloud, with a living man atop him. Behind that horse came a second, living also, as dapple gray as the first and high-stepping. And on this second horse was a woman dressed not, as the first rider, in leopardskin and boar's-tooth, but in a scale armor that glowed like carp in a pool, and skin of ruddy-glowing hue. This woman led a third horse like a sable shadow behind her, and far behind that horse could be seen, if any had been there to see it, the rough hills of another land.

The lead horse's hooves touched solid ground. A spark jumped free at the contact. This spark seemed to set the very funnel of cloud afire. Then as the first, the second, and the third horse emerged, the whole cyclone became a tunnel of flame.

The horses danced away from the flaming arch. Their riders did not try to stop them, just hugged their necks and let them run, looking back only once at the flaming cloud that had brought them here and the fading landscape far within its tunnel.

When the fire had entirely burned out, the two riders were sitting on sweat-drenched horses, a hilltop away, looking back the way they'd come.

"Where are we, Tempus? What accursed place is this?" said the woman whose hair and skin glowed as if the fire had left her some of its light.

"Accursed is right, Jihan," said the man, who was full of shadow, sinewy, and bold as unending time. "We're at the end of everything, or at least of this place." He motioned with his free hand to the devastation of what had once been a town and a great house with castle's walls. "Not even its name is left." His voice was so much like shifting gravel, and so full of foreboding, that the gray horse under him snorted restlessly and pawed the ground. He looked over its withers at the ground and saw there a single, glistening carp, here where there was not so much as a brook or a stream, only the end of a town's life.

Jihan, beside him, sniffed and rubbed her eyes with the back of her hand. "I do not like this. What do you mean, the end of everything? *Every*thing cannot end."

"*Everything* is a relative term, Froth Daughter," said the immortal vagabond to his inhuman companion. "This place is full of death; it's the end of the world for all of those who knew what to call it."

"How can you be so calm about this? We don't know where we are, or why, or how to get—"

"It's happened to me before. It's happened to you, truly. The world that spawned you wasn't the world of men where we met. Nor was it the world I was born into."

"I'm . . . frightened." There was a revelatory awe in the Froth Daughter's voice. "For Niko, who is mortal. Of . . . all of this."

"You are frightened of the unknown, nothing more. So let's go make it knowable." He reined his horse rightward and it came up on its hind legs, so anxious was it to do his bidding.

"I'm frightened at nothing but your obtuseness, your stubbornness, your damned quarrels with the very gods of heaven," she yelled, following as closely as she could while ponying the spooked, riderless horse of their absent companion. "I'm most frightened of your bad manners, and what will happen to this poor dying land if you don't find your lost protege, Nikodemos, quickly enough to suit you."

"Even you, Jihan," he said, half turning in his saddle to flick a severe look across her face like a slap, "must realize that there's a reason we've been lured here."

"Lured?" she said.

"Lured," he said as he kicked his Tros horse into a lope. "Sometimes, when things need a decent burial, someone like me comes along to see to it."

"You hate death," she accused. "All your bravado and all your years, and you've never gotten used to it, or accepted it. Why else would you take a mortal like Niko into your heart, where fate can pull his strings and reach you thereby?"

"You know, you learned too much and not enough on the misty isles. Didn't the adepts there teach you that all men flee death and chase dreams?"

"But you are the avatar of death, the herald of strife, the minion of the Storm God himself . . . And you don't dream. You don't even sleep. So don't talk to me about dream—"

"This place is a dream of mine," he said in a low, clipped voice that made his horse's ears twitch. "A dream I've had that I thought I wouldn't live to see—no matter how long I lived."

And this revelation frightened the Froth Daughter more than the flaming cyclone or the loss of Nikodemos, the third horse's rider, in the clouds, or even the ruin all around them. "What do you mean?" she demanded. "What is this place? Is this the work of the witch who haunts Niko? Is that what you're worried about? Black sorcery and unnatural death?"

"I told you, I've dreamed about this place. If I'm right, we head west, through that forest where the cyclone cut a swathe, and we'll find a sea."

"How can you know so much about somewhere you've never been?"

Again, his teeth flashed. "Blame it on my curse of immortality. Blame it on the weather. Blame it on man and mind and the whims of the gods, if you will. But we've come here because our mortal charge was lured here like the bait he is, and that should tell you something."

"What?" she nearly screamed in frustration. "What, Riddler, *what?*"

"That this is where the world ends—this world, anyway. And though it is not our world, we were bound to come here eventually, being immortals in a universe of mortals."

"*Will you speak plainly?*"

"We've come into the future—ours, theirs, drawn by Nikodemos, whose lot is to see the worst and the best of men. And see it he will, and we will—even the sea that laps the final shore: the sea at the end of time."

"It's not fair that you know so much. You're scaring me."

"The Storm God tells me what I need to know," he reminded her. "Even when I'd prefer not to know it."

"Does your god tell you whether Niko is all right? Whether we'll be—"

"Safe? Triumphant? No." He stopped his horse now, and hers followed suit because it had followed his so long that it did what it had always done. The big man leaned on his saddlehorn and faced her squarely. He said, "Jihan, remember: this is the future, the end of this place, and the place where all things end. Take nothing for granted here. Beyond this place is . . . nothing. To leave it, we must go back, not forward. Keep this in mind, should we be separated."

"Did the lord of dreams, your enemy, do this to us, then? Or Niko's witch? Or—"

"All the enemies we left behind are as nothing here. This place is balanced on a pinpoint of eternity. The god has a thing to do here. I have a thing to do. Niko does, for he preceded us. As for you, you can always go back to the sea which spawned you. Don't be afraid. Fear is a waste of energy."

"Easy for you to say," she muttered at his back as he kneed his horse and it loped toward the wide swathe in the trees.

Following his leopard mantle into the dusk, Jihan could not bring herself to wish she hadn't come. But a sadness overwhelmed her, a sadness to do with ended lives, wasted lives, lives eaten up by hates and petty quarrels, and all the other proclivities of mankind that she'd seen in her journeys among the worlds of men, but did not understand.

CHAPTER 3: A STRANGER'S WELCOME

The man who'd fallen from the sky lay in the chief stableboy's bed while all the palace buzzed with the news of his coming.

People came and went, asking him questions he couldn't answer. Faces faded in and out of his sight and, among those, the one he liked the best was that of a fair-haired girl with freckles and amber eyes. Whenever the girl would talk to him, he tried to answer, but the language in his mind wouldn't reach his lips.

She sometimes came into his room with a young man of similar visage, and he told himself they must be related, so closely was her beauty restated in the other's face.

There were others who came, and these were less pleasant visits. One of these was fair-haired also, a man with hunched shoulders and a rough complexion, a sturdy man who brought bowls with him that did not have soup in them.

This man would take his unresisting hand and put

it in a bowl of this or that, and sprinkle salt upon it, and shake his head when he looked into the palm he'd salted. And he would hover, hands in his sleeves, just at the edge of vision, talking in low tones that couldn't quite be deciphered.

Another man came with this one, twice, and then came one time alone. This was a dark man, and the darkness was more than that of complexion. Some people have a veil about them, as if they eat the light of day. And to the man who'd fallen from the sky, such veils were self-evident, such men the pawns of magic, or accursed. He'd been too long among the mages and the witches not to know one when he saw one. When this man offered him drink he closed his lips. When food came from that hand he would not touch it. As soon as he realized who stood over him, he always feigned exhausted sleep.

A third visitor came when the candles in his room were lit. This one had a way with light, as well—the candle's flame lived in the hollows of his cheeks and danced in his hair, which was like forged bronze. Seeing this person come with the night, the injured man relaxed and thought of sleep. He held out his hand when the man came near and said, in a language he hoped they'd understand, "Enlil loves the traveler in his service. Life to you, priest, and everlasting glory."

That man squeezed his hand, but when the name of the Storm God was spoken, he dropped it. Among a tirade of gibberish, the name of Enlil was picked up by other voices in the room.

Until that moment, the man who'd fallen from the sky didn't realize that all the people he'd seen were in the room at the same time, or that there was any succession of time to be considered here, or what it might mean to utter the name of the god in the house of men who might be enemies.

A surge of fear rushed through him and brought

him strength. Caution followed, wiping the cobwebs from his mind. His fighting nature made him struggle to sit up then, and it was the fair woman who helped him, putting pillows behind his back.

They were all speaking a language that teased his mind, a language he hadn't heard spoken since the early days of his training, when as an apprentice he'd learned the dead language of the god he served. He'd learned it just well enough for ritual and blood-bond. He'd learned to say the god's prayers by rote.

This realization—that he was among speakers of a language that no man spoke anymore—chilled his spine. Strength came into him as he found need for it. He wanted to turn his head. He wanted the soup the girl had offered. There was a word he knew, for offering food to the god. He used it, and hands hurried to give him the soupbowl.

It was the woman who brought it to his lips. He grasped her wrist to steady it.

She leaned down close and their eyes met. This time, he had control of his lips and his tongue, even if the words came hard. In an ancient language of ritual, he ennunciated slowly: "Thanks to you. I ask the safety due Enlil's servant in a pious household. I am Nikodemos, called Stealth, from . . ."

He couldn't say where. He didn't want to try. He knew, but it didn't matter here, something told him. And the taint of magic was still heavy in the room, its practitioner too close. He shouldn't have given his true name with the wizard present, but he'd wanted to tell the woman who he was. It mattered, somehow.

She said, "I am Tabet. You are in the palace of my father, King Genos, lord of the city."

He had soup in his mouth as she said that, or he might have responded wrongly. He swallowed, attributing what she'd said to the strangeness of her dialect and the antiquity of the tongue they both used. The City of Genos was a myth from the beginning of time; the descendents of Genos had been lost forever. If she'd truly said that, then he was still dreaming.

Which was fine. Even with an evil magician in the dream, it was a dream which included pillows and a soft bed, warm and sustaining soup, and a girl of bright eye and comely form. When he really woke up, he was going to be disappointed to find himself on his sable horse, journeying interminably through the clouds with Jihan and Tempus, neither of whom would admit that they were lost . . .

When he woke again, the dream was still real, and the clouds through which he'd been traveling were starting to seem like a dream. Surely he couldn't have fallen from his horse, snagged by a viper of ectoplasmic strength, and been half drowned in wind and water and fish. . . .

One didn't question. One waited. He felt better on this second awakening, in the dawn. He felt twice better when he realized that the young woman named Tabet had spent the night by his side.

But then the men came, the men he remembered from the night before, a threesome dour and robed and formal, mincing along with parchments and scrying bowls and astrolabes and all the paraphernalia of judgment that a mercenary learned to keep shut of.

They started to ask him questions.

He hid behind the language barrier, which was flimsier than he dared admit. He pointed to himself. "Niko," he said, and smiled his most winning smile, which had melted many a woman's heart.

But these were not women. These men had the air of a tribunal about them. The girl had been sent from the room. She'd promised to come back later with clothes for him, which proved only that she expected there to be a later.

He was not so sure. The room around him was white-washed mud brick and smelled of stable. If she was the descendant of fabled King Genos, the family had fallen on hard times. There was no poverty evident in the dress of the three men who seemed determined to question him, no matter how dumb he played.

He put them off one day, and he put them off that night.

He went to bed knowing that, the next morning—if he was still there—he would have to answer their questions. He'd heard them speak of "The Test," among themselves. "The Test" must be given to him. Something they all cared about hung on the results.

But that was tomorrow. Tonight he could still try to flee, if he gathered his strength. There was a window by his bed. If he could just get up, he could see the lay of the land through it.

He should have been able to: there was nothing wrong with him that he could find, except for bruises and a bump on the head that made him a little dizzy. But there was a lethargy in his limbs which he couldn't will away, and there was the matter of his clothes.

He couldn't understand where his own clothes had gone. He wanted his gear: his cuirass and breech, his greaves, his swordbelt; his scabbard and beltknife and throwing stars and helmet. He wanted, more to the point, his horse and his shield and his crossbow and all the accouterments of his trade.

But he had none of those. He had not a stitch until the young woman called Tabet came with a chiton and pantaloons for him. Behind her was a handmaid, a fat one.

He said, as Tabet smiled and pantomimed that she'd put the clothes down and leave him with the handmaid, who'd dress him, "You stay. I have questions."

Her whole bearing changed. She shoved the handmaid bodily out the door and came to his bedside.

"Yes?" she prompted.

"Those men? That test me? Who, and for what?"

"Oh, NikodemoscalledStealth, do not fear the Test.
I myself will speak for you—"

"Call me Niko. Speak for me how? Why?"

"You are a man of the Storm God, you have nothing to fear. We test strangers, that's all. For the
god."

He nodded, though he didn't understand what she
meant. If it was for the god, it would not go ill.
"Then I will do it, if you like."

"It's not me. You must, you see—" She pursed her
lips and changed the subject: "That's all for tomorrow. Tonight, I'll have them bring up food and I'll
stay with you again and you can tell me all about the
Outside."

"The Outside?" The syllables were meaningless to
him, since the only definition he could find for them
seemed senseless.

"The World. I've never been out of the city."

He nodded and she reached for his hand. He let
her take it, felt her fingers tracing the callus on his
palm. He knew what to do with her, and perhaps she
could guide him through this. He needed food and
sleep and he needed to remember how he'd gotten
here. He kept seeing fish in his mind's eye—though
it made no sense, he'd come here in a rain of fish, he
now remembered. But the memory was confused.
He knew how to clear his head and regain his strength,
he told himself: let the girl help him—she was a
princess, and an easy ally; eat; drink; let the god
show him what to do.

When the men came back with their test in the
morning, he'd know what to do and how to do it.
He'd get the information from the girl or the god.
His spirit was already balanced enough to tell him
that.

So he tried to relax and enjoy the naive play of

letting the princess dress him and feed him, and
perhaps undress him later. But something nagged
him. Something in the wizardy eyes of the dark man
riled his gut and wouldn't be banished, no matter
how much hospitality the daughter of the king offered him.

During that evening, he told her that he was a
mercenary by profession, that he'd been a paired
elite fighter, and for whom, and saw all of it fall on
deaf ears.

She told him, when he asked, how he'd "fallen
from the sky in a rain of fish," and steadfastly denied
that his gear or his horse had fallen with him.

But about the test and the three men giving it, she
would tell him nothing more, saying only, "That
wouldn't be fair. In the morning, we'll all find out.
But I'm sure you'll be fine. After all, Enlil sent you,
didn't he?"

CHAPTER 4: FATHER AND SON

"Father." Macon spoke to the tight-shut door at the top of the city's highest tower. "You must see me." The prince's voice was louder than it should have been, he knew. But dawn was nearly breaking and, in these extraordinary times, this was going to be an extraordinary dawn. "Please."

The stout wood before him did not so much as shiver. Was his father asleep? He pounded once again upon the door with his fist, pounded so hard that the torch in its sconce by the door seemed to shake and the flame it held danced wildly.

Extraordinary times. Times of double rainbows and floods of fishes, times of naked men who fell from the sky and entranced his sister. Times of warlocks running wild and seers exalted and priests of somnambulent gods claiming to hear messages from heaven.

What was wrong with Father, anyhow? What was wrong with everybody? What, especially, was wrong with his sister, Tabet, who heeded no advice and no decorum, just hovered over the sky-fallen stranger as if she were not a maiden princess, but a serving wench? Staying the night—staying two nights—alone in the room with a man. It was unheard of. It was unacceptable. The man was naked, without credentials, suspect . . . a stranger. A creature from beyond the city walls. If only their mother had stayed with the city, then perhaps Macon could have found an ear less bristly than his father's.

But mother had left long ago, with a stranger who had come for a fortnight, and none of the family had ever forgotten that. . . . It couldn't happen again. Macon wouldn't let it.

He had talked to the seer about his sister's behavior, and stout Crevis had said only, "The future is unfixed, busy forming. Your sister has free will."

Having gained no comfort from the seer, Macon had gone to the priest of the Storm God and asked, "How is it that a storm of fish has brought this man here? And what does the god say about my sister attending him like a serving wench?"

The priest, Jamad, had bowed his head and clasped his hands, staring at the empty altar of the god in the temple's quiet sanctum, all walled with frescoes from ancient times. The frescoes had never bothered Macon before, yet now the bloody scenes of primal violence seemed to stir in the light of the god's thousand candles as if the walls were alive.

The priest, when at last he raised his head, had said, "Do not fear the god, my son," as if Jamad were enough older than Macon to be calling him "son." Which he wasn't. A linen robe and a ceremonial necklace didn't entitle the priest to treat Macon like a child.

"You listen to me, Jamad," said the prince. "My sister's in thrall to that naked reaver we've got sleeping over the stables, and I expect somebody to help me do something about it. Go down there and tell her she can't stay the night with him—that the god forbids it or something."

"The god doesn't forbid it, Prince Macon," said the priest with a level stare and emphasis on the word "prince" that Macon didn't misconstrue.

"Not even if my father were to tell you to *say* he did?" Macon said, his temper out of control. "What use is a palace priesthood, if not to enforce the will of the king?"

"You are not the king. The king is too wise to ask such a question," said the young priest, who turned away from the empty altar and headed for the frescoed walls. "Since you *are* asking such a question, I will give you the answer you must hear, if one day you are to be king in this city. Come."

Macon stomped stifflegged along beside the young priest until they stood before a wall where the god was depicted with his sandaled feet spread wide over the city and his armaments in his hands, fighting a dragon from hell. "The Storm God protects the city from evil without. Only with the god in your heart can you protect the city from evil within. To hear the god in your heart, prince, you must silence your own voice."

"I *had* catechism, priest," said the prince. "I know the routine. What I'm asking isn't religion, it's politics."

"It is personal preference, which is not politics. The newcomer will undergo the Test, and when he has taken it, perhaps the altar of the city will not be empty." The priest turned to Macon. His eyes, catching the glimmer of the surrounding candles, seemed to magnify it. "This is a delicate time for us all. Go to your father. Perhaps he will explain it. As for your sister, should she learn anything from the stranger, we will be glad to know it."

"Fool," said Macon to the priest, and stalked away.

That left only the sorcerer, of whom Macon always

was careful. The magicians had their own fortress
within the city's walls. Macon seldom went there.

As dawn began fingering the night's skirts, he got
up his courage: though he was leery of the wizards
and their ways, whispers in the palace had it that
Macon's father listened most of all to the warlocks of
late.

So up he went into their lair, where polished black
granite made his feet cold through his sandals. There
he demanded to see Seth, the highest among the
warlocks, and was ushered into the presence of the
dark man.

Macon couldn't think of a thing to say. Couldn't
imagine why he'd come here. If his sister wanted to
sit with the stranger—caress him, kiss him, make
love to him and bed him and shed her virgin blood
on his sheets—then what difference did it really
make to Macon?

"Yes, prince?" prompted the warlock in his dark
and unadorned robe of office. The warlock's walls
were covered with scrolls on shafts of bone and clay
tablets on shelves of stone. There were no frescoes
here. There was hardly a torch burning. The windows of the warlock's study were open to the end of
night.

"I came about the stranger and my sister."

The warlock nodded commiseratingly. "The family
ties, yes. What help would you from me, Prince
Macon? The stranger has yet to take the Test. If he
fails it, the world swings one way. If he passes,
another. Surely you do not wish to falsify the
outcome?"

A shiver ran down the prince's spine. "I don't
want that naked fishman touching my sister."

"He has touched her already. Their hands have
joined. She has given him sustenance. She has given
him—"

"I know that. I don't want her with him, is all."

The words seemed to spit themselves out of Macon's mouth of their own accord. "If she's going to be like that with anybody, it should be—" He'd almost said, "It should be me," but he bit it back, horrified. It wasn't that. That wasn't what he wanted. He just didn't want her with the stranger, who was . . . wrong . . . somehow.

"It should be someone of suitable degree," said the warlock smoothly. "Someone from the city, yes. Well, Prince, to interfere you'll bear a heavy cost. Can you pay it? Will you pay it?"

"Yes," said Macon without thinking.

The warlock didn't blink and Macon couldn't look away from those steady eyes. "And, too, there is the Test, and its outcome to consider. As well as the workings of sorcery in these matters—"

"What is this damned test?"

"You don't know? You really don't?" The warlock came from behind his desk and toward Macon. A cold preceded him that pimpled the prince's skin. "If the stranger is the god's creature and the god demands it, the altar that has lain empty so long will have his heart upon it. That should solve your problem, though not entirely."

Macon couldn't believe his ears. Certainly the warlock was speaking in riddles. Human sacrifice in the city? It was unthinkable. Decreed by Jamad, the young priest with his high and mighty airs and his flaunted morality?

"Not entirely? If I understand you, you're saying that the Test can lead to human—"

"It never has before, and the priest is anxious for a candidate that the god will accept. He may be so anxious that he will choose the wrong one, in order to have chosen someone."

"But how could the stranger's death fail to solve my problem?"

"The stranger is . . . not like us. Your sister has

fallen in love. The grave does not always cure that illness. And, if my eyes do not fail me, with such a one, there is more danger in his death than in his life."

"What is he, then?"

"A mercenary. A blood child of a thirsty god. The beloved of a dark power greater than mine. In your terms, he is—"

"Evil." Macon crossed his arms.

The warlock smiled as if at a precocious student. "Not evil, but a tool of certain forces. When men face forces beyond their control, whose desires are different from their own, they often call those forces evil. Enough about the stranger, for we must give him the Test and see what comes of it. Let us talk about your sister and yourself, and what you will pay to set her heart free."

"I . . ." Macon thought back to what the warlock had said earlier. "I will pay whatever price you ask. I don't want my sister leaving the city with that man. I don't want her marrying below her station. I want her . . ."

"For yourself?" suggested the warlock softly.

Macon's neck grew hot. "No! You know that's not right. I want her for the city, that's all. For the family. I don't want to lose her like we lost my mother." As the flush crawled up to his face, anger joined it. "It's my business, what I want her for. What do *you* want, Seth?"

"A student. A prince who will be king, who knows the ways of my art and has pledged allegiance to our . . . ways."

"You have it," said Macon without another thought. "As long as she doesn't—you know."

"I know. And you'll have what you can't admit you want: the power that was your father's; the honors that the priesthood steals from the city's rulers; dominion over—"

"That's the whole price?"

"Well, not all, but enough for you to know right now. And we must discuss the method . . ."

Macon's mouth was dry; his heart had stopped beating. "The method?"

"Magic and sorcery are phenomenal—the science is one of process, artifactual. To take a thing away, one must put something else in its place."

"I don't understand."

"You don't? You are not willing to say you want your sister for yourself, is that so?"

"Of course it's so. What do you think I am, a—"

"In the old times, I would have answered that I think you are a king. In the city's youth, the blood of kingship flowed through its women. To have children who could inherit the throne, a man would marry the Queen, even, as with your father, when the Queen was a blood relation. Or a princess—"

"You're saying my mother was my father's sister?"

"I'm saying you should study the city's history. But I'm saying also that, to dismiss a lover from the heart of a woman, you must have another lover to put in his place. Now, who shall that be? Or must we leave it up to fate and the meddling of unctuous gods?"

"I—" Macon took a step backward. He shook his head. Was he really having this conversation with the warlock? Did he think that Macon was fool enough to believe that the warlock could make his sister love whomever he chose? Or Macon chose?

As if reading his mind, the warlock said, "These are extraordinary times, calling for extraordinary measures. Go you to her rooms, and bring me a hair and a piece of undergarment. Since you cannot bring yourself to proclaim the truth, then you will not mind if I, in your stead, claim the lady's heart."

Something in Macon relaxed. The warlock had

almost had him believing that a spell could make his sister love whomever the caster chose. Now it was a more realistic thing the warlock was asking: permission to sue for his sister's hand.

"I'm only the prince, not the king," Macon reminded the warlock.

"That is true today. Who knows what might be true tomorrow? And you are also my student. Give me your answer, student, from the depths of your heart—and be bound by it."

"Yes, fine. You have my permission to court Tabet, without any objection or obstruction from me."

"Good." Out stretched the hand of the warlock and Macon felt compelled to take it. "Come in the evening for your first lesson, after the evening meal. By then the Test will be under way."

"Under way?"

"Enough for now, student. Leave me." And the warlock turned his back on the prince as if he were dismissing a stable boy.

Macon had come up to his father's tower from the sorcerer's, straightaway.

Here it all seemed like a dream. Like a mildly bad and suddenly inconsequential dream, he kept telling himself. The warlock had made a tool of him. The warlock had gained an apprentice, so Seth sought, an entré into the inner circles of the family. But Macon had gained an ally against the stranger, and tit for tat was the way of grown men in the city.

So why was he still uneasy?

"Father!" He pounded once more on the door of his sire, telling himself that, if the door did not open, he would go right to the room over the stables and drag Tabet out of there by the hair, shake some sense into her while the stranger took his test, whatever that was. Thus, no matter the outcome, Tabet wasn't going to run away with a stranger the way their mother had . . .

The door opened with no warning. His father stood there, long-nosed, sunken-cheeked and somehow smaller than he'd ever been.

"What is it, son?" said King Genos.

"I need to talk to you about Tabet and the stranger," Macon blurted. "And about my mother—was she really your sister?" He found his fists balled on his hips and his voice raspy in his throat.

Genos looked at his son and his eyes seemed to mist. His hands upon the door whitened. He said, "That was so long ago. You don't understand. Come in, Macon. Don't judge what you can't comprehend." And the king of the city stepped back to admit his son into the high-tower room, where none of the children had ever been.

It was like a monk's cell. There was nothing in it but a single feather pallet, a rough board table, and some scrolls upon the floor under a window open to the west.

Genos closed the door after his son had entered and said, "What is it that troubles you—the stranger or your sister or my wife?"

"Tabet won't leave the stranger alone. He's evil, Seth told me. And he may pass the Test, then what? She'll run off with him—Tabet will run away like mother did. Did mother run away because you made her marry you? How could you marry your sister? I don't under—"

"Hush, Macon," said the father in a voice that tried to be kind but which was full of anger and sorrow and the weight of thousands of years. "You cannot find the answers to so many questions all at once."

His father went to the window and stared out of it. Shoulders hunched, back turned, he said, "The city was founded so long ago that there were different strictures. The royal line was thin. The blood had to be preserved. We made a city so vital it has endured unchanged by time. We made choices no one else has ever made. There is no sickness here, no misery, no strife anymore. We have warlords who fought their last battles so long ago you could not count the years. We have magic so strong the world has not diluted it. We have knowledge so powerful the world cannot contain it. Do not be swayed by the warlock." Suddenly the father turned and glared at his son. "You haven't been, have you?"

Startled, Macon blurted, "He said he'd teach me some things."

The father closed his eyes and opened them. "You have bargained thus?"

"Yes."

"For what prize?"

"Tabet. So she won't run off with—" His voice sounded young and shaken and falsely sure of itself, even to his own ears.

"For your sister's soul? How could you?" The father sat heavily on the windowsill. "It is my fault," Genos said softly after a time, as if speaking only to himself. "I did not undertake to teach you the games of men. We thought we had all the time in the universe, your mother and I—and that was untrue. I made the same mistake with you. I must think on what to do about this."

"You don't have to do anything; I'm fine. It's just a course I'm taking from the warlock, nothing more."

"This place where the city is now," said the king very slowly, "is not a normal place. I didn't tell you even that—we didn't, not wanting to trouble you, or your sister, or the people, with problems you couldn't help and couldn't solve. At this place, the city's life hangs in the balance—the future, or lack of one, for us all. Now, what you have done cannot be undone. It must be surmounted. Do you hear me? Listen closely. You must make your own choice, and Tabet hers."

In his inner ear, Macon heard the warlock promising to sway Tabet's heart and he shuddered. But he said only, "Yes, father."

He repeated that simple phrase a dozen times before King Genos had finished lecturing him, and by then he knew it was too late to explain what else he'd done. As he knew it was hopeless to ask his father to intervene between Tabet and the stranger.

If the man before him was allowing this Test, and looking for a person to sacrifice on the Storm God's altar to save the city, then King Genos was no longer the father he had known. After Genos' lecture, he could not even find it in his heart to confront his father with the horror of what he'd learned from the warlock and the priest.

For the first time in his life, Macon looked at his father and saw a dangerous man, a pitiable man, a gullible man, and a man who might be wrong.

When the prince left that tower room, his whole world was changed. Nothing looked the same. The city was a caricature of itself, and his heart was full of barbs.

The only ray of hope in all of this was the warlock, Seth, and the bargain they'd made. In a city riddled with hypocrisy and underpinned with evil, founded on incest and lies, surely sorcery was the only hammer strong enough to wring the changes long overdue.

As Genos' eldest son, Macon told himself, this revelation and this moment had always been his fate. Here at the end of time, having found out the truth at last, his path was clear: he must take into his hands the weapons that the warlock had offered him and, with them and his sister beside him, supplant his father. The old man had lost his wits and the city had lost direction because of that.

The guilt of what Genos had done was going to destroy them all, otherwise. The son who was no longer content to be a prince hurried down the stairs, through the palace, and into the dawn, where everything was different now; where nothing could be trusted.

Overnight, he had been shorn of all his fantasies. Overnight, he had turned from a boy into a man. And that man wanted to be king.

CHAPTER 5: ANOTHER DAY, ANOTHER DREAM

When Tabet had crawled under the covers beside him, just before dawn, Niko had pretended to be asleep. Her whole length burned against him, and his body knew exactly what she wanted, but something cautioned him. It was too soon.

There was too much he didn't understand about these people, or their city. And in his heart there was *maat*, his discipline of balance and equilibrium, to be listened to. He was weak still, but not too weak for what she wanted. Yet he was in the hospitality of strangers, and under the scrutiny of alien wizards. His loins could not be allowed to override his heart, which felt unease.

Something was wrong about this place, about this Test which she said he'd take when the sun rose. He needed time, and he needed her to gain it. He played with his breathing; he rolled against her when she insisted on cuddling, always without letting on he was awake.

He prayed she wouldn't reach for him. He counted

on his intuition that she was virgin to keep her from it. And he counted the minutes until the rising of the sun. Her breathing deepened next to his. Her young nipples scalded him. It took every bit of discipline he commanded not to simply throw a leg over her and let nature take its course, but he managed.

He needed another day, and she was going to secure it for him. Every instant of contact between them promised Niko she would. Her need was clear and the pleasure of lying, skin to skin, flesh to flesh, with her was nearly overwhelming. As he felt it, she must, too. Young girls, he knew, had a natural ability to get their way. He needed her protection.

Her infatuation would give it to him, he told his passion. If he took her, he could not count on all she held in check as he could if she must wait for him.

So he lay there, breathing, burning, and when the first creak came upon the stairs she burst from the bed in a flurry of covers.

He let the sound of her dressing seem to be what waked him, so that he could watch her dress. He said, "You're very beautiful," as softly as he could. It wasn't original, but it was true.

Her hands went to her breasts and she blushed. He said, "Don't cover yourself," to make things clear.

She muttered, "I must; someone's coming," and she blinked away tears as she scrambled into her shift.

"What's this? Why are you sad?" he said, still nearly whispering. "You're too lovely to cry."

"The Test . . . I don't want you to take it," she told him as she fumbled with the last of her buttons.

"Then stay with me another day. Another night. I'll have my strength back soon."

He couldn't be more overt than that, not with words, so he reached for her just as the footsteps made the landing.

"Ssh!" she ordered, and he remembered that she

was a princess of the city. Of the Lost City of Genos. Of that city which, by the evidence of his senses, had lived unchecked since ancient times.

In came the priest again, representative of the Storm God—of his god. With him was the dark presence of the warlock, Seth; bringing up the rear was the sturdy seer with the bowls and implements of his vocation.

All three stared at Tabet. Instead of blushing now, she raised her head and said, "He is not ready. He needs another day at least to get his strength back." She crossed her arms over her breasts and slapped one bare foot against the floorboards to punctuate her words.

"The Test cannot wait, dear princess," said the warlock.

"The omens are favorable today," said the seer, much more deferentially.

"The god will protect him," said the priest.

"Jamad," said the princess to the priest, "the god had better." She turned to the seer. "The omens will be as good tomorrow; you'll see to it." And to the warlock she said, "I am no one's 'dear', *dear* Seth, but my father's. I demand that Genos be present for these proceedings, as he has always been before when strangers were tested. And that the test be held in the palace, as we have always held it. Which means, of course, that our guest must be able to walk the stairs and stand in the great hall. Anyone can see he's not up to that yet. Another day in my care is what he needs. And I will brook no argument." Her breath was coming fast; her voice trembled with command; her back was straight.

Niko chose that moment to sit up in his bed and say, "I'm afraid she's right—if this involves standing for long, I'm not yet strong enough. Why don't you tell me what it is you'll want me to do?"

The warlock ignored him, staring at the girl, and Niko took note of the proprietary look on Seth's face.

The seer said, "I'll just check the omens quickly for the morrow," and started setting out his bowls.

The priest came forward and stood at the end of the bed. From that distance he squinted at Niko as if a wide valley were between them. "Who are you, really?"

"Nikodemos, called Stealth, late of the Stepsons, once of Abarsis' Sacred Band, partner of the Riddler—a mercenary fighter, sworn to the Storm God." Truth never hurt. "If you are a man of the god, ask in heaven about me." He dared a weak smile.

"Do you know why you're here?"

"*Not now!*" ordered the princess. "I told you, Jamad, not yet. Tomorrow."

"The interviewing can be done today without harm."

"Is that up to you to determine?" She walked up to the priest and said, "I want my father here for this." Then she faced the warlock, "Please, Seth, tell them it can wait. I dreamed a dream I must discuss with someone, before this Test is done."

The warlock smiled then. He nodded. "Given that the princess has had a dream, we should wait at least until we've heard it. Surely you agree, Jamad, Crevis?"

Crevis, the seer, looked up from his bowls then. Niko saw the salt floating there, but could make nothing of it. "We must make a start today—perhaps the interview will count. Tomorrow, there will be clouds and interruptions."

"Crevis! Can't I get the omen I need from you?" demanded the princess.

"Not, my lady, if it is not there."

Anger flooded the princess's face and she turned again to the warlock. Seth offered her his arm and said, "Come tell me your dream, Lady Tabet. Crevis, you too should hear the dream, in case it needs interpreting. Let's leave these two adherents of the

Storm God alone together. Do your interview, Jamad, and make it brief. The princess does not want her guest exhausted."

Out went the princess with the warlock and the seer, leaving the priest alone in the room with Niko.

"Well, priest," said Niko in a tired voice, "tell me what this is that's happening here, and why the god needs a test of one of his own. Everywhere else in the world, my guild would house me and my priests would shield me from what I smell leaking out from that wizard and his palace puppeteers."

"This is not the world, soldier. This is the city, older than anything but time itself. The rituals you know are from a later time. The god here is much younger, his ways strange to you. You must let me guide you."

"Fine. Then tell me about the Test: what its purpose is, whether it is dangerous, and how to surmount it. It is my right to seek counsel from one of Enlil's priests."

"I—" The priest seemed to fold onto the end of Niko's bed. "I'm more worried right now about what dream the princess might have had. We seek a heart to appease the god, one for his altar." The priest's eyes came up, burning. "Thus it was told to me, long ago. Testing the strangers who have come to us has become our custom of late. But never has a man of Enlil come through here . . ." The priest trailed off.

"What is it you are not saying? Enlil loves his own; war and death are his altar, honest battle in the field. Anything less is a travesty." Niko's uneasiness came out in his words. "What is the problem here? Can I help?"

"The city is threatened. Perhaps that's why you've come. It surely is what we're trying to ascertain."

"Others will come after me," Niko said with a certainty come from his maat: he could see Tempus in his mind's eye, and Jihan. "If you wish, we might labor in your cause."

"First, the Test," said the priest implacably.

"Then describe it to me."

"Who is interviewing whom? Tell me about yourself, about your business here, how you came to fall from the sky in a rain of carp."

"I was with my commander, my partner, on the way to join fighters of like mind for a sortie into unknown lands. We had a . . . sprite . . . with us, a female creature of power. We used the god's clouds to travel and I . . . fell. Off my horse, out of my clothes, and into that fishy maelstrom." Niko shrugged. Speaking of it had brought back memories of the ectoplasmic viper that had snared him. Thinking of it made him miss his lost gear and his horse and his companions. "I didn't ask to come here. The god delivered me here." He shrugged again.

"Does this happen to you often?"

"I've gotten into this and that bit of sorcery, over time. The god works as he wills. It's not up to me to figure it. I rode for a priest, once; fought a warrior priest's battles in a dozen lands. In heaven, my record is written and there are souls that will speak for me. Ask there before you do me harm."

That was clear enough.

The priest blinked and got up from the foot of the bed. "Perhaps I will, soldier. You see, it's different here. We have no work for your kind. Or at least, we didn't until . . ."

"Until?"

"Until the city became ensnared here, trapped in an evil I don't understand."

"Ask the god, not a mere soldier. Or my commander when he comes. Which he will."

"Time will tell," said the priest, having had enough of this interview that was going nowhere. "I must find out what dream the princess had, and see if

King Genos will find it convenient to attend your
Test on the morrow."

"Find out, while you're at it, priest, how much of
your troubles are the wizard's fault. Look there first.
Give *him* your Test."

"Ha! Seth? Our warlock is immune to such tests as
the god and I can give."

"Perhaps to yours, but not to the god's if Enlil
really is here."

That stopped Jamad in his tracks. Niko had the
distinct impression that the priest only imagined,
envisioned, and implored the god; that he had never
met, dealt with, or even been disciplined by Him.
"Memories of the Storm God are not Enlil Himself,"
Niko's maat made him say aloud. "Bring the girl back
to me, when you find out what her dream was.
Dreams come from a place where I have powerful
friends."

And that shooed the priest finally, leaving Niko to
sweat over what he'd said until the princess might
return.

He heard voices talking outside his shut door for
far too long, and one of those voices was female.

When the door at last opened, it was Tabet who
came inside, but she had the warlock with her.

"This dream I had," she was saying as they entered, "is too important to go uninterpreted. I must
stay here with our guest, that is clear from it. If you
can't tell me what it means, then leave me to my
meditations, Seth."

The warlock would not be chased out so easily. "I
must finish with the patient—sorry, with the guest."
He peered sharply at Niko. "What would you think,
mercenary, of a guest who comes into a city and
causes the eldest and most beloved princess of that
city to dream of violence and sex, of treachery and
blood, in a place where none of those things exist?"

"You'd have to find a place where none of those things exist," said the Stepson.

Tabet giggled, then sobered. "You can see he's too tired, Seth. I will send word to you when he's rested."

The warlock was trying to be patient, but the titter had raised his ire. "You do that," he told the princess as he swept toward the door.

Reaching it, the warlock rounded on Niko: "And you, stranger—the Test will elicit the truth from you, never fear."

"Fear the truth? Truth's not what worries me, wizard."

The slam of the stout wood door was Seth's only reply.

In the wake of it, Niko and the princess took each other's measure—boldy, silently, both well aware that they were finally alone.

He said, "Perhaps you'd better tell me about this dream you had, Tabet," and patted the bed beside him.

She said, "And perhaps I should not," but came to perch on the edge of his bed.

He looked up at her. "Why not? Dreams are for sharing."

She looked down at him with half-lidded eyes. "This dream wasn't one I dreamed," she confided in a whisper, "But one I made up to confound the warlock and the priest." She smiled tenderly and raised a hand to his stubbled cheek.

He caught her fingers there. "Tell it to me anyway. It came from somewhere—a daydream or a nightdream, a dream's a dream."

She tugged against his grip halfheartedly, looking away. Then she said, "I told them I dreamed of a ravager, a man who was not a man, on a great horse like smoke, who came to purify the city in a bath of fire. He had a blazing creature with him, female in form, and the heavens opened at her command. And amid it all lay you and I, locked together in an embrace of . . ." She lowered her head, then raised it. "I told them you became my husband in the dream. But I did it only to forestall them." Now she tugged harder on his hand and he let her fingers go.

This was difficult for her, he knew. At the end of the room was an old cracked bronze mirror, veined with the green of neglect. A sunray struck it through the window as he watched, and he saw the two of them there: the bright-haired maiden with her demurely downcast eyes and shoulders hunched protectively, her arms hugging her belly, her knees tightly closed, as if all her womanhood could be held in abeyance by the simple mechanism of staying perfectly still.

And he saw himself too, as he hadn't for untold days, and was shocked at how young she seemed beside him. Years in the Riddler's service had stolen the youth from him; his hazel eyes burned, sunken deep, into an angular face stubbled with beard that had the scars of wars and too many sorcerous battles graven there.

When he'd been remarkable for his boyish prettiness, a prodigy of arms among more seasoned soldiers, he'd longed for a face like this, for shoulders full of knots and skin weathered by wars. Somehow those marks of his profession had come upon him unnoticed, while he was busy fighting witches and other men's wars and trying to stay alive.

How long had it been since he'd seen himself in anything but a pond or a running stream, a polished piece of wood or the advancing shield of an enemy? The girl beside him seemed like a child in the mirror, too young to touch, if his soul had matched his face.

But it did not, he told himself. She was here for

him; she'd chosen him, not the other way around. If he refused her or rejected her, now that she'd made herself his protector, things would go much worse. She'd lied for him, falsified a dream for him, she thought.

Yet she'd dreamed a waking dream of things to come, if he'd needed more of a hint from heaven about what to do with her than his loins could give.

He said, "That dream's not one to fear. I know the two you speak of, and as for the rest . . ." He let his hand brush her thigh and she didn't shy away. He let his palm rest on it, and she didn't move away. "You're the princess, here. Tell me what you want, lest my heart make me overstep."

She hung her head, mute.

His pulse was pounding. He let his hand slide up. "You lied for me, you think. You didn't, you'll see. There's truth in everything between us . . ." And the rest was a matter of promising not to betray her trust, or to hurt her—or to rush her.

Young girls were Niko's specialty, but this one had a palmful of fate. Her skirt came up above her thighs and she let him lift her onto him, only the covers between them. Then she was stiff and still as if frozen there, and he heard her whisper, "The door, it isn't locked . . ."

That was all he needed: her brother bursting in, or worse.

But risk is seductive, in its way. He let his hands go still on her buttocks and reached for her lips with his own.

She wanted a husband; he hadn't misheard that. She was the daughter of the legendary Genos, or so she claimed, a princess of a mythical city from the beginning of recorded time, where all the mysteries he'd studied had begun.

What would his teachers have thought, if they could see him here and now? All the secular adepts of the misty isles who pored over ancient books from here, what would they say if they knew that Genos' daughter was offering Niko her long-held virginity?

And that thought startled him and worried him, so that he said against her cheek, "How old are you, Tabet?"

She whispered back, "Old enough."

"Old enough to know what we're fooling with here? You've never had a man, am I right?"

She sat up on him, suddenly astride. She pushed hair from her face. "Of course not. What do you think I am?"

Tabet blushed and would have left him, but he pulled her back down and rolled, bedclothes and all, on top of her, and kissed her again, this time letting his passion loose for a space of a dozen heartbeats.

When he lifted his head, her lips stayed parted; her breath was coming fast. And then he answered her question: "I think you're a princess, and I think a man who falls in love with you had better consider that. You're not one to take lightly, to love for an evening and leave of a dawn."

Her hands came up and locked behind his neck. "Love me, Nikodemos," she murmured, and closed her eyes while her locked arms sought to pull him close.

"For how long? If legends are true, this city is immortal. I'm not."

"Stay here with me and time will pass you by," she said and it had the ring of a promise in it.

When he didn't answer, she opened her eyes and he saw only an infatuated girl in them—no witch, no covetous lord of dreams trying to steal his soul.

"You don't know anything about me," he warned. "I have burdens in the World . . ."

"This is not the world; this is the city. Stay here with me, as my husband, and not time or the warlock or the priest of the silly god will dare to harm you."

"Tabet, you don't know what you're saying," Niko muttered. There was a strength in her that seemed to draw all his away, so that he bent to the pressure of her arms and came up on his elbows. Wherever their bodies touched, heat scoured him.

Stay here with me . . .

There was no harm in it, he told himself. There was no harm in her, his flesh was sure. Her skin was soft and it tasted sweet. She offered something he hadn't known he'd been starving for, and the price of it receded as his need increased.

At the last possible moment, he pulled back. Rearing up on straight arms, he looked down at her and said, "Are you sure, Tabet?"

And she was.

Afterward, she promised him whatever he asked. She would take him throughout the city, give him a tour of "our domain." And more: "You will be happy with me eternally, Nikodemos. You will see. Stay with us and no harm will ever befall you." Her face was beatific.

On the far side of his passion, questions lurked and doubts massed. Now that he'd embarked upon something he hadn't meant to do, it seemed more than foolish—it seemed dangerous, a velvet trap into which he'd stumbled.

Niko said, "There's much you've got to tell me. About this place and you and what's ahead. There's still the Test, isn't there? What we've done can't make any difference to—"

"My father will protect you, once he knows. We must go to him, after we rest." Her eyes blazed like the eyes of a sprite or a river witch.

He was suddenly exhausted, yet too restless to lie back with her the way she asked. "The door's not locked, remember? And you promised to show me the city and tell me of it—and your family."

Could they do that? Walk out of here, hand in

hand, when they'd postponed his test by saying he was too weak?

She saw no problem in that. She was all princess now, headstrong and wild with some weird joy. She wanted, he realized, to be seen with him, to show her conquest to one and all.

Even her bloodstained skirt didn't give her pause.

"It's not that I don't believe you," he said, holding back as she pulled him toward the door. "But a bath would be welcome. And clothes—for us both."

"You're right," she giggled. "I'd forgot. You don't have any clothes." She was a woman drunk on love, he realized, and tried to bring her back to bed.

But she would not be swayed. She strode in her stained shift to the door, where she called imperiously down the stairs for a groom.

When the groom came, she gave orders—for clothes to be brought, for a bath to be drawn, for quarters to be prepared "next to mine, in the palace. And tell my father it's time for my bethrothal feast, to arrange for it this very night!"

She slammed the door on the openmouthed groom and came back to him, her whole face shining. "Now we are alone, let us do the deed again, to seal our joined fate."

Tabet knew nothing of men or their limits, he realized then. As he took her in his arms for a second time, he found himself staring out the window at the stableyard, beyond which was the ancient, timeless city whose princess had just claimed him as her own.

CHAPTER 6: TOKENS

Macon was just stealing hurriedly out of Tabet's rooms when Matilla, the old handmaid, caught him. He stuffed his hands in his pockets and prepared to explain himself: to lie, for he had no intention of explaining why he'd stolen hair from his sister's hairbrush and a soiled stocking waiting for the washerwoman to collect it.

Matilla fixed him with a glare that had subdued the children of the king from childhood and worked her rubbery lips. Her fuzzy chin jutted. She stood up to her full and crooked height and Macon found himself wondering just how old Matilla might be. She'd been an aged crone as long as he could remember—since the city was born, his father had once said.

"Macon," she said in her nasal and wavering voice, one word that went through him like a fever and sounded like the wind wailing through the towers on a winter's night. His name, coming from her, sounded like an indictment. Or a curse. He stiffened and clutched the wadded stocking in his pocket, squeezing it as if he could hide its bulk. But it was no good. Matilla was glaring at him as if he'd stolen the god's meal from the temple altar, the way he'd done once on a dare as a child. She was wise, was Matilla. She could read his guilt on his face. She'd probably already divined that he was on an errand of the warlock's, and for what foul purpose.

He was opening his mouth to confess when the old woman spoke again:

"Your sister's locked herself in the room above the stable with the stranger." She smacked her lips and a disapproving noise punctuated her revelation. Her eyes began to well with tears. She blinked them back and bore down on Macon severely. "You'd better do something about it, boy. Your sister's virtue is at stake and you're lurking here like a thief."

Macon's hand tightened on the stolen goods he held. "She's . . . infatuated."

"Tsk. Don't you think I know that? We can't have these goings on. You talk to her, boy. Hear me, or there'll be hell to pay. She's no business hanging on that drifter, a stranger, trash of the world, flotsam from—"

Macon closed his eyes in relief. Matilla had never taken a husband, it was said. The entire natural world was foreign to her, the ways of men and women a mystery. She was like a priestess of the god without a god to serve. Everything that smacked of pleasure or indulgence, she hated. Every human failing was her enemy. The coming of age of Genos' children was a certainty she fought as if it were a battle or a feud with nature itself. So it had always been, so it would always be.

He said to the old woman, whose grief and misery were real, whose face showed a struggle between her love for Tabet and her oldmaidish horror and despite of human passion and those who flaunted it: "I'm trying, mothermaid. I'm trying. And you may help me, if you'll be wise and silent, and do what I ask without comment." Surely, Matilla's collusion would come in handy before the deed was done.

"Just tell me what you want me to do, Macon. Tsk. Tsk. Tsk," said Matilla, a mantra and a curse.

"I want you not to mention to anyone you saw me here, and have Tabet's rooms completely cleaned before sunset." Macon was thinking on his feet; he had nothing for Matilla to do now, and yet he must give her something.

"That's all?" said the little woman who'd ruled his youth with an iron claw.

"For now, yes," said Macon. "I'm on my way to find out what more we can all do. I'll see you this evening. And remember," he said softly over his shoulder as he passed by the dejected and outraged ancient on his way to the stairs, "this is our secret. What we do for Tabet, no one must learn. Or we'll be able to do nothing, and off she'll go with the stranger the way mother left us, never to be seen again."

Where had that come from? On his way down the stairs, two at a time, he upbraided himself for a loose-lipped child. He wasn't as calm as he should be, not as clever—not by half. Thus on the stairs he passed a stableboy, going up, and thought little about it.

He heard the boy confront Matilla on the landing, but not their words, only the handmaid's scandalized tone.

Whatever it was, he'd find out about it later. Now was the moment to slip through the back rooms of the palace, choosing the ashlar grimness of the servants' floors over the red/black/white splendor of the palace proper, and the risk of encountering someone with the right to ask where he was going.

Would the warlock be displeased that he'd been

seen by Matilla—caught in the act, almost? He worried about it all the way to Seth's sanctum, where he burst through the door without even bothering to knock.

Seth must have been expecting him. The warlock sat behind his table, facing the door through which Macon had just come.

He was smiling slightly. Seth's smile was cold and bereft of humor, a twist of lips and a squint of eyes.

He waved Macon to a chair and said without preamble, "Put the tokens here." His long dark finger tapped a spot on the table between them.

Macon said, "I was found by Matilla, the handmaid, but she didn't see me take the tokens. She'll help us, if we—"

"Put the tokens here," said the warlock once again.

Macon couldn't seem to get his hand out of his pocket. His fist was locked around the stocking, which was wound about with his sister's hair, and the whole bundle seemed too big to go through the opening in his pocket. Clumsily, he struggled with it, not able to take his eyes away from the warlock's.

Those eyes showed no bit of pleasure, or of approbation, or of any emotion except dire purpose. "Apprentice," said the warlock again and this time his words grated on Macon's ears, "the tokens, freely given."

A shiver ran through the prince. His wrist was snared in the cloth of his pocket; he must look like the fool he felt. Yet the act of giving forth those tokens would not be consummated, as if the very universe decried it, as if nature itself obstructed him.

Finally, he unsnared his fist and brought out the wadded stocking. He tried to drop the hair and the soiled stocking where the warlock was pointing, but his fingers would not obey him.

"Drop it," ordered the warlock. "Now."

Macon's fist opened like a wound. The stocking

sprang forth and unfurled. The hair from his sister's brush glistened in its folds.

Macon sat down hard in the chair, breathing heavily, weak and chilled as if something in him had come unstrung.

"Good enough, apprentice. Now go back to the palace and learn what you can learn," said the warlock, not looking up at him.

Macon had expected something more—better praise, an explanation, initiation into the rites he was helping to facilitate. The warlock hardly acknowledged him, now that the deed was done.

"That's it? Just go back to the palace?"

"To the palace," said Seth absently, and waved a hand to shoo him.

When Macon left the sanctum, the warlock had not moved an inch or said another word. He merely sat before the wadded stocking and hair of Tabet. Even when Macon said farewell from the doorway, Seth didn't look up.

Chapter 7: The Interlopers

"There is no such place as this," Jihan breathed as their horses came out of the copse and the city stood revealed. "Not in the world of men. There cannot be." Her throaty voice was troubled. Her head was raised to the distance—to the white and shining city and the blinding sea beyond.

The city was on a hill finer than any other on this windswept coast, and that hill topped a promontory skirted with mist. Between the city and the copse, at whose edge they'd stopped their horses, was a sweeping plain, regular and rectangular, dotted with villages, like a great and idyllic dell.

Where the ground swept up on the plain's far side, a curving waterway shimmered. And beyond it were other waterways, like wheels within wheels, concentric circles joined by spokes that ringed the city as if she were their hub. The final rim of the final wheel was sunk deep into the blinding sea.

"This city like a wheel, what do you mean when you say it is stuck?"

"Look for yourself, Jihan. The wheel of the city is mired in the sea."

"Not truly. There is no city which is the hub of a wheel, not when that wheel is made of earth and water . . ."

"You are a creature of an enchanted sea and yet you talk to me of mundane rules of order?" Tempus tried to smother his irritation. Jihan was always challenging him; she was an everpresent question in need of an answer. Nothing was ever sufficient unto itself for her. Jihan was visiting the world, he reminded himself, not a creature native to it. Thus she wished to see lines sharply drawn, black and white boundaries everywhere, and a nature as orderly as her own was not. She wanted, he sometimes thought, to be the only numinous thing in the universe, the only supernatural manifestation, the only wonder.

But she was not, not in this world she'd come to, where he'd inherited her as a sort of talisman of his curse. She was immortal, yet she wanted everything else to be mortal. She was more than human in beauty and in form, yet she wanted nothing else to share her grace. Her tiny waist and her broad muscular thighs tight against her horse as he danced on the edge of the downslope were as real as the sod under them, yet she wanted the city they sought to be unreal.

"It's as real as you, Jihan. It's as real as time. And it has come to the end of its time."

"But you yourself have told me that all things are an everliving—"

"Don't misquote me, Jihan." He kneed his horse, who snorted a complaint but bunched its hindquarters, lowered its wedge-shaped head, and began picking its way down the slope. "The city *is*."

"But is what?" She kicked her horse savagely and it squealed in protest before it began following Tempus' down.

"A wheel, I told you. Stuck in the mud of the sea at the edge of time." Suddenly he realized why the city distressed Jihan so: the roaming city was eternal, yet changing; not a thing of stasis, but a thing of evolution—like them both. And yet the roaming city faced its end here.

Those that live a span such as Jihan's, or his own, disliked confronting the backside of eternity—the dark punishment of nothingness, the end of forever that was not extinction, but fossilization.

She sensed a personal danger in the city's plight, a peril that could touch her and change her as no mere death of her worldly form could ever do. He and Jihan had faced witches and warlocks and demons and fiends, swirling maelstroms from awful hells that men had made, but never anything like this.

He felt his own knees tighten against his horse's barrel. This was no place for Jihan. Or for him. He'd held the thoughts in abeyance since the god had sent him such signs as enabled him to know where Niko had disappeared to, if not why.

The Froth Daughter beside him was a creature spawned of water; she was immune to anything the world could offer, as long as the world offered days and nights and forward motion. She'd battled forces from beyond the imagination beside him and he'd never tried to shield her, for even should she die, her essence would be returned to the dimension that spawned her. Her father would have gotten her back, a creature of the waves once more.

How many times they'd risked themselves and each other, always sure of their souls' survival and willing to lose all else. This was what had kept them together, she playing at becoming human and he trying to become something more than a human cursed by wizard and god to live forever.

But here at the edge of time, forever could end. He'd wanted death when it was unattainable. Now he realized he'd wanted only sleep, another grace denied him. He was tired to his very bones, but there was no rest at the end of time. There was no honorable fate in being trapped like a frog in amber.

He let his reins hang loose, one hand grasping his saddle's pommel with all his mighty strength. His eyes roamed to the city and seemed to stick there, as if the very image of the place had a desperate allure.

It glimmered white because its towers were gilded with electrum, with silver, with the purest gold. The roof of its palace would be shingled with ivory and no man within would count those things as wealth.

He knew the legend. He knew the stories. He was even curious. And he knew that Niko was there and that the presence of his partner must draw Tempus through those gates as surely as if the god's welcome were written there by lightning and graven on every cobblestone. Yet he was hesitant, and not only for Jihan's sake.

So he shouted into the breeze, "We'll stop at the first village we find. There's no rush. We'll rest the horses and talk this out."

"Talk what out?" she called back. "These horses don't need rest, and you know it. What is it you're not telling me, Riddler?"

"That place ahead might be dangerous to your health," he told the wind that was fiercer now, that caressed his face like unseen hands. To her health, and his own.

"And not to Stealth's?" She used Niko's war name, reminding Tempus thereby of all the demands of the honor code he'd taught her to live by. That he lived by, in lieu of anything better in all the annals of man. Without honor, there was only disappointment and chaos and the endless sullying of the gift of life. They lived it and they taught it and they hoped to teach man and his universe by example. You protected those you loved. You demanded right action from yourself and from others. You fought the slight evils as firmly as the great ones: you betrayed not, nor did you forgive betrayal. You were constant in demanding the best from yourself and from those around you. You accepted no compromise, even when compromise made life and love possible.

By those rules, in the world he'd come from, Tempus had no choice: Niko was his to teach, his to challenge, his to endow with the freedoms that experience brings. The man called the Riddler could not leave Nikodemos to the eternal city, when that city might never roam again. If the world needed anything, it needed Niko, as many Niko's as it could find. But right now, there was only one Niko, and he was trapped in a place that could destroy him with its immortality.

Jihan was immortal by dint of never having been human; her body might die, but she would live. Tempus was immortal by dint of curse and god; he sought death, but life would not give him up. In the place beyond the valley and the plain, where the wheel's spokes met and the sea was not a sea of life, but a sea of memory, Jihan could lose her self and Tempus could lose his lease on life and his chance at death.

It had been so long since Jihan asked her question that Tempus had forgotten it until she yelled again, "And not dangerous to Stealth's life?"

"Most dangerous, Jihan. When we stop, we'll talk about it." He had to look into his heart and find the god there. Then he would ask of himself whether it would be worth all things to both of them to free the mortal fighter named Stealth from a curse of deathless life and lifeless death.

All the way down the slope, Tempus worried the thoughts rolling through him as if they were plaguing demons on a battlefield. Niko had been offered immortality by the lord of dreams, and turned away from that idyllic half life. He'd been courted by a witch whose power shook the very bedrock of a simple world, and never flinched from the horror of her, because he'd seen the love in her.

Where Tempus and Jihan were souls transfigured by their anger and abroad in the world of men to teach lessons long overdue, Niko was man's own lesson in the making. What forging the gods had in mind for the ore that was Nikodemos, Tempus had never known for certain.

The Storm God wouldn't say and the other powers who vied with gods in the world did not confide in Tempus. That had always been a matter that Tempus was willing to leave alone.

But now, looking at the city stuck in the sea at the edge of time, Tempus felt his own life-force shudder. Was Stealth worth the price of entering that city? Was the wisdom in Nikodemos great enough to risk Jihan's life in the world, and his own, to save it?

Mortals could become immortal in the city, legend said. But what happened when immortals entered it? Neither he nor Jihan were sustained by the same rules as the men who'd founded it.

A superstitious chill crawled up the Riddler's back to lodge where his spine met his skull. Death, should it come, he would welcome. Agedness, infirmity, senility or stasis. . . . these were other matters.

How old was Jihan, by the world's measure? As for himself, he'd stopped counting long ago. He must think carefully and go slowly.

And when that was done, he must tell the Froth Daughter, who thought he knew everything, that he did not know even if, upon crossing into the city, they would have bodies with which to help Nikodemos if he needed them.

For all Tempus knew, when the shadow of the city fell upon his horse and its rider, all that would remain in the saddle would be crumbling bones and ashes too old to scatter on the wind. Jihan might become a gust of salten spray, soaking into thirsty earth.

Or, worse, they might be put in thrall by the city, or end up lifeless yet undead in its museum. Or, worst of all, become mortal where they stood.

Their temporal candles could start to burn. They could lose everything that made them effective in the world, that made it possible for them to teach the tribes of men.

They could, in short, begin to die with the city the moment they entered it. And, unlike Nikodemos, they might find themselves, from the first moment they stood there, with no hope and no escape.

As the gray horse picked its way down the hill, Tempus mused up at the city and it stared back at him, gleaming, content with his decision to come or stay away. His eyes ached from looking at it, as if the city's light was pulling them out of his head.

His hands slipped on his reins, and not simply because of the marsh gas and the mist in the hollows of the flatland that shouldn't have been so extensive. The closer they came to the city, the farther they realized it was.

If hope had wings, Tempus' own soul had made it so. He needed to bed his horses, eat a meal with a hot posset, touch Jihan where she hated it, and in general affirm himself in life. Then he would go out and see if he could talk to the god about this matter.

Although he could never tell if the god would answer, he had no doubt that Enlil was here. There were too many men and too much strife in this place for the god to pass up his chance.

If truth be known, there was enough disquiet in Tempus' own heart to summon gods and devils from near and far—even so far as the depths of his very soul.

CHAPTER 8: TOUR OF THE CITY

Tabet took her beautiful stranger out into the city through the Horse Gate when the sun was high. Light loved the city, always. Today it seemed the very heavens caressed her beloved home and the man she'd found to share her life in it.

Sunrays split on the castle's electrum ramparts and cascaded from its gleaming ivory cornices to the pavings below. Shadows were banished memories underfoot. Silvered windows reflected an eternity of sky and cloud and boy and girl walking the street between. Everywhere she looked she saw herself and the tall stranger, hands linked, strolling in the light.

The city was a hall of mirrors today and she had never loved it so well as when it showed her the man of her dreams by her side. For Nikodemos was no boy, and she must remember that. The bounced reflections on the broad Processional Way showed her that truth, as it had always showed truth to the rulers of the city when they sought it.

Here the chariots rolled on Festival Day, multi-
plied by the facing facades into great armies. Here
the king walked on New Year's and Harvest and
Remembrance Eve, and became a thousand kings,
head of his line of reflections as if head of a dynasty.
Here the gods awaited their meals on every solemn
holiday of thanksgiving when the temples of red and
white and black stone were filled with worshippers
bearing gifts.

And here Tabet would be married to the stranger,
Nikodemos called Stealth, as soon as Father could be
persuaded and propriety allowed. So it was not scan-
dalous that they walked the hallowed, cobbled way
while the sun was high and all time held in abeyance. It was not anything but a fine omen of things to
come. While the sun was high, the heavens could be
persuaded to a royal will, so the family who ruled the
city had long believed. When the sun was high and
shadows banished, the world was like the city—
eternal, unchanging, and perfect, without bias or
slant, stripped of everything but the pure fierce joy
of being.

Thus her father would forgive her for walking this
hallowed street with her beloved, even though the
enactment of this ceremony had not yet been sanctified by king or god. They would stroll this way again,
holding hands with high-held heads, while all the
people watched someday.

Someday soon. Perhaps tomorrow. Today, Tabet
did it for herself, and for the god, and for the universe she'd grown to think of as a friendly force that
heeded every hint she gave it of what fortunes and
what future should be hers.

A third of the way down Processional, Niko asked
softly, "How is that we haven't seen a single soul
here? What kind of place is this? It feels . . ." He
shrugged when she looked up into his eyes and he

finished a different sentence than he'd begun, ". . . odd, being the only ones on the street this way."

"It is the noon meal," she scolded lightly, not lying, simply beginning her answer with a different truth. "Everyone's at home to eat and rest and ready for the wane of day."

"The wane of day? The day's still young." There was a slight frown between his brows, and she saw habitual lines there from squinting into distances she could only dream of. She looked into his hazel eyes and thought she saw a glimpse there of chaotic battlefields and feats of valor in pools of blood.

She closed her own eyes and looked away. Thinking of where he must have been and what he must have done in his young life made Tabet uneasy, yet what was hidden in his past excited her. Here was a man from beyond who was a hero, a warrior, a fighter who had fought the gods' battles in the world.

This she was not imagining. He had spoken of fighting for a priest, and her own priest, Jamad, treated him with special care—with caution, and with respect. This man who had so much boy in him had an edge of iron to him so sharp that all the men who had the city's welfare in their care were whispering together about what to do with him.

Tabet smiled at the thought and saw Niko's brow smooth. She, Tabet daughter of Genos, knew exactly what to do with the stranger. And she had done it. He was theirs now. Hers by right of blood shed and betrothal given. If he was fearsome, he would be fearsome in behalf of the city, not against it. If he was an omen, that omen would read forever in the favor of Genos' family.

She knew she'd done the right thing, giving herself to Niko. It had been so clear to her that no word or thought or danger could have prevented that moment when they lay, flesh to flesh, on a bed above the stable and became one as the sun rose high. It remained only to tell her father and teach the city's wisest that there was wisdom in their princess. She was no longer a maiden; she was no longer a child. With this boy—with this man—beside her, she would take her rightful place among the city's steersmen, as she'd been born to do.

Their uninterrupted walk down Processional Way confirmed it. The sun smiled upon them. The windows of silver gave back reflection upon reflection of them, making them a multitude of lovers in an eternal light of purity and grace. Even the bronze mirrors, down where the Storm God's temple was, showed them without ripple or distortion or even the slightest hint of heaven's displeasure. If it had not been right with the universe that she and this man be walking the Way together, legends said that clouds would come to obscure the sun and mist would blow in the streets and the very weather gods would have fogged the mirrors of their souls.

For that was what the refractions and reflections and diffractions of Processional Way represented: the soul of the city was bared in this place; the life of the city was prognosticated here at holiday time.

If their love had been wrong, someone would have come to stop them, if nothing more numinous occurred. No one had. No one had even noticed them on this most hallowed of ceremonial byways. No one had come shooing them from the palace or the sanctuaries of the city's gods or the wizard's lair which opened onto the square they now approached. Not even a hawk or eagle had circled above them as they strolled the entire length of the Way. If a bird had come, she would have had to think again: to take note of its passage and direction, or whether it circled or dared to swoop, and whether its shadow crossed their path. But there had been no shadows, beyond those in Nikodemos' change-color eyes.

Looking into them, she realized she had to say

something, that he was waiting for her to respond. She said lightly, "The day's still young, as you said. But the morning's done. Its shadows have disappeared. Its hegemony is over. It has, in essence, died. It is the magic moment of zenith, when the city and the world are one, when there are no shadows to say which way time goes or which way the world turns or if it turns at all. We believe that when the shadows come again, the day begins to die."

It was a long speech. She smiled at the end of it uncertainly. Had she revealed too much? Were her beliefs too different from his?

His face was very grave, yet held a boyish curiosity that made her heart glad. "Surely there's more to your beliefs than metaphor. It takes more than metaphor to keep men off a street as fine as this."

And without thinking, she stepped into his trap and told him the truth, without fear as to whether the truth would frighten him away from her. "This is a ceremonial way; we use it only for royal and religious processions. And for high rites of passage such as investitures and accessions and—"

"Marriages of the royal sort," he finished for her with a shake of his head that made slate-colored hair fall across his forehead. He took his hand from hers to rake it back. His angular face was carefully arranged. "Tabet, I told you, you know nothing about me. And I know nothing about you or your city or what demands your culture might make—"

"We will have the Storm God, your lord, sanctify the matter as you and I have sanctified the act." She spoke carefully and firmly, knowing her future as she now envisioned it was at stake.

"You know that I was not—that I do not—trifle with you. But there is the test, and so much unspoken between us." Again he squinted, and she saw the first shadows of the afternoon take root below his eyes, as if the sun were moving away from them, displeased at his words.

"This is no place for such talk," she admonished him, suddenly cold. "The heavens listen to what is said on these cobbles. Laws of man and nature come together here. Here you must be firm. Here you must be true. Here you must have only the result you desire in your mind, or ill shall come of it. Here you must say again that you love me and you are my husband, in the gods' eyes and the eyes of man."

"With Enlil as my witness, Tabet, I made a wife of you back there and I won't turn away from that—not the responsibility, not the consequences." His voice was tight and his lips hardly moved as he spoke.

His eyes, though, seemed to go beyond her, to something in the distance, something back the way they'd come, toward the Horse Gate and the palace. "But by the Storm God and my oath as a fighter, I don't know the rules of this game. And you're not helping. What does this mean?"

And he put his hands on her shoulders and turned her with ineluctable strength, so that she was facing back the way they'd come.

Three men were coming toward them, robed men walking abreast down the holy street.

"It means," she said, not knowing why she did, "that we must get off the street. We don't want an argument under the eyes of heaven; we don't want the ears of fate to be tempted by overhearing discord."

"Fine. Where to?"

"There! The temple of Enlil, where the rules you speak of should be the same for you as for me." Hearing his voice and not seeing his face to temper the impression, the latent violence in him came through to her as never before. And yet, she told herself, he was simply responding to her need and his sense that she felt threatened.

He took her by the elbow and nearly spun her

around, moving her toward the temple three doors down so quickly and firmly that she didn't even protest that turning their backs on the approaching threesome might not be the best idea, after all.

As he led her up the tiled stairs of the Storm God's temple she nearly tripped upon a single orange carp lying in her path. She kicked it with her heel as he hurried her, and it flopped a little as it fell to the stair below.

Then there was no time for wondering about fish where fish shouldn't be, for the dark majesty of Enlil's temple enfolded them like a cloak.

Talk about shadows! Here was nothing but. Overhead were great wheels on fire with a hundred tapers in each, and a vaulted roof above, where the great god fought the terrors of the underworld for the greatest prize of all—the free will of humankind.

Enlil fought the dragon, and Enlil won. Enlil fought the ravening demons of the battlefield, who grabbed at his chariot's wheels and died under them. Enlil fought the stone giant conceived by a jealous god who was his enemy, and Enlil subdued that giant with his mighty arms and his fine-forged weapons. And Enlil, in that moment on that ceiling, had the face of the boy/man called Stealth.

The very visage of Nikodemos, proud and full of war, stared down at her from the heights of a ceiling whose paintings were as old as time itself, and Tabet felt her knees grow weak.

There were benches in the chapel, and she reached out for one as Niko let her go and stood spreadlegged. "Now what?" he asked her in a hushed voice.

With the cold stone bench beneath her, solid as the ancient rock it was, her nerves steadied. Yet she hugged herself as she looked up at him, and beyond him, at the god with his face so high above. From this angle, the resemblance was inarguable and she began to shiver.

"Now what? Now we wait. When they come, we listen to what they have to say, and we say what we have said to one another." Who was this person who spoke to Niko? She'd never been so bold in all her life. Though her legs were still weak from the enormity of what she'd done and what she'd seen, her determination was so strong that it seemed to her she was guided by another, stronger will.

She looked up, beyond Nikodemos, so much like the god in the chiton and robe that a stableboy had brought for him, and saw the god in his manifold feats above them, and the god with his wife in their supernal home. And this buoyed her. What was there in life but choice, and risk, and the taming of chaos?

If the god had sent this stranger to her—even if the god had come to earth disguised as someone named Nikodemos—then that was no more than confirmation of all she'd felt. If fate had a hand in her life, then she must realize it and not be afraid. But she knew then that when she'd lain with Nikodemos, she'd done so as a child and when she'd arisen from that bed, she'd done so as an adult. She was no longer a girl, a mere princess, for mere princesses did not enter into the temple of the god with a lover who bore the god's visage.

She straightened her shoulders as the three men who'd followed them crossed the threshold and turned to see who they might be.

"Father! Crevis!" What was the seer doing at her father's right hand? "Jamad, I brought Nikodemos to see the sanctuary of his tutelary god . . ."

The priest fixed her with a blazing glare. "Princess, this is not a feast day, when women are allowed in this temple. If you'd be so kind as to leave—"

"Oh you're wrong, Jamad," she said with that strength that seemed to come from deep inside her. "This is a feast day, and will be one henceforth. It is my betrothal day." She stood up and approached the three men.

Her father was letting the seer whisper in his ear. He hadn't spoke a word against her yet. There was still time to make this moment her own, to show the heavens what she, Tabet, required of them.

"Father, I have walked the entire Processional Way with my betrothed of the heart, Nikodemos, and no shadow fell upon us. No person interrupted us. No evil befell us. When you appeared, we were already at the end. I sent word to you—"

"Tabet," said her father, a hand on the seer's shoulder to silence the whispers, "how could you do this without consulting me first? Go back to the palace and wait there until I return." Her father crossed his arms, slipping his hands in his embroidered sleeves.

"No, I won't," she heard herself say, and she found herself at Niko's side. His hand pressed against the small of her back.

The stranger said, "King Genos, I wish we'd met some other way. I'm Nikodemos, called Stealth, man of the Storm God, sojourner in the World, and I ask your hospitality in the name of Enlil."

Genos scowled. The seer whispered once again in his ear. Enlil's priest moved away from the king and leaned against the temple's doors. His eyes kept flicking from Tabet's beloved to the painted ceiling high above, and back to Niko.

Then her father said, "By formula and ritual, you are welcome in the house of the god which I, the king, keep for Enlil's pleasure and his glory in the eyes of the people." The ritual phrase uttered, the king's voice deepened: "But you are a stranger, about whom we know nothing, and it is our custom to test strangers here."

"I have been told that. I do not seek to shirk my fate," Niko said.

Tabet could have boxed his ears. She stamped her foot and said, "Daddy—"

"Hush, girl!" Genos replied. "Then so be it. But how then, can you boldly stand here and touch my daughter in my presence, knowing that your fate is uncertain?"

"The fate of every man is uncertain. My lord king, you know nothing about me, and I understand your concerns. But sit with me and I will answer all your questions. Be assured that the god is in my heart and my intentions toward your daughter are honorable—"

"Tabet," interrupted Genos, "you cannot expect to announce your betrothal to this stranger before all my questions are satisfied and he has passed the Test; even he sees that."

"Father," she said, "I am already betrothed to Nikodemos, not merely in spirit, but in flesh. If truth be known, here where words go no farther, Nikodemos has already become my husband." Her head was high as she spoke, but her hand went to her belly. And her voice trembled as she added: "You cannot prevent me from marrying this man before the people, since my body has already married his. No matter the outcome of the Test, I demand my right not to be shamed or refused the husband of my choice."

"You'll likely be a widow before the ceremony," said Crevis—outrageously, bluntly, and without a thought for her feelings.

She looked askance at the seer and then at her father, wide-eyed. "Are you going to let him say such a thing? How can he say such a thing? I demand that my betrothed be moved into the palace immediately, as I sent word to you. I want this Test business settled properly and I do not want you, Father, to listen to this old . . . mummer. . . . this fakir, this fortuneteller above the wishes of your own blood daughter."

"You know I can't do that, Tabet," said King Genos. And: "Now apologize to our noble Crevis, who has only your best interests at heart."

"My best interests?" Tabet echoed on a rising note. "What if I am with child? What if I bear a prince? Does he not have the right to a father's name? Is this man, a warrior of the god, not a suitable father for my—"

"Tabet," Niko said and she stopped as if his one word had dried up all of hers. "This is now a matter of negotiation between men, of custom and decorum. Please let me speak for myself."

"All right, then. So be it. I leave you men to your drink and your talk and your power games. But hear me, Father: I want my betrothed comfortable in the palace by nightfall. And you, Crevis: obstruct me and you'll make an enemy you'll not be able to take lightly. And you, silent priest of the god under whose eyes all of this flummery is taking place: if you are not craven, a corrupt creature of politics, you'll listen to the god's will, which I have heard in my heart, and protect Nikodemos, his sworn adherent, with every fiber of your being and every means at your command."

And she stomped out with a backward look at Niko; by Crevis with her lip curled; past her father with a wet and blazing glare that promised tears in a river should he disappoint her, and out the door of the temple.

Down the steps into the day she strode, and paused.

The fish was still on the steps, but its bright scales had faded to a muddy brown. Everywhere, the light had gone out of the day. A mask of cloud hid the sky like a featureless veil.

She didn't go back the way she'd come. She was too wise to risk the results of retracing her steps, dejected and alone, and having that reflection fed back along the many-mirrored way. She cut into a side street and came out near the market, where she shopped for bright silks before she headed home.

When she did finally enter the palace, she had the makings of festival garb for a marriage couple of royal blood under her arm.

She would not settle for less. The Test would not harm her beloved. She would not allow it. She would get help—from her father, from the priest. And if not from them, from the warlock, if necessary. There was nothing fixed under the sun, and no force in heaven greater than the will of a princess of the city who had fallen in love.

Chapter 9: Understanding

"Is this how you repay my hospitality, stranger?" King Genos wanted to know.

At least they'd left the god's chapel. There was something about having arguments over deflowered daughters and dangerously obscure tests where the god could hear that made Niko nervous.

He'd dealt with distraught fathers before. He said, "She would not be forestalled, my lord King." The dignities came hard to his tongue, after so long with Tempus and the armies, but he'd met his share of monarchs. He kept trying to tell himself that this one was no different, that he had nothing to fear here beyond the exigencies of the Test and the normal machinations of power that abounded in city-states.

But he knew different: he could feel it with his *maat*—something here was very dangerous, in the way that a witch who loves you or a dream lord who seeks your soul is dangerous. He was sweating under the light chiton and cloak that Tabet had found for him, here in the back rooms of the temple of the god.

He wondered what Tempus would say if he could see Niko now—lost in a city that time had forgot, dealing with men who lived as if civilization had just begun, who let the old ways and the old rites guide their lives, and who never for a moment thought themselves out of touch with the grace of the gods they served.

A soldier who'd been sorely tested, Niko could feel the certainty and the desperation in these men and it frightened him. They were men whose orderly lives were threatened, men who had lived a manifested mandate from the elder gods, undisturbed, for centuries while progress passed them by. They had been untouched by the World for millennia, and now the World was reaching out to touch them. Niko, who'd tumbled into their midst at exactly the wrong moment, was fast becoming a symbol of the chaotic forces that threatened them.

He could see it in their eyes. He'd looked into the eyes of the lord of dreams, into the eyes of revolutionary priests and fighting warrior-monks, and into the eyes of madmen and those whose souls were possessed by evil, and he'd never seen anything more unpredictable than the three before him, with their surety and their fear.

For long moments after he told King Genos that his daughter had forced herself upon him, there was silence around the bluestone table.

Then the monarch cleared his throat. "That may be, soldier, but you see our predicament. We know nothing about you but what you tell us, and that is precious little. My daughter wants to make you a prince of the realm. You must admit it's . . . unlikely . . . that someone from your world should come into mine and become a member of a royal family which has existed for . . . so long."

"For thousands upon thousands of years?" Niko said softly. "She seems a mere girl. Are you telling me she's older than these hills? That—"

"You will not understand time as we perceive it," said the seer as if he'd read it in a scrying bowl.

"Niko," said the priest, "again I say to you, you must answer our questions, not interrogate us."

The king held up his hand. "There will be time, once the Test is done, for us all to learn what we must learn. The Test is what counts."

"I don't know yet what you'll ask me to do."

"Survive," interjected the priest of the Storm God, and for the first time Niko thought of him as a possible ally.

"And the betrothal?" Niko pressed what advantage might lie in the uncomfortable silence that had followed the priest's blunt observation. "Tabet, your princess, is right—there's no need to make her suffer. Surely a widow's better than an unwed mother, even if the mother's royal." He didn't want to marry the girl, especially; but then, he didn't want to take the Test. And if there was any way out of the one, it involved the other.

The father's aura came clear to Niko suddenly: troubled, full of red and green, palpable anger and doubt. "I'll move you into the palace, stranger, that I will. Under guard, you'll be. You'll not see my daughter again without a chaperon. And you'll cooperate with your priest, here, and my other advisers. We'll take this marriage under consideration." Genos pushed himself to his feet. "Under close scrutiny. Meanwhile, you and your priest will prepare a list of credentials, at the very least, that show you worthy to be my son-in-law."

He turned his back on Niko and headed for the door.

The seer rose to follow, caught his king, and whispered once more in the royal ear.

The priest raised a hand a few inches from the table when Niko opened his mouth. He closed it without bidding the king farewell.

At the door that led into the temple proper, Genos turned. "There'll be no cancelling of the Test, Nikodemos called Stealth, no matter how my daughter schemes or cries. Whatever you think you're doing here, the Test is the reason the gods sent you. You may think you've circumvented me, but hear this: my whole city, every soul and all its history, weighs upon the balance scale on one side; the Test and its taker weigh on the other. We stand to lose it all, and we'll fight to keep what no other city has: our special graces, our wisdom, our perpetuity. Against that, what my daughter wants is as a leaf in the wind. Be warned. The Test you must take, and in the end it matters not at all to the greater scheme of things if you take it as a bachelor or take it as a married man."

With a swirl of his cloak, King Genos turned in the doorway and was gone, his seer trotting along beside him.

When there were no footsteps resounding in the temple, the priest put his chin on his fist and grinned slyly at Niko. "Well, stranger, shall we get at it? Let's find something about you the king will like, and find it before dinner."

"I think it's time you tell me about the Test, since it's all the king cares about."

"If you're a true man of the Storm God, Enlil will tell you what you need to know, judge your heart, and scourge it if you're found wanting. Don't they teach it so out there among the barbarians?"

"My commander would say that the barbarians are everywhere, but especially here," Niko pointed to his own heart. "And there." He pointed to Jamad's.

The priest did not smile. "Let us begin, Nikodemos called Stealth. The man who deflowered Princess Tabet can not come to a palace dinner the way he came into her heart—naked and full of trickery. There must be something about you we can say when we introduce you to the people."

Niko thought, Tempus, this calls for your skills, not mine. He wasn't much with words. He said, "My war record's good enough, if your people care about that. Sacred Band fighters are consecrated pairs, under the Storm God's aegis . . ."

Explaining the World to someone who was no more a citizen of it than the secular adepts who'd raised Niko apart from it—this was an impossible task. Explaining more was unthinkable. He gave a list of battles and glorious units, skirting his brushes with magic, and saw no flicker of recognition, let alone satisfaction, in the priest's eyes.

So he said, after an interval of dutiful recital during which the priest scratched on a clay tablet with a stylus, "What I am, priest, is a weapon of the god. It's what I was trained to be in the World; it's what the World makes me whenever I step into it. Here, I could be something else, I think."

"Something else?" said the priest, and his head came up sharply.

"I was a student of the old ways; I still am. If this place is as its legends say, I could bring a certain grace here, from disciplines I've studied and mysteries I've pursued. I'm no master, but I am a diligent student. In a place where time is not the enemy, I might bring some worthy knowledge."

"You really don't understand, do you, mercenary? Can we hire you to unmire the wheels of our city from the awful swamp into which we've sunk? We're facing destruction, here. Later, I'll take you to the tower and show you the sea. Perhaps then you'll understand. If we cannot find the heart the god wants, all is lost—all we know, all we are, all we ever might have been."

Niko said, "If the god brought me here, it's for

that reason." He met the priest's eyes squarely. "To save this place or seal its doom. It's up to you, the citizens, not to me, to make that choice. I told you, I'm merely a weapon of the god. And I'll tell you this: in Enlil's place, sitting with a consecrated priest, I should be getting the help I need. Think on that, friend, and what it means to the future of you all."

CHAPTER 10: RITE OF THE VIRGIN

Seth was first among the warlocks of the city, wisest of the wizards, the only one among them to have seen opportunity in disaster and seized it, when the king had called his advisors together that day the city had materialized on the shore of the neverending sea.

From that day, the warlocks had all but run the city in the king's stead while Genos sequestered himself in the tower. From that day, Seth had been preparing for this moment, when he would consolidate his gains and face his fate.

He fingered the stocking on the desk before him, and a sweat began to break on his brow. He stroked the strands of the princess's hair that her brother had brought him, and his concentration became so great that the dark sanctum about him seemed to fade away.

Prince Macon was a fool and a doomed fool at that, to give up his sister to the warlock, even after the boy had realized he wanted to supplant his father.

For that was part of what was at stake here: the kingship of the city. Whomever married Tabet could claim that right of succession, if the husband but knew the ancient laws and had the will to enforce them. Having all but ruled in Genos' stead since the city became enmired at the end of time, Seth had acquired a taste for ultimate power.

In the face of imminent doom, it inspired him. For that was the rest of what hung in the balance as the city teetered on the edge of destruction at the end of time. The prophecy was unequivocal: the city must be made fast against invaders, lest the soulless one of legend come and suck the very heart from the city and it become trapped forever in the mundane world—dying daily as did all the lesser haunts of men, and all its population with it.

Immortality had seemed Seth's birthright; he had known nothing less. He could not give it up. Power had seemed his due since the day he'd donned the robes of a novice and begun his climb up the rungs of his order's structure; he knew lust for nothing else.

Nothing else had ever moved him, until this crisis presented him an apprentice in the form of the king's eldest son, an apprentice who came bearing gifts.

Should Seth succeed in marrying Tabet, he would be a wizard-king, a warlock whose word was law not only unto his lesser mages, but unto the city entire.

And though the city might yet be doomed, no wizard could refuse an opportunity like that. If the stranger, Nikodemos, was the soulless one, then the city must fight a flaming battle to survive, should the prophecy hold true. If he was that one, it had been an error of gargantuan proportions to let him live even this long.

But the error had not been Seth's. Under his stewardship, the city's gates had been locked and no stranger admitted without careful scrutiny and immediate testing. A man who fell from the sky in a rain of fish was not a man one could keep outside one's walls.

One's walls. The phrase echoed in the warlock's inner ear and disturbed his concentration. The room about him, dark and filled with shelves and scrolls and shards of bone and pottery, closed in upon him, solid and real once more.

The battle for Tabet's heart was between him and the stranger, since her brother was an idiot, a principled fool who could not admit his own lusts even when the warlock faced him with them. The boy had had his chance, and chosen to become Seth's apprentice to save his sister, rather than admit he longed to wed her.

The bloodline that had ruled the city since creation was growing thin. A warlock's seed would be a strong infusion. If one read the prophecy with a certain bias, one could interpret its words to mean that the city would be transmuted, transmogrified, not destroyed utterly. A heart was at the center of it, that was certain.

That heart could be a woman's heart, not a man's. The heart of the city must not be sucked out by a stranger. *War will be in the hearts of men. And death will fly over the city as She has not done in millennia. Pluck a heart from a stranger, if the king loses his, and give it to the god if it is not his already.* This had been the true wording of the prophecy. With prophecies, wording was everything.

Death was something Seth could not conceive. He was a true child of the city, born to live forever. He was a warlock to that end, the city's true protector, sworn to its continuance. If the time had come for a warrior of the city to rule from its high towers, then so be it.

If that meant marrying a princess of the realm, then he would sacrifice even his eternal celibacy to that end. And Macon's life, for that would be the sure result of a royal wedding, when the prince realized what his dim wit had overlooked.

And death *would* fly over the city—Macon's death, the stranger's death, perhaps even King Genos' death.

Seth stirred his fingers in Tabet's stocking, suddenly uneasy as the path before him became clear. He was becoming a motive force of the very prophecy he sought to turn to his purpose. He was acting in harmony with a reality he sought to avoid. But he knew better than to attempt to forfend fate, or underestimate the magic of belief.

Everyone in the city had seen the endless sea; all felt their peril. So many frightened minds summed an inertia of unstoppable force. If Seth had not been a warlock of talent, he might have quailed at the task before him, that of harnessing the steeds of fear who drew the city's chariot to the brink, and turning them onto a path he had chosen.

He was an initiate of a brotherhead as old as the sky, as strong as the earth, as fated as day following night. For untold years, the city had lived in peace and her magic had been dedicated to maintaining that harmony. But other magics were taught to warlocks. Magics of conflict; magic of confluence; magic of sympathy; magic of the dark night and the darker mind of man and god.

There was no true peace without war. The city knew the value of strife; she had fought her way to peace and gotten a stranglehold on eternity, early on. She had rolled through the worlds of men and shaken off their misery with a flourish of her skirts, but never been ignorant of it. The city's greatest prize was her special gift: the gift of life among the cities of death.

All the wisdom of the city's years resided with her warlocks, those few souls who were all that remained of her warrior class. It had been thousands of years since the city had needed a champion to fight for her. Legend had it, when last she had, that the man had been a warlock as well as a warlord.

The city's shape was that of a circle; her waterways spoked out from the round hub of her metropolis, to end in a great rim of sparkling current. She was every cycle of man except the end of all cycles: death.

The warlock whose soul had been dedicated to a war with death itself could not turn away from this battle, from the final turn of the great wheel, for it was his job to keep that wheel turning, if he must grease it with his own blood.

He sighed. For the first time in hours he moved more than his fingertips along the pilled silk of Tabet's stocking. He moved his whole right hand from his worktable, into the drawer beneath.

From that drawer he took an obsidian blade, as old as the city itself. The man who'd chipped it from its quarry, who'd used flint to flake an edge on it—that man was dead and gone when the city learned to cheat death. Some said he'd been its first warlock, that it was his death that had given the city life.

The blade had no hilt, no ceremonial handle, no pommel of jewel or bone. It glittered in the torchlight of Seth's sanctum with a light as old as time itself. He fingered it gingerly, holding it at eye level, his fingertips meeting where it flared widest.

He rubbed it for a time, his fingers always carefully far from its razorsharp edge. He fancied that in its rough surface he could see the city's past, as many warlocks before him had thought they'd seen the banished days of strife there.

The city had learned to live forever; it had not always been even so much as a city; it had not always known the magic of peace. Peace had come from wisdom; wisdom had come from the hearts of its rulers, and then from the hearts of its citizens. Greed

had been banished first, then foul fury had been
driven from the gates. Grudges had followed, with
vindictiveness slithering behind, hissing like a beaten
cat. Thievery and murder had gone last, hunted from
door to door and cast out like lepers, into the world.

It was said that the city had spawned all the ills of
men and loosed them upon the world as it cleansed
itself. It was said that what had been driven out
would someday return.

It was said, too, in whispers in the back rooms of
the warlocks' fortress, that the gods were responsible
for the evils of men, and the wizards born to fight
them.

For years those ancient writings had seemed rote
lessons, for there had been peace within the city and
strife banged vainly on her gates from without. During
those years, Seth had always been restless, never
content. He'd known in his heart he'd been born for
some great purpose.

Now he knew what that purpose was. He was the
warlock of which the secret writings spoke, the man
who would fight the final battle for the heart of the
city, and walk through the flames of consuming passion
to defeat the soulless one.

Or not.

No prophecy had been written beyond that point.
No wisdom had been given for what might lay beyond
a final confrontation. Most of his order thought the
prophecy apocryphal in any case.

But they had not, as Seth had, felt the fatededness
in their own souls.

He sighed deeply and brought the ancient blade
close to his lips. He kissed it once.

It was warm, not cold.

His breath moistened it, and as he drew it carefully
away from himself, keeping it level the entire
time, he thought he saw men fighting there, among
the hills and valleys of its fashioning. Everyone is

born for some purpose. For most, the purpose is death. For Seth, the purpose was the war against death.

"Death," he spoke in ritual phrases he'd learned without wondering if he'd ever utter, "thou art my enemy, my vassal, my servant. When I say to Thee, 'Go hide thy face,' Thou shalt obey me and begone. When I say to Thee, 'Come, strike down mine enemies, my will shall be Thine. My commands shall be as Your leash and as Your harness. My words shall guide You to the fields for Your tilling. Wherever I point, there Thou shalt descend upon Thy black wings and unmask Thy horrid face. Thine eyes will blast mine enemies. Thou shalt be my sword and my shield, my vassal and my slave. Forever."

And he let the fingers of his right hand close around the obsidian blade from the beginning of time. "This virgin, Tabet. let her be mine and mine alone." Then, holding so tightly he cut his palm, he drove the blade in his right hand into his left, which he held over Tabet's stocking.

A scream rang out, as if from a thousand voices. One of the voices was his, but his throat was only one throat of many throats whose anguish he could hear.

He clamped his lips together and the sound stopped.

He looked at his trembling left hand, from which the obsidian blade protruded. He forced himself not to faint. He grasped his left wrist with his right, to stop his wounded hand from shaking.

The blood must fall in exactly the right place, in exactly the right fashion.

He felt no pain, though the obsidian blade protruded from the back of his hand, and from his palm. He felt nothing at all, as if the hand belonged to another, as he centered it over Tabet's stocking, on which hairs from her head, carefully arranged, glinted in the candlelight.

He took another deep breath, and it roared in the silence of his sanctum.

Then, abruptly, for his stomach was beginning to churn and his vision was growing grainy, he brought his left hand down, hard and fast, upon the stocking wound with hair, saying, "With this blood, I thee claim. With this knife, thy virginity I pierce. With this spell, I thee wed."

The force with which his palm struck the stocking and the table beneath should have sent the knife up and out of his flesh, caused it to exit cleanly, the way it had come.

His right hand was poised to catch the blade as it flew out of his flesh.

But it did not fly from him. It remained, its point driven through the hair and the stocking and into the wood beneath, his hand joined to all by that means.

He tentatively tried to raise his left hand, and a sudden pain washed over him, nearly stripping him of consciousness.

He had nailed himself to his desk with the obsidian knife of antiquity. It would not come out of his hand.

He tried not to panic. He could pull it out, of course. He would endure the pain. He would pull the bloody obsidian up through his left hand, using the fingers of his right.

He would. He could. But it was all wrong. Something had gone wrong with the spell. The knife should have sprung up when it struck the stocking, and landed cosily in his waiting right hand. The lesion in his left hand should already be healing. All that should be left were a few drops of blood upon Tabet's stocking—a single sign that the spell had worked.

But it had not worked. Something was dreadfully wrong. More than just the pain, which shouldn't have been there. More than just the fact that he'd impaled his hand. More than the difficulty of getting the knife out of his flesh when his righthand fingers were sticky with blood and the obsidian so slick.

Something was wrong with the ritual.

Seth swallowed hard against rising bile. In his mouth, saliva spurted so distinctly he could feel the jets of it coming up from beneath his tongue.

Before he dealt with the repercussions of an ill-cast spell of such antiquity and power, he had to free his hand.

Biting his lip and not knowing he did, he wiped his right hand repeatedly on his robe while sweat rolled down his forehead into his eyes.

He took deep breaths, his gaze fixed unblinkingly on the horror of his impaled hand. Then, with all the discipline his order's training had given him, he began levering the blade from his flesh.

He had to work the tip loose from the wood. He had to rock the blade back and forth, using his left hand as well as his right, which was clenched around the flaring edge of the blade.

He could not look away. His fingers kept slipping. He could feel the blade grating against the small bones in his left hand. He feared for his tendons, and felt the knife lick against them.

There was no other way to do this but the way he was doing it, short of cutting off his own hand or calling for help. Neither alternative was acceptable. So he sat for what seemed like hours, rocking the blade back and forth, pulling with his right hand and trying not to further injure his left.

Finally, he felt the tip loosen, somewhere beneath his flesh and the stocking. He continued his circular, pulling motion, trying not to consider how much bigger was the hole in his hand than when he'd started.

He cursed a steady stream, but did not notice. He never thought of what it might mean to curse everyone and everything involved with the warlock's own training, while in thrall to a spell gone bad.

He controlled his pain, every surging, redhot wave of it—that was enough. He controlled his temper, all its ice against the fire of his blood. He controlled his fingers, where some other man might have lost the capability for fine motor skill.

And eventually the blade came free. It popped loose and burst upward through his flesh in response to his fingers' demand with a sudden and surprising force that caught him unprepared.

The slippery blade slipped from his grasp and went flying through the air to shatter against the corner of his scrollcase.

He stared at it in horror, his wounded hand, wrapped in Tabet's stocking to control the bleeding, cradled against his chest.

But he didn't get up to retrieve the pieces. He was dizzy. He was uncertain of the consequences of what he'd done. He was more frightened and more angry than he'd ever been in his whole long life.

He sat for a time, staring at the shards of the priceless obsidian blade, of the token from antiquity that had always seemed to symbolize the warlocks' mandate in the city.

Then he cleaned up the blood on his desk, and wrapped the now-red stocking more tightly around his wounded hand, picking Tabet's hairs out of the sopping folds before they were sealed in his wound by serum and clotting blood.

Finally, he collected the shards and when he was done, he went to the window and called to an acolyte:

"Fetch Prince Macon here, immediately. Accept no excuses."

The sun was setting. The sky blazed like the pain in his hand. Blood seemed to smear the clouds.

Seth waited for Macon with black murder in his heart, too overswept by emotion to remark its sudden coming.

He understood now why the spell had not worked.

The price he had paid to learn a squallid truth was one that not he, nor all of the city, could afford.

It was so simple, it had never occurred to him to ask, or to check, or to make the dithering prince find out the truth of it.

And now he had destroyed the talisman of his order, opened himself to unknown peril by trying to cast a spell where one could not be cast, and nearly ruined his own left hand in the process. If he needed an omen, his ravaged hand was more than omen enough.

When the prince arrived, the fury in Seth had not abated, for it was a fury that had come to him with failure, and with error, so complete a fury that there was no part of him not consumed by it. Therefore, no part of him could even remember a time when it had not been boiling inside him, except as a time before extraordinary measures had been called for.

Thus the warlock snarled at the prince, before the youngster had even crossed his threshold, "You fool! Do you know what you've done? Do you know how you'll make up for it? Do you have any idea what price we'll all pay for your folly and that of your whore of a sister's?"

Macon stopped. His open, friendly face flushed and then drained of blood. Clutching his cap, he stepped over the warlock's threshold, strode up to the desk, and said, "Take that back . . . what you said about Tabet—"

"Take it back?" Seth rose to his full height, all dark fury such as the city had never hosted since it began to roam. "Take it back? You fool, the spell went wild because of her whoring! You're an apprentice, now. Do you have any idea what kind of price all involved will pay?"

Macon reached across the desk and caught the warlock by the collar of his robes. "Take that back, I say. My sister's—"

"Your sister," croaked the warlock as, with a shrug and a deft movement that brought his forearms up to break Macon's grip. "Your sister isn't a virgin, fool! That soldier's got to her. Or perhaps it was someone else—a stableboy, a lardseller . . . perhaps it was you!"

Macon stood, openmouthed and frozen, his fists clenched in midair over the warlock's desk. "It's not true," he whispered in horror.

"It's true. And it's going to take some extraordinary measures on your part to put things right . . ."

"Then there's still hope? For Tabet? For me? For you and her, I mean. For the city . . ."

When the boy had stopped blithering, the furious warlock said, "There's always hope for the city, fool. Unless and until it becomes a city of fools, there will always be. When last we met, Prince, you said your maidservant, Matilla, would help. Find out where the soldier is now, tell the maid to bring all his soil to you—every bit—and to watch him, whatever he does, wherever he goes."

"That's all?"

"Then come back to me, apprentice, for your next lesson. And find your courage, wherever you've hidden it. Blood will spill, I assure you—more than the blood on Tabet's thighs."

"But . . . shouldn't I tell my father? The stranger, he's violated my sister. He's . . ."

"Tell no one. Find out who knows what, if you must. But this a matter for wiser heads, for magic and fated purpose, not for the meddling of—

"But he's raped my sister!"

The warlock seemed to ignore the Prince's outburst. "A matter for men, not boys. This is my wife to be, we're discussing." Seth's face seemed to clear of suffused blood. He looked at the prince very pointedly, without blinking. "If Tabet was raped, we'd know of it. We must assume the circumstances to be otherwise."

"That bastard. That seducer. I'll kill him. I'll—"

"He will take the Test, never fear." The warlock came around his desk, took Macon by the arm, and hustled him to the door. "Go instruct the handmaid. And find out what you may, while telling no one anything. Then come back to me with word."

The prince left with only a bit more prompting.

Seth was content to wait, pleased with the interview. His fury was under control now, well banked and giving a great, exhilarating heat.

He almost lost control of it again when Macon returned, stuttering that there was to be a feast this very night, a feast for Tabet.

"And for the stranger," continued the prince miserably. "She's calling it a 'betrothal feast,' my sister is. And my father's going *along* with it, and so's Jamad, that snivelling priest, and even Crevis, the seer. And they all *know* she's not a virgin anymore, I can just tell by the way everybody's acting!"

"I wish I had known," said Seth under his breath. Then, louder: "We shall go to the feast, prince. Did you do the other things I asked?"

Macon nodded and confirmed that Matilla had agreed to help.

"Good. There is time. There are widows, not in the city, but in the World. The stranger is from the World, a mortal with a test to take. A Test, I promise you, he'll fail. A Test with death at the end of it, as prophecy demands and honor dictates."

This time, Seth didn't have to dismiss the prince. Macon was backing away from him, young eyes wide, stammering promises of fealty and excuses that he was wanted at the palace.

No matter. Seth would see him there, by and by.

Chapter 11: The Betrothal

The betrothal feast was laid out in a massive chalcedony hall full of art and craft whose splendor could no longer be equalled in the World.

Nikodemos had been enough places to know why: the colossi of horses and rams and bulls and wolves were made by sculptors working in a harmony whose knack was lost among the squabbling peoples beyond the city's walls. Community of effort had produced the vibrant rugs of millions of knots which floored the place with subjugated demons whom the king of the city hunted through wooly hill and dale filled with mythical animals. Consonance of heart had fashioned the great electrum inlaid doors and polished the massive cedar columns which held a roof painted with every star a man could see in the sky, each in its proper place, as if the collected wisdom of the city had come from every hilltop on all the earth, and all her wanderings had been recorded by faithful scribes.

It was the most magnificent room Niko had ever entered. In it he felt the nobility of not just the city's dwellers, but the whole heritage of man. The melancholy that swept through him as he entered that chamber was so deep and wide and tender he nearly wept. On the misty isles where he was trained, adepts struggled throughout their lifetimes to regain a glimmer of what the city knew; to rekindle a spark of the fire that burned in the hall's gargantuan hearth, where logs rested upon the backs of glass-eyed dragons with smiling snouts—for it was a fire totally in balance, like the room around it, neither destroying nor creating, but warming with what seemed like a sentient pleasure at its task.

Like the fire, the entire room and everyone in it appeared complete, content, controlled. Their hospitality, so rich and warm and gracious, seemed an effortless expression of the continuity they represented.

What the adepts on Bandara would have given to stand where Niko stood, to gaze upon this place whose loss the whole world grieved, without even the wit to know it did so. This city was a secret that had opened to him when its princess embraced him, and in the celebration hall he felt none of the threat that he had in the Storm God's temple, when the king had demanded his credentials.

Yet Nikodemos called Stealth was not fooling himself: he could die for reaching so high above a soldier's station. He was not so overwhelmed by the beauty of the hall (and the softness of the carpets and the antiquity of the statuary and the melodies of the harpists and the pipers) that he underestimated his peril.

But danger was what Niko ventured into the world for, always. Often, with less reason. Until he had come here, he was without so much as a glimmer of hope that his effort, or the efforts of all men like him, could ever make a difference, restore even a spark of the light that lived here to the darkness that was without.

In his heart, a slow and like fire to the one in the far wall's hearth began to burn. It was a fire of rejoicing, that the city existed. No longer did he doubt that Tabet was who she said, or Genos who he said, or the city what it claimed to be.

He had seen his own face on the young Storm God's likeness in what was arguably the first temple of Enlil ever raised by man. Niko was not one to discount omens; since the balance of *maat* had come to inhibit him, consonance and coincidence had special meaning to his soul.

If the city were all that his senses told him, and all that his education proclaimed, and all that its dwellers thought that it was, then it was in as much danger as was he, here at the end of time.

Ever since he had become a Bandaran fighter, a man of the Storm God, Niko had risked his life as a matter of course—never gladly, but in clear understanding of the necessity of someone risking something so that everyone did not lose what some did not even know they had. It was his burden in the world to do so. He'd risked his life for no better reason than physical survival. He'd risked his soul's survival on matters of principle and honor that mattered to no one but himself—and perhaps to his commander, Tempus, who tutored him. He'd risked his access to Bandara, his spiritual retreat and his soul's lifeblood, for friendship with a mage. He'd risked his place in heaven for the love of an evil witch. He'd risked his spirit's restplace, his sacred soul's retreat, when he'd flouted the very lord of dreams. And he risked the Storm God's displeasure and a warrior's afterlife, trying to balance all of those.

Yet none of that was significant—not the pain he'd gained for it or the scars he wore from it or the wisdom he'd learned because of years spent fighting the battles of *maat* and god in the physical world—

when weighed on the scales of his belief against the city's survival.

For it was *the* City—the beginning place, the eternal place, the place where all the good that gods had allotted man resided. The first would be the last, so legends said—when the city died, all that made man deserving of an immortal soul would die. The hopes of the World lay in the city's survival. The fact that it languished here, its great wheel mired in an endless sea, was what had brought the melancholy sweeping over Niko, so deep and so wide that he had stopped in his tracks, gazing at the hall with eyes that had never seen so sad, yet so wondrous, a sight.

He trembled now, blinking hard. Sometimes a sunset would strike him thus, and he must gaze at it, mark every instant as it changed, blazed, faded and died in such eternally ephemeral glory.

He could not stand by and see the city's sunset, be here only as a witness, one from outside who'd topped a hill at the right moment. His *maat* knew his fate when it saw it.

He wasn't frightened, though his pulse beat fast at the enormity of the responsibility, and the task, before him. He was elated that here, at last, was something truly worth risking eternal night to save. His god was here, young and virile, if Niko had needed more proof, wearing Stealth's face in a temple older than the language which had given him his warname. His commander would be here, when the time was right, as Tempus always was where fate was supposed to be.

If Niko lived that long, to look Tempus in the eye and ask the Riddler to solve this riddle for him, then Nikodemos would be blessed.

If not, to fight for the city in the service of his god would be an honor. To marry its princess, more so. To take the Test and live through it or die from it was no longer, in his mind, an option or a matter of choice—it was a duty.

He'd been tested all his life. Sometimes he'd told himself it all must be for something, that the universe did not torture him for fun and spite, but for its own good reasons.

But he'd never let himself believe it. Not until now. Now that the reason for his years of conflict and loneliness, disappointment, suffering and loss had all, in a moment, been revealed as training for *this* moment; now that he had found the place he'd never thought to find, that his studies had told him no man found except in afterlife—now he could not take a step farther into it. He was rooted to the spot.

Tabet tugged on his arm. People were watching them: long eyed folk in gauze and velvet; folk with ancient faces; folk with knowing eyes in which fear had found a place, but never crowded out grace or honor or generosity.

These folk of the city would make him welcome without proof of who or what he was. They would fete him and greet him and put him to the Test without demanding even that he save them, through life or death or force of arms.

They . . . *were*. They simply were. And they knew the joy of that. Niko could see it in their auras, all the blues and golds that rippled through the crowd as men and women moved about.

They felt, they longed, they tasted and listened and ate and laughed; they satisfied their hungers of the flesh—and all with such attendance on the moment that Niko's heart beat fast as he put his arm around the princess's waist and let her lead him through the crowd. They were present and accounted for, and in fear only of fear.

There was a tinge of that fear around their auras' edges, where the shine of them was laced with dark. All their long spans they had husbanded the races, kept the faiths, learned their lessons and taught them widely, if secretly, through emmissaries they sent wandering in the world and worldly wanderers who stumbled on their secret place. They knew life and loved it. They were not obsessed with becoming anything, but they wished to continue to *be*.

This love of being, this full and complete art of living that showed on faces all about him, should not be lost. They knew it.

And he hoped they knew that he knew it.

There were eyes that slid away from his, in case he should die in their Test. There were eyes that dwelled on him too long with sympathy, empathizing with his burden, as if they'd known him in the world.

And there were eyes that simply could not leave anything unseen, eyes that drank your heart and yet left it fuller.

What risk was too great to save a roomful of folk such as these? If there had been one person, in the World entire, so wise and so alive, so free from despair and yet so comprehending of life's anguish, Niko would have settled at that one's feet and stayed there, never lifting up a sword, to learn a different art than war. But in the World there had been only Tempus, the Riddler, the black immortal who taught that war and death were humanity's lot and that personal honor was the only prize in a world full of men who continually disappointed even themselves and failed to meet even their own standards.

In the wizard-ridden towns and in empires of barbarian kings, in the black mountains where unnatural enemies lay in wait for unwary human souls, on hilltops housing gods and in valleys hosting demons of hideous aspect, Tempus' way and the way of the misty isles had become one for Nikodemos: there was no better truth than the Riddler's; nothing but the inner peace of your restplace and your soul's survival was worth preserving.

The City had been a legend, a wisdom tale for telling round the cookfires of arduous campaigns, a sea story come from far beyond Innanna's distant shore. Tempus and the god they both served were all too real, abroad in the night and formidable in their might.

The World was wide and full of woe and mystery, but the world had room for only one legendary City and it was clothed in myth, else no one would ever have done anything but trekked their way to here. The pilgrims would have circled the earth threefold, and nothing would have been as now it was, beyond these walls.

Within them, Tabet's honeycolored hair tickled his nose as she swung around to face him: "Here comes Father! Remember what I told you."

The shadows in her eyes struck him like a demon's tail. The rulers here carried more than their people's burden: more cares, more travail, more pain and less willingness to accept their fate.

"Don't worry, Tabet. I've been on the sword's point my whole life, and never been mortally cut."

Tabet's wisdom was farther back behind her eyes than that he'd seen in the others: she was a young girl in love, and even here love made demands to weigh down the lightest heart with impossible longings. He forgave her that, even before she responded to what he'd said.

When she did, it was after three blinks of those hungry eyes that seemed to want to take him inside her on the spot. "You are saying that you will triumph, because you always have? *We* have always been the guardians of the city, of wisdom's flame, the everliving proof that man can shed his baser natures—and look what has happened to us now."

"Perhaps all of you are not so pure," said Niko honestly, remembering the warlock. "Magic is a tricky ally. It corrupts . . ."

"Power cannot be unused; its proper use is man's true lesson; its benefits cannot be lost because of its dangers; its connections are what make us a society; its responsibilities cannot be shirked because its conduits are degraded."

"The city's catechism?"

"Some of it," she replied. "The warlocks serve the gods in men, as the priests serve the discrete gods outside us. Without magic, what use would we have for our divinely-given will? What is healing, but magic? Architecture? Art—the bringing of a vision into concrete form—is magic. And the working of one will upon another . . . that is the wellspring of individuality and its power, through the conduit of the god-knowing mind."

"Right," he said, to forestall her. The wisdom of the city was rarefied; hearing it from a girl who'd snuck into his bed, scheming to be deflowered, confused him. Women, in the world, did not think so deeply. In Tabet was more contradiction than Niko liked.

But then, if he were to marry anyone, it never would have been someone less. Yet a mind behind those eyes was something he hadn't expected, even though he'd seen the like in the city's women among the throng and not been startled.

Tabet was a king's daughter. She was wise beyond her years in all but matters of the flesh. She had chosen him as her champion with a naivete and a surety which at once attracted and repelled him. He knew at that moment that he'd have married her if she'd been a shepherd's daughter.

But no shepherd's daughter could ever have spoken those words to him. He searched for her hand, laced his fingers in hers, brought those fingers to his lips. "I'm honored to be your choice," he said. He'd never been much with those sorts of words.

She flushed and looked away. He thought he heard

her say, "You're the city's choice." But he wasn't certain, for she was dragging him, by the lacing of their fingers, into the crowd of her friends and neighbors.

Everywhere she led him, people smiled at him with those smiles that asked nothing more than acknowledgment in return. People offered their names like gifts and he strove to remember each and every one. He met a weaver and a silversmith and a stoneworker and a farmer of millet and a farmer of hogs. He met the royal baker and the royal vintner. He met the family servants, who were as regally dressed as any among the crowd and who offered him to eat and to drink as if the palace was each servant's home.

Which it was, he realized.

He was settling into the rhythm of the festivities when he saw the warlock enter, then the priest he'd met, and then Crevis, the seer. Each had others of his kind around him, and these looked at Niko as a man might look at a lion he'd captured to set loose in the forest to rid the glens of tigers, but who might yet raid the stock pens instead.

The whole mood of the hall changed. People seemed to draw into themselves. The music became more somber. The fire in the hearth seemed to dim. Sconce flames flickered wildly as a gust blew through the hall.

And all of that was nothing, compared to the chill that overcame him when Tabet's grip upon his arm tightened and she said, "So, we must see who among them are our allies, yes?"

She was not a girl tonight; she was a diplomat. He had to remind himself that she was a princess of this realm, accustomed to court intrigues, or he'd worry that all since he'd come here had been illusion—that he was in the clutches of a consummate witch.

But she was no witch; she was Genos' daughter.

She'd told him that the city valued power in its leaders. He mustn't assume that this was a city of wizards, a city of adepts, or a city of ghosts. In it were only men—men at their best, perhaps, but men nonetheless—with hierarchal structures and complex codes of behavior that harnessed, but never eradicated, those very strivings which in the World often brought out the worst in mankind.

In the warlock, the worst was well defined. Or Niko's jaundiced view of magic cast a pall over the man. In the priest, Jamad, he saw more hope. In the sturdy seer named Crevis was only fate and the whimsy of the gods.

It was these three who would administer the Test. That was why his skin crawled when he saw them, Niko told himself. But crawl it did. And his euphoric musings on the best of the city collided with his pragmatic distrust of the three courtiers and made him stiff as Tabet dragged him over to greet them.

"Crevis," he said to the seer, choosing him as the first, acknowledging the unknowable result that the diviner represented. "How did your omen-taking go?"

"For the morrow?" said the seer. "Storms and interruptions, Nikodemos, as I said before. Fete while you may, man of the Storm God. For your sake, I hope you're all you proclaim."

"Yes," said the warlock. Seth did not wait for Niko's acknowledgement, but inserted himself both verbally and physically, stepping close so that Niko and he were nearly nose to nose, his hip brushing Tabet's as he did. "Your credentials, I hope, will please King Genos. From my meditations, it seems your presence disturbs certain . . . powers here."

"Those powers are always disturbed by men who seek balance and harmony," said Niko carefully, unable to ignore the sorcerer's challenge.

"It is the god's choice of Nikodemos which matters," the priest interjected in a deep but hushed voice. "The god and the rising sun and the city's life will all come together with the dawn. A storm is fitting, don't you think, Princess?"

Tabet's hand tightened on Niko's. "My betrothed will please not only my earthly father, the king, but my father in heaven—the gods of the earth and sky and storm and the gods of wisdom and perpetuity."

"Please is a small part of what is at stake here," scolded the warlock.

"Nikodemos," said the priest at the same time, "I must talk with you before we sit to dinner—about your speech."

Niko hated to leave Tabet with the warlock and the seer, but that was clearly what Jamad wanted, and the priest was his only clear ally among the administrators of the Test.

"Excuse me, then, all," he said and went with the priest, off into a corner where great tapers were impaled on tall, free-standing holders of iron fashioned like giant oak trees.

"Did you see the warlock's bandaged hand?" Niko asked the priest. "What could have happened to him that magic couldn't protect him against—or heal immediately?"

"Our magic may be different from that of the World, Nikodemos—I'm no expert on anything but the god's will, and sometimes, I think, a novice at divining that. Tonight, let's worry about your statement. We'll worry about Seth tomorrow."

But the whole time Niko was refining his speech, his introduction and presentation to the representatives of the city gathered to hear of the princess's betrothal and meet her intended, he kept his eye on Seth, who never once moved away from Tabet. Never once.

Three times did the warlock put his bandaged left hand to the small of the princess's back, where it rested against her spine far too long to be considered decorous in the world from which Niko had come.

There was no chaperon to stand between those two, as there had been, all day, whenever Tabet would contrive to see Niko once he'd been moved into the palace at her father's command.

Until they'd come down to the fete hall, they hadn't had a moment to themselves.

And now. . . .

Niko nearly left the priest to intervene. He hardly heard what Jamad was saying; a dark instinct of sorcery suffused him. He felt the breath of witchery on the back of his neck. His *maat* rustled in him, disturbed. From his restplace, down deep inside him, a superimposition of storm clouds masking awful shapes flashed before his eyes.

He said, "Jamad, I must—"

But at that moment, King Genos entered the hall from some secret door behind the hearth.

The band stopped; the drummer beat a great copper kettle spread with skin; a fanfare rolled over the room.

And the people, instead of bowing or kneeling as might a court out in the World, clapped their hands together softly, and welcomed their ruler as one might a returning warrior or a long-lost friend.

Genos wore a long coat of colors, strips of rainbow hue radiating out from its collar. That collar was set with ornamental stones in a sunray pattern. On his head he wore only a plain gold circlet. In the crook of one arm he carried a scroll.

He bowed his head in ceremonial fashion, an acknowledgment to his wellwishers, and strode alone, at measured pace, to the center of the hearth.

There he turned his back on the crowd and slowly knelt before the fire. Still with his back turned to the people, he said in a voice that carried throughout the hall: "Hereupon to the fire I give the list of the city. May it burn to heaven. May every name upon it reach the ears of the gods."

There was a silence among the courtiers now, broken by only a single murmur, as if from one throat, that told Niko how unexpected this burning of the list was.

Still kneeling, with his coat of colors spread out like the rays of a prism set before the sun, silhouetted against the blaze in the hearth, Genos continued: "My daughter, who is Tabet, daughter of Tebat, favorite of the Earth Goddess, beloved of the Adad of Heaven and the Adad of Wisdom, Princess of the City, is a child no more. As the list that contained her as a maiden and ward of the Host of Heaven is destroyed, so let the restrictions set upon her as a maiden priestess of the Earth Goddess be destroyed. Let her freedom be lifted up to Heaven as the smoke of this list is lifted by the winds of the Storm God."

Genos paused; his arms and shoulders shifted. Niko could just see that he took something—another scroll—from beneath his robes.

King Genos continued, in the silence marred by not so much as a cough or a whisper, "Let the list of the city reflect this truth: Tabet, daughter of Tebat, daughter of Genos, favorite of the Earth Goddess, consort of the mighty warrior, Nikodemos, the Valiant, lord of Bandara, man of the Storm God, is Queen of the city from this time forward. May the Adad of Earth and the Adad of Heaven, the Storm God and the God of Perpetuity and the God of Wisdom, bless this union and make it fruitful."

Suddenly, in a ritual fashion, Genos turned toward the dumbstruck throng. He took the scroll he held and put it to his forehead. He kissed it with his lips. He held it out in both hands, parallel to the floor. And he said, "Queen Tabet, rule beside me forever." Then he took one hand from the scroll and held it out to his daughter.

Tabet cast one look at Niko, a wide-eyed look he couldn't read. Then she slid away from Seth, who was whispering in her ear still, and walked at processional pace toward her father.

Niko sidled over to Jamad and whispered under his breath. "What's this? What's happening?"

"You were just betrothed," Jamad whispered back through unmoving lips. "The hard way. Genos is no fool. He's made her Queen in her own right. They're co-rulers. If you marry, you might become a prince, but not a ruler while Genos thrives. Right now, you're a consort in the king's lists of the city—good enough for a stranger who may die on the morrow. Solves the propriety problem, in case she's pregnant. But it doesn't necessarily advance our cause."

"Our cause?" Niko hadn't been aware that there was one.

"If you pass the test, or fail it, the Storm God should reign supreme among the deities of the city— only the Storm God can save the city, as I read the prophecy. Tabet's tutelary deity is the Earth Goddess." The priest shrugged. "Whomsoever she marries, it would be well if that one were a favorite of Enlil. Of course, if it's Genos she weds, then the god would be satisfied."

"Genos?" Niko's voice was too loud. Several of the court glanced at him askance, then away, to where the newly crowned Queen minced forward to greet her father, the king, as co-ruler for the first time.

"Genos can marry his daughter, the Queen—ceremonially or actually. It is well within our laws to do so. It may be the thing the gods demand, for all I know—the true sanctification of his kingship, a ratification the city needs of his right to rule. Our last queen ran off with a creature of the world."

"She can't marry her father," Niko said, and crossed his arms.

"Then pass the Test, soldier," advised the priest. And: "Of course, now that she's queen, there will be other suitors—Genos is no fool. He's taken the advantage by this move."

Niko didn't care about royal politics. "Other suitors?"

"The queen's husband is powerful—more powerful than a princess's. Look at Seth; he'll ask her, at least, to consider him in your stead. Then there's the prince, who'll never rule as long as his father does. . . ."

Nikodemos felt a sharp pang at the absence of his sword on his hip and his throwing stars and the dagger, all his panoply come from the lord of dreams. Though no whetted edge could have helped him win this day, he missed their comforting weight: they were part of the world he'd left. Even on the misty isles, when he buried them beneath the ritual gravel, he'd known they were there.

He longed, too, for his sable horse and the wind in his face and all the things of a life that seemed to him lost forever. Marrying Tabet was his to do; the god had put him here, decreed it in a rain of fish and fate. But this strange city with its ancient codes was changing him with every breath he took here.

He didn't like it. The wisdom he cherished was here in force, but it was wisdom from another time, and for men of finer sensibilities than his own, it seemed—men that could condone ritual marriages of daughters to fathers or brothers, and co-regencies between the sexes. . . .

What had he fallen into, here at the end of time?

Tabet reached her father's side and took the scroll from Genos. She faced the crowd and smiled, but the smile was a frozen one like a death mask or the wide smile of a fox run to ground as he makes his stand against the hounds.

Her stare came to rest on Niko and the force of it was a physical jolt that moved him a full step backward. By the look of her, she'd had no idea that Genos would make this surprise move.

That was something, anyway—she was still the girl

who'd thrown a leg over him above the stables, not some wily, ancient crone in a child's body who'd seduced him and tricked him and now meant to sacrifice him to her hungry eyes and the city's gods.

She said in a voice that trembled only slightly, "People of the city, I, your queen, greet you. Under the tutelage of the gods, I beg you pray with me that my rule be fruitful, my judgments just, and my mind guided by the God of Wisdom in all things."

She closed her eyes and bowed her head. Genos followed suit. As did, it seemed, everyone in the hall but Niko.

Then he caught Seth staring covertly at him. So there were the two of them, watching while everyone else in the room watched only their inner images of the gods.

Seth raised his hand to Niko from across the room and the challenge in that salute was unmistakeable.

Niko answered it. When he turned away he saw that Tabet, too, had opened her eyes. She shook her head at him and frowned.

Then she closed those eyes once more and intoned, "With your blessings, my people, all things good will come to our city during my stewardship."

"*Long rule to Queen Tabet,*" the crowd intoned without any discernable cue.

"*Long rule to King Genos,*" they added, and Niko realized how old this ritual must be.

Then Tabet said, "People of the city, you know we are in times of travail. Let me introduce to you my consort, Nikodemos called Stealth, a lord from a world away, who has been brought by the gods to aid us."

So much for Niko's little speech. Genos had precluded everything they'd planned to say, changed all the rules to a game in which Niko had not been coached by his priest.

"Get going," Jamad muttered urgently.

"Up there. Look, fool, she holds out her hand to you."

"But what about—"

"Forget all that. Do as she says. She's the queen now."

He knew that. He walked, stiff-kneed and self-conscious, through the courtiers who made way for him like a sea parting, and up to Tabet and her father.

He took her outstretched hand and let her maneuver him, as gracefully as she could, until he stood on one side of her and Genos on the other. Then she said, "Nikodemos will take the Storm God's test tomorrow. May your prayers and ours go with him." She took her scroll and pointed it at Niko.

Then she closed her eyes. The crowd did the same. Then they said a solemn prayer for his success —or for the city's deliverance from peril through "his strength, his heart—the heart of a stranger—and the divine aegis of the Storm God who has given us leave to test a man upon his altar."

He couldn't tell if Tabet were playing some role, or if she really was different, somehow.

When she opened her eyes and signalled with a pious word an end to the prayers, she returned the scroll to her father, who brandished it once and said, "Let the betrothal feast begin."

At once the musicians resumed playing. The people chattered to each other. Servants grabbed up trays of food and drink. And three men in palace robes came to take the scroll, dragging a little golden wagon with a velvet pillow on which Genos carefully laid it.

"Dance with me, Niko," said Tabet, a cool smile on her pretty face.

He took her in his arms and over her shoulder saw her father, with the seer and the warlock clustered

round him. The three stopped talking as soon as the
priest of the Storm God joined them.

Niko said, "Why didn't you tell me?"

"Betrothed is betrothed, isn't it? Anyway, I didn't
know. No one knew, except perhaps Macon, since
he declined to come and is somewhere sulking. It's
not nice to offend the new queen by denying her
your presence on her betrothal night."

"Your brother might have been detained by some
detail . . ."

"Macon is a spoiled brat. No longer can he lord his
male primacy over me." He craned his neck to look
at her and she was beaming with a wicked satisfaction as she continued: "Seth told me that Macon had
refused to attend when Daddy told him. He'll come
later, of course—he must begin consolidating what
power remains to him."

Niko nearly stepped on her foot. Things were changing too fast for him.

She said, "Don't look so grim, beloved consort.
Now we can sleep together and no one will talk.
We'll need no chaperon. We have a night of pleasure
to enjoy together."

"And in the morning?"

"The Test." She shrugged in his arms. "You know
you're fated. You told my father's advisors so. And
me. I couldn't have stopped that in any case. Nothing matters as much as the fate of the city. As you
said, you've lived on the sword's point all your
life. . . ."

He pulled her close so that he didn't have to look
into her eyes, which now kept him out of her thoughts
as concertedly as before they'd tried to pull him all
the way into her.

Most were sitting down to eat when Macon arrived, bleary-eyed and obviously half-drunk, with an
old serving wench by his side. These two went straight
up to Seth and the serving wench led the warlock

from the room. Macon ignored his sister, sat down heavily in King Genos' empty chair, and called for, "Wine! Wine, more wine, and still more wine! This is a night to remember that I want to forget as quickly as I can."

Macon cast a threatening look at Niko, and a furious one at his sister. She merely twirled with Niko on the dance floor and pretended nothing was amiss.

Niko didn't know what to make of it. His powers of observation were useless here, where the implications of the events he witnessed were too foreign to be understood.

But he knew that a Queen was different from a princess. And he knew that King Genos was looking at him with amused satisfaction, with a conqueror's gleam in his eye.

Something here had gone Genos' way—everything had. And Niko was less and less sure that any of what had occurred here tonight boded well for him. His priest, Jamad, was downcast and solitary, clearly fretting.

Near daybreak, as the crowd was thinning and the revellers beginning to stumble in their stained finery, Niko saw his chance to take Jamad aside and ask some hard questions.

But no sooner had he slipped away from Tabet to collar the priest than there was a commotion outside.

A herald picked up the cry and called from the doorway secreted behind the hearth, "Strangers, King Genos! Strangers at the Lion Gate!"

And everything stopped in the great hall.

CHAPTER 12: WEAPONS OF THE GODS

Stormclouds were massing above the city in the predawn light as Tempus and Jihan waited to be admitted.

The walls of the city were tall and as thick as the bodies of three men. Legend had it that three men were buried under each gatepost, to make sure the walls would stand.

But those men, if they ever existed, and that legend, were memories from prehistory. The city was now. Real. It towered above Tempus as if sprung from the solid ground beneath his horse's feet.

The promise of unnatural storm, massing in the sky overhead, was almost comforting, compared to the manifestation of the city in this place. In his path, Tempus amended gloomily, trying not to listen to their horses' screams or Jihan's ranting.

The horses were merely reacting to the storm blowing in off a sea that was lord of land and time and space itself, a storm just barely holding itself in abeyance so that every hair on Tempus' body stood on end and his skin felt as if a multitude of insects crawled upon it. Niko's horse, ponied behind Jihan's and carrying only the lost warrior's gear, whinnied loudest of all, riderless and skittish, its sable ears pricked forward at the walls like ready arrows.

Jihan's carping was another thing. She didn't like being made to wait while sentries consulted higher powers before admitting them. Nor was that all that troubled the Froth Daughter:

"I don't understand, Riddler, why you brook such insults. We shall ride up to the gates and I shall freeze those men to living icicles. Then we can enter where we will—if we choose." She turned to him and her eyes glowed fiery in the first rays of dawn, which ran along her scale armor and her gleaming skin and made her seem a woman of molten bronze, lining every muscled inch of her inhuman beauty. Her threat was not idle: she was a creature of the sea and it was a cold sea, the very sea beyond the city's back. Her father, when he'd send her to dwell among the living, had endowed her with power over water, and over heat and cold. And there was a lot of water in mortal flesh.

Tempus couldn't have her freezing the denizens of the city willy-nilly, destroying it out of hand with a plague of ice. Not with Niko in there. Not until they'd done whatever the god wanted here.

So he said, "We must wait, Jihan, to be invited. This is an ancient city, filled with ancient folk, not the sort to offend—or to confront unnecessarily."

"Hrmph. You may be afraid, Riddler, but I am not." She crossed arms on which light ran like water along muscles better suited to a soldier. When Jihan was angry, she attracted him most of all. Her hair whipped around her face and made the sprite seem even wilder. Or proximity to the endless sea did. Jihan was yet a water creature; her father's power was close here. Her temper and her nature too had grown fiercer as they approached the citadel on the shore.

The white walls of the city towered over him, mute and taunting. Was it a final resting place, in there, for his ancient bones? The Storm God, when Tempus had asked him, did not say so. What the god thought, or what the truth was, were other matters.

On a hilltop back a thousand leagues, across the interminable plain they'd crossed in thrice the time it should have taken despite the ability of their horses, Tempus had consulted with the Storm God as he had not done in ages.

He had opened his heart to the god and his mind to the god and his body to the god. And Enlil had come to speak with him. The Storm God had brought his lightning and his thunder and his violence to reside within Tempus once again. The presence had wracked him and filled him with unslakable lust for life and war and carnal knowledge. The god had come into him and everything was clear, for one awful moment before Jihan had crossed his path.

Then lightning had licked around the two of them like a pack of hounds and all things degenerated into lust.

But in that moment, when the god's mind and his mind became one as happened only in the most awful battle or the most sacrosanct of ceremonial couplings, he had confirmed all he'd needed to know: this path was fixed, which had led him to the city; Niko was somewhere in its heart. And the Storm God wanted entry there, in the person of his avatar, Tempus.

The use that men made of their gods was not always what the gods desired. The Storm God, lord of war and rape and bloodletting, was hungry for the city's repentance, angry at the eternal place, and desirous of redressing a list of deific grievances.

Thus Niko, like a beacon, had been cast onto this shore for Tempus to follow. But the god was not careful of his creatures—not of Tempus, not of Nikodemos, a sworn servant, not of Jihan who had come from the sea. When Tempus asked Enlil what it would mean to his own survival to enter into the place, the god had laughed in his head so loud he thought his eardrums would burst.

Then the lighting which had made a bed for him and his unearthly mate had raised up a hundred heads like snakes and bitten him, driven him off while Jihan slept, and herded him to the hills' highest top above their bower.

There the god's roaring voice like thunder had formed words that echoed in his soul: "*How often have you begged to leave me, Servant? How often have you lusted after death and sleep and all the weaknesses of mankind? Now you petition me to protect you from mortality? Where is your vaunted humanity? Where is your courage, you who are the sword in My hand? Should the blade become eaten with rust, then what must I do with it? Go you into the city, and make reparations there. Bring back pious worship in its place, or neither the city nor yourself shall enjoy immortality anymore. All the gods will turn their faces from the city, and it will crumble. I will turn my face from you, and you will be less than dust upon the land. And all together, you unnatural children will perish. The underworld will open to eat you up. Demons will reach up from the sod to take you. Your horses' hooves will sink into My mire so you cannot flee. Disappoint Me, immortal mortal, and you will be as nothing, your memory itself lost to time, your soul ceded to all your enemies in Hell who burn sacrifices to secure it!*"

For the Storm God, that was a long speech, and an angry one. The god never made empty threats; the god was Threat itself. And as if Tempus were some fool who needed proof, Enlil had showed to his inner sight the horrors that awaited a fool who'd made a bargain such as his, should that man fail the god he served.

The vision, or portent, or fortaste of what might come to be, had not been pretty. Tempus had seen Strife upon her chariot, drawn by maddened, winged lions with claws of fire and ice. He had seen bodies ground under those wheels catch fire, and those flames lick up to consume the white walled city where it stood. He had seen Fury come down from heaven and smile at him through carbuncle eyes. He had seen every soul he'd sent to the afterlife queued up to greet him before the gates of Hell.

He'd seen his sister, riding in a litter with the lord of dreams, and she was beckoning. And Greed was there, wide-mouthed with sharp white teeth. Blind Cowardice ran before them, cringing, with Vengeance in hot pursuit. Deaf Vengeance wore the crown of Heaven, and had the faces of all the gods on a head that spun like a cyclone.

The many-eyed crone of Jealousy danced behind, surrounded by the hounds of Lies all in a pack. The hounds were driving a herd of fools beside them, and too many of those tortured faces were ones Tempus recognized.

When, in the vision, the lot had reached the city's walls, he'd found himself alone, shaking where he'd gone to his knees among the thorny bushes of the hilltop. He'd slumped down there, exhausted, drained as he always was when the god left him. But the god had never left him with such a vision before. Or with such true and deep fury in His heart.

Tempus did not misread signs. He knew himself too well, and the phenomenal world had always been his study. He had sat there through the night, resting, watching the city so near and yet so far. And when Jihan had come to find him, he'd said nothing more of what he'd seen than that Niko was surely behind the white walls they sought.

But Jihan could never accept a flat statement. All the while they'd traveled, she'd deviled him for explanations.

Now, as they waited for admittance before the tall cedar gates that had stood for thousands of years, she continued to demand answers he didn't have, to questions he would as soon not have broached.

Before the god had wrenched him from one dimension to another, from one reality to the next, life had been simpler. Among the vicious children of his last sojourn, he had been overqualified; an avatar, an adjudicator, a force like unto a force of nature.

Here, he was not sure what he was. Or if teaching lessons to these people would be so easy—or easily survivable. In former times, when he had been a power like unto the Storm God's in the land, a representative of heaven's darker side fighting incarnate evil and sorcerers of note, he'd amused himself playing with Death, thinking he wanted it; thinking his misery made him long for it; thinking life and love were curses and his accursed soul above their joys.

Now he was no longer certain that sleep and death were any answer. The god had lifted him—and his— bodily out of the world in which a sorcerer had cursed him loveless; even if the god had not, in the last few years he'd come to think that eternal loneliness was preferable to eternal sleep.

Jihan had taught him that. And Niko: Nikodemos, called Stealth, his rightful student and inheritor, the son he could not beget upon a woman, no matter how many women he got with child. Niko had taught him that in humanity was the spark he'd despaired to see: the eternal flicker of moral courage that made a man more than a beast.

Tempus no longer wished the curse of life removed from him. He wasn't even sure he hated the god and his raping lust anymore. This new place was full of mystery. If the city had not been there, he realized, something else would have raised up from the earth to daunt him. He was the god's servant abroad in the land, if he was anything at all but mouldering bones.

Here, there might be hope, where in the last place he had wandered, there had been only Nikodemos to presage it. And if the god were wild and thirsty for blood and vengeance, it was only because men were so disappointing to the supernal mind.

As mankind kindled its fires with each generation, as the previous generations' embers burnt out, nothing was lost if everyone remembered. This was never so clear to him as when he sat his spooky horse before the city which sat mired by the sea at the end of time and Jihan asked interminable questions not even a god could answer.

"But why is the city stuck here?"

"I don't know."

"Why did you say to me that I should avoid the seaside at all costs?"

"I'm not sure. Because your father might reclaim you there, perhaps. Then I'd have to pony both your horse and Niko's."

"Not because you love me, Riddler?"

"Love is denied me; you know that. Those I love will spurn me; those who love me, perish, if they are mortal. So beware, inside the city's walls." He was no longer so sure that this was true. The curse might well be lifted; or if not, a dimension between might counter its effect.

But it was his legend, part of his mythology, and he used it like a shield to save him trouble with Jihan, who when the moon was full wanted babies and a husband: him.

Her face grew petulant, her eyes downcast. She changed the subject: "How can you be sure that Niko's in there?"

"Listen to his horse scream a welcome, if you distrust my intuition."

And that was true enough. The sable stallion behind her gray was yelling his heart out, muzzle thrust up into the air and quivering.

"What does the god want us to do here? Save the city?"

"Maybe. Or say its last rites." There had been fire in his vision, fiery clouds and fire-built towers and fires that the god's lightning started.

"But don't we need to know why we're coming here? What if they ask us?"

"We're weary travelers, in search of a lost companion whose horse we lead. What more do they need from us?"

"If they are as you say—wise and ancient—they'll see through that."

"To what, Jihan?" He asked one question of his own; then another, out of pure exasperation: "What would you have me say? That the city's time is up? Could be. It needs a lesson, one the gods are teaching."

"You mean, that it got stuck here?"

"Or perhaps that we've been brought here. Inside it, don't lose sight of me. Don't let their wisdom sway you—it is a wisdom from the beginning of man, for man, and of man. They haven't been able to spread it on the Earth, so don't you take it to heart."

"You're saying they have come to this pass to be disciplined by angry gods?"

He forgot, often, how quick she was. He underestimated the inherent knowledge of a sprite of nature. She was not more than a driver in that female body, a manipulator of its charms—charms to which his own flesh attested at the god's whim and every other opportunity.

"Jihan, follow my lead in this. What is wrong in there, if it does not affect Niko, may not be our problem." The god rustled in his head and his gut cramped so that his stomach growled. "If the gods have been affronted," he amended, "then the Storm God will make it clear to us what to do."

"As they did when we helped bring down an emperor? When we set a mountain warlord up as ruler of a land wizards had held in thrall? If we're here for some purpose, Riddler, tell me straight out."

"We are here," he said very slowly and quietly, else he was going to bellow at her and jump from his horse to hers and wring her neck, "to reunite with Nikodemos, make a sacrifice to the Storm God as propriety demands, and get out without losing anything—not our souls, not a piece of gear, not our lives."

"You still worry over that, though you maintain the people within are immortal?"

"The *city* is immortal. When its people leave it, they leave that grace behind. Watch that when you leave it, if you do, you don't find yourself on the road to aged, wrinkled cronehood."

He loved to bait her. It was one of life's true pleasures. He'd denied it to himself because he'd been unclear as to their peril, and thus uncertain of himself and his ability to deal with what lay ahead— with what he was leading her toward.

Now, the god had confirmed his worst fears, and that made things easier: he asked nothing but to know what was required of him. Now that he knew it was mortal risk, a new game with high stakes and newer rules, he no longer felt the need to shield her. She was, after all, no weak woman, but a power in her own right.

"If entering through those gates makes me ugly, Riddler, I shall make a eunuch of you and petition my father that the offending parts never be allowed to grow back." She bared white teeth at him, while under her, the skittish dapple danced sideways and the sable beside it let out a barrel-shaking squeal that made Tempus' ears ring.

"Promise?" he called to her. "It would be worth it, to be rid of your pawing and posturing and the allure of your inhuman flesh, all at once." The god had, so far, let him regenerate whatever wounds he took.

Whether that would continue in the city, he could not fathom. But he knew what he sought here: Niko. And he knew what the god wanted there: a lesson taught. And he knew how to teach lessons, and how to tailor them to the quality of his students. It was what he did in life that had brought him to this pass.

For an instant, as a sentry leaned down over the wall and sunrays broke atop it, before the man called out "You may enter with the permission of King Genos and the best wishes of our newly-crowned Queen Tabet, who invites you to her coronation festivities,"—for a tiny, isolated moment before that, he wished he'd come alone.

It was enough to do to find Stealth and bring him out of there, while teaching the lesson of an angry god. To have the Froth Daughter's welfare in his hands, when he did not know how much of the god's threat was real, was more responsibility than he would have liked.

In that instant, he resolved to separate himself from both companions, should he emerge from these gates successfully, with both of them in tow.

Then the gates did open, a long slow process of winching and the pushing of many men.

What lay revealed behind those gates took his breath away. He'd been in the ruins of ancient cities, but never thought to see one standing in its prime, let alone filled with carousing folk.

There was a gatepost on each side of the gate itself, great square towers with arrow slits for archers who no doubt watched them closely as they rode their horses through. There would be an inner wall behind the outer wall, and a moat of rubble, he knew from his travels, between the two.

Once they were within the inner gate, twelve men closed the wings behind them, and an officer of the guard came up on either side of their horses.

One said to Tempus in the same ancient tongue the sentries used, "Queen Tabet and King Genos welcome you, strangers. If you'll come with me, we'll secure you lodgings, you'll have your interview, and then the queen has extended to you her hospitality on this day of rejoicing. Festive clothing will be provided, and you may join the celebrating of the queen's betrothal."

"We have come on a happy day," said Tempus as the officer of the guard reached up to take his horse by the bit and the gray snapped at the man.

The officer's shadowed face tightened. "We'll take your horses, lord. And your weapons, of course."

"Not of course," said Tempus. "These are ceremonial weapons, and priceless ones. Our warhorses will do damage to anyone but us. So lead on to the stables, captain. And then to our quarters." He threw a leg over his horse's poll and slid down it, to make it clear that no offense was meant.

Jihan, too, dismounted. She was as tall as the officer who stood on her horse's off side. To him she said, haltingly in the unfamiliar dialect, "Tell me about the queen's good fortune, and about your marriage customs."

Tempus winced inwardly. The very mention of marriage was going to start Jihan on an unwelcome tack.

It was that soldier who told Jihan, innocently enough although picking his words with obvious care, "Our new Queen Tabet, daughter of King Genos the Mighty in Wisdom, has chosen a stranger like yourselves for her acknowledged consort. Should she not be wooed away from him in the next seven days of revelry, the marriage will be consummated. If he passes the Test, of course."

"Test?" said Tempus to the captain beside him.

"Stranger?" said Jihan to the officer who walked with her.

Niko's horse let out a blast of welcome, rearing up on his hind legs, which surprised Jihan's horse, who shied. Only Tempus' mount stayed calm in the ensuing melee of horses' hooves and the scramble of folk from their paths.

When they had the horses calmed, the tether undone from Jihan's saddle, and the sable walking meekly between the two grays, Tempus asked again, "Test?"

The captain said, "You'll find out soon enough. We have a ritual test for strangers. The consort has not yet taken it. Once he does, I suppose it will be your turn, if he fails."

Tempus was about to ask what kind of test this was, when Jihan demanded of the man beside her, "Just who is this stranger that the queen is marrying? We're here looking for a friend of ours, the man whose horse this is. And you can see by the horse's behavior, he thinks his master's here."

"I don't know about that," said the soldier with Jihan uncomfortably, and looked for aid to the captain who walked with Tempus.

The captain of the city guard stared levelly at Tempus and said, "One Nikodemos, called Stealth, from the outer world. If this man is your friend, and that horse his, and those weapons also, then perhaps we should go straightaway to the palace."

"Then to the palace it is," said Tempus, still careful to cause no trouble, though he felt the walls of coincidence and fate rise up on both sides of him, higher than the city's, which seemed, from inside them, to touch the cloud-wracked morning sky.

Even from so near the gates, he could see the

ramparts of the central palace, and the street of temples at whose end the Storm God made his home.

And he could see Jihan's wide-eyed, voiceless query, which he answered with a shake of his head: *no more questions; go along with this—with me*. That was something to thank the god for: Jihan, in this most sensitive circumstance, kept her mouth demurely shut.

Niko's betrothal to the city's queen was another matter, for which no thanks were due to heaven.

CHAPTER 13: STORMCLOUDS AND INTERRUPTIONS

Macon stumbled into the warlock's quarters, more drunk than he'd ever been: his sister had named the stranger who fell from the sky as her consort; this was reason enough to get drunk.

It was reason enough for a prince of the realm to question his chief warlock without false and cloying courtesy, as well.

"So, Wizard, where's all your fine talk now about wooing my sister and keeping her in the city? Where? When will your fearsome magic dispell her infatuation? I'll be old from waiting, is when. Like when I'll be king. Father's made her *queen*, you know. He can marry her himself, so everybody's saying. Is this what your magic's wrought—"

Macon tripped over a stool in the shadowy chamber whose windows were covered with skins, righted himself only because he fell onto a reading stand, and blinked into the gloom. "Seth? Revered master of the arts, you in here? Your apprentice's come to call." He hiccoughed. His stomach lurched.

In the shadows, things were stirring. Seth was there, he was certain. Looking into that weird and unnatural gloom through drink-blurred eyes made Macon queasy, as if the floorboards under him were decking, as if the ground below were rolling like a ship at sea.

He blinked again into the dimness. Outside, the dawn was breaking. In here, all was mist and dank and indistinct. He thought he heard a mewing, like a baby's or a cat's.

He thought he saw a figure beside the one he was sure was Seth's. That figure was old and stooped and familiar—Matilla, the handmaid.

He was sure it was she. But the warlock and the handmaid were locked in a terrifying embrace and all around them thick smoke snaked, as if pythons slithered from shadow to shadow.

The mewing came again. The darkness in the chamber seemed to thicken. Macon's palms were sweating. They lost their grip on the reading stand and he nearly fell to his knees.

Arms outstretched and swinging to help him catch his balance, he stumbled forward.

And stopped as if he'd walked into a solid wall.

There was nothing there, but something solid would not let him take another step. His face was pressed against a nothingness so firm it felt like a wall of glass. His eyes strove to make sense out of what he saw.

He couldn't, for Seth would not be making love to Matilla, and Matilla never was so young or so fine as the woman Macon now thought he saw. And both of them were ignoring the prince's intrusion, and the ectoplasmic vipers from beyond the grave, and the creeping solid shadows which now took demons' shapes and clapped clawed hands like some delighted audience.

None of this could be happening, Macon told himself. He must have fallen asleep in the fete hall. He must have.

But the words he uttered as he burst into the warlock's chamber—angry words, insolent words, incautious words—still echoed in his ears.

And mixed with them were the mewing cries of the woman, or whatever it was, in Seth's embrace. Macon had never seen a man do what Seth was doing to a woman. What was natural to animals in the fields, and beautiful in blood horses in the stud barn, was ugly and horrid here.

Human limbs seemed too white and too hairless; human bodies seemed ungraceful, contorted, full of conflict as they joined.

It was the woman's body which troubled him most of all. It seemed to flicker, to shift its shape, to change as he looked on, a voyeur caught frozen in the act.

He felt remorse, embarrassment, and something deeper—a mortal fear of the unknown rite he'd stumbled onto. If he could have moved, Prince Macon would have snuck away like a scullery maid, down the back stairs and into the clean and honest light of day. He tried.

His feet were fairly rooted to the spot. He couldn't turn his face away. His neck muscles ached and cramped from trying. His eyelids would not close, nor could he focus anywhere except on the entwined bodies of warlock and woman and ectoplasmic snakes.

The woman could not be Matilla, Macon told himself with wordless fervor. She was too young, too blond, too fair of limb—too much like Tabet in her form. She could have been Tabet, but Macon knew his sister wasn't here.

His breath was coming fast, affrighted in his chest. For as he stared, the woman grew younger still. She began to shrink. Her limbs grew small and frail; her breasts receded; her hips lost their flare.

All over her, the smokey snakes slithered, and he caught a glimpse of her wide-eyed face, its mouth open in a silent scream.

The sorcerer was suddenly free of snakes, holding the woman against him without visible constraint—except the snakes like ropes thick as a strong man's arm that bound her.

Her legs were wrapped around him, and she was shrinking still. She was no larger now, and no more maturely formed, than a girl of eight.

Soon Macon realized she must be even younger. Her head was full of baby fuzz and she clung to the warlock, squalling, her chubby fists pounding at his chest, her fat little legs kicking at his waist.

A gasp and a groan went through the room; an awful sound that might have been made by the whole tower settling. It was a sound of expulsion, a sound of completion, a sound that seemed to resonate straight up from the tower's cellars.

The volume of it had a presence and a weight. It slapped at Macon and pushed him back from where he stood. It slapped at the snakes who nearly covered the baby in the warlock's arms, and they began to slide away, into dark corners, into the very walls, it seemed.

And the baby who had been a copulating woman fell to the ground in a heap of twisted, broken flesh, as if she'd been pulped by the coils of smoke. And grew. And grew more. The broken limbs lengthened and the baby cheeks spread, and wrinkled while he watched.

As Macon stood transfixed by the transformation of broken baby into broken, aged handmaid, the warlock clothed himself in robes as dark as shadows.

Seth waved a hand and the shadows themselves receded. He looked at Macon and said, "You have a question, apprentice?" He smiled at Macon and the smile was as cold as death.

Macon reached out to touch the invisible barrier and no barrier was there.

He took a hesitant step forward. "Yes, I have questions. My sister and the stranger, what are we going to do about it?" He was frightened, sobered by what he'd seen. He was a prince of the city; he must remember that. But he could not ignore the broken body on the floor, as the warlock seemed ready to do.

Seth, tying his robe at the waist, stepped over the motionless body. "You've seen my solution—at least part of it. This crone whom your sister loved has provided us a special service, at great personal cost. Now, help me with her."

"Help you with her?" Macon was horrified. "But she's—broken."

"Dead is the word. Surely you've seen death before. Looked out your bedroom window, at least, and spied upon it from a distance."

"But that can't be, not in the city—"

"Sorcery is deadly, when it must be. These are extraordinary times. Matilla was something your sister dearly loved—and she offered any service I desired, to save Tabet from this awful marriage, even a marriage in Hell if it would help. So we performed it."

The warlock reached down and took the broken body of the handmaid under its arms. "Get her feet, apprentice. This is your doing as much as mine."

"My doing?" Macon was nearly dumbstruck. Death. . . . He couldn't touch a dead thing. Even the animals for city feasts were slaughtered outside the walls.

"Your doing. You gave me leave to court your sister; you had not the courage to admit your lust. Lust is the requirement, you dolt—the only bridge over her infatuation is a greater one. Now *take her feet*. When something is banished, something else must take its place."

Macon shuffled numbly to the far side of Matilla's corpse with tears in his eyes. He bent down and found he couldn't touch the broken ankles. What did a corpse feel like? This crushed thing looked only a little like Matilla. The empty husk of her was a poor shadow of the original, now that life had fled.

"Take her feet!" commanded the warlock, and this time Macon's hands obeyed their master as if trained to do so.

"Good," grunted the sorcerer. "Now, to the window. The storm will break any instant. When it does, we'll cast her out the window. The broken bones will be seen as a result of her fall."

"And her . . . death?"

"As an omen against the marriage. I'll see to that. And it is one. On your sister's account, I have had to marry a wizened crone and kill her while I deflowered her. I'll bear the price of that someday. Now all that's left is to make the gain worth the cost. . . ."

"But death in the city. . . . They'll know it was us." Macon hesitated.

"*Lift*, prince. *Now!*" The warlock grunted and Macon was reminded of the sound that had sent the smoke-snakes slithering for the farther walls.

He lifted. The crushed body of Matilla that swung between them was surprisingly light, as if more had fled with life than spirit.

They half-carried, half-dragged her to the window. Seth spoke a word and the skins over it drew back.

Every hair on Macon's body rose up and shivered, each upon its own. He tried not to look at Matilla's staring eyes. The handmaid had been their virgin mother. A death that was a rape and horrid, a death during which she grew younger and younger as she died, and must have been so frightened, so terribly hurt. . . . What had he gotten himself into?

He dropped Matilla's ankles. He stepped back three paces, saying as he did, "I can't be a party to this. You're evil. This whole thing is evil. I never meant to bring death to—"

"It's too late, boy. You're in up to your crown. A murderer by sorcery—it was you who decreed I do what was necessary to save your sister from leaving the city with the interloper. Anything, you said. Any price. This is only the beginning. *Now pick up her feet and get ready.* When the first thunder cracks, we drop her."

"But—"

"No buts," said Seth in a quiet and commanding voice much more frightening than his loud tones. "It's too late for buts. You are a prince who would be king—who will be king, if your heart is strong enough. And I am a warlock who will marry your sister, or be damned for trying. Our bond is stronger than life, stronger than death, and forged eternally now."

"But I didn't understand."

"You brought me Tabet's hair, and her stocking. When you did that, if your word wasn't enough, then the tokens sealed your fate—and hers. Only if sorcery fails, will you suffer more than you can stand, this I promise you."

Macon couldn't think of anything else to say. Remorse choked him. His gaze kept returning to the corpse of Matilla, who'd loved him and cared for him, who loved the children of the king like her own, those she'd never had in order to care for Genos' brood.

How could he live with what he'd done? He slumped against the wall, still holding Matilla's cold and crushed ankles. They felt like bean bags in his hands.

"Think of your sister, deflowered in the arms of the stranger. Think of the omens. Think of the city's plight," advised the warlock as if reading his mind. "Think of the city's future—it was your father's mismanagement, his sad excuse for rulership, that made the city an affront to its gods. You can change all that."

"Make the gods love the city again?"

"Ha! No, not the gods, apprentice. The gods are forevermore forbidden you. It is other powers, henceforth, that you serve by serving me."

"Serving you? I thought you said it was my fault about Matilla because you were serving—"

"A figure of speech," soothed Seth. "You serve magic's gods, the gods within, who will be better allies for a city whose time is coming to an end. Trust me, Macon. Have I not said I'd make you king? A king who is a warlock is a formidable king, a king even gods will think more than once before flouting."

"I don't mean any of this," Macon tried again to say. "I just don't want my sister—"

"—In the arms of a stranger. She will be magic's queen, and that should please you. She'll be the consort of dark power— mine, yours . . . the city's, once it is reconsecrated."

"I don't understand you. I can't hurt my people, or the city, or Father, or Tabet—"

"They're hurting you. Anyway, it is too early, and too late, for that. Our bargain is made. You'll do what you're told. This death will be an accident come under the omen of storm and interruption, as Crevis predicted. Do you hear?"

"Yes, I hear."

Outside, Macon could see the sun break free and scald the streets with light. Then a cloud attacked the sundisk and enshrouded it. People scurried. Down by the Storm God's temple, there was a gathering of some sort. They were too far away for Macon to make out individuals, but there were horses there.

"Get ready," said Seth, who'd performed some awful rite in Macon's name. "On the count of three."

"One."

Macon told herself that this was all a bad dream,

that what he'd seen hadn't happened; that Matilla was so old she'd simply . . . died, and Seth was taking advantage of drunken gullibility, a flaw in Macon's nature.

"Two."

Macon told himself that the warlock was not powerful enough to bring death to the city, that he was really holding some animal slain outside, and the spell was only one of masking—of changing one thing to look like another. That was it. He'd go back to the palace and Matilla would be there, humming away through pleated lips as she made his bed and scolded him that he was old enough to pick up his own dirty clothes.

"Three."

Just before the thunder pealed, Macon assured himself that the warlock wasn't strong enough, or wise enough, or fearsome enough to command thunder or to know exactly when it would clap.

But clap the thunder did, an earsplitting peal of it.

And as if forced by a power more than mortal, Macon found his hands and arms swinging in concert with the warlock's as they heaved Matilla's broken body out of the window of the tower of wizardry.

Then Macon blurted, "It will fall right below your window, you arrogant sod! Right below your sorcerous lair, and then the blame will fall on you—and me—also! Oh why did I help. . . ?"

"Will it?" Seth answered Macon's question with a question of his own, and added, "Watch."

The body had not reached the ground below. It had not splattered on the pavings. No crowd had gathered.

Seth's hand was extended, palm up, out the window. The body floated, halfway to the ground, high over the people's heads on this shadowless day when the sun's face was obscured by storm.

"And watch," said the warlock with satisfaction.

He moved his palm; he flexed his fingers, as if shooing a fly.

The body of Matilla, suspended in the air, seemed to waft on a breeze. It drifted on the storm currents. It floated down the street.

Macon watched the body glide over the heads of the cityfolk, unnoticed, until it reached the citadel, the very tower where his father had secreted himself at the palace's highest point.

And then Seth said, "Still watching?"

Macon's indrawn breath was answer enough, as the warlock abruptly brought his hand down to his side and the body fell, as if from his father's tower, careening off ramparts.

Where it landed in the courtyard, Macon could not see—the walls of the palace intervened. But it had fallen straight and true. It would be in the central, private garden court.

He closed his eyes. He was going to be sick.

The warlock said, "No time for boyish reactions. You're a prince who will soon be king. Find the king in yourself, or we'll find some spell to put one there."

Macon opened his eyes and looked at the handsome, ageless warlock without a flicker of hope. It was too late to do anything but continue what he'd started.

When he was king—if he ever was—he would deal with this warlock, this murderer, this affront to man and god. Now, he must play along. He had neither the wisdom or the strength to fight wizardry. And he hadn't the courage to tell his father, Genos, what he'd done.

It was Father's fault in any case, if you really thought about it, he told himself. It was Father who had let the city become enmired here, who'd locked himself away in the tower, leaving the business of kingship to his advisors, when things had gone bad. And who'd let Tabet run wild and free, so that she'd gotten involved with the stranger.

At least, whatever the horror he felt, if Seth made his word good, neither Nikodemos called Stealth nor Genos himself would marry Tabet.

And trading one horror for another, he'd been taught, was what manhood was all about.

The corpse fell to the ground at Genos' feet. He was alone in the garden, trying to meditate, find some way to mediate all the sudden changes come upon his city, after so much had been changeless for so long.

Matilla came crashing down in a horrid heap of smashed flesh and baleful omen.

He was an old man, was Genos, still with a body and mind undulled by the infirmities of age. He was old in wisdom, but old in his ways. He was old in spirit, too.

He had an old man's love for long-lived friends, and an old man's care for aged servitors.

He found himself crying over Matilla's corpse, though he hadn't cried when his wife left him for a stranger and death in the world.

He found himself fearful of the horror in Matilla's eyes. What had she seen, when Death had come to take her at last? What had she found, beyond the unknowable barrier at life's end?

Genos found himself paralyzed with worry, when he was drained of tears, over what the seers and the priests and the warlocks would make of this. All his advisors turned natural events to their advantage. This event—unnatural for the city, and surely a foretaste of no good—was not one that could be nudged into another shape.

It was simply and completely the worst thing that could have happened, on the day of the stranger's Test and the first day that Tabet reigned as queen.

When King Genos got up off his knees, he was hurrying. As he went, he called for his heralds: "Send

a runner to the Storm God's temple! Have the preparations for the stranger's test halted! There must be
no Test today, tell the administrators! And bring
them here: Crevis, Seth, and Jamad. And my daughter the queen, bring her also! Immediately."

The summoned did not immediately arrive. When
Genos had pulled himself together, left the garden
and locked it, posting two sentries there, he learned
that strangers had entered the city's front gates.

"We didn't want to bother you with it, Sire. Queen
Tabet is taking care of it. They're at the Storm God's
temple, awaiting the Consort's arrival, with the rest."

Strangers? Did no one tell him anything anymore?
More strangers!

Genos made his way slowly to his throne room and
there he sat, chin on fist, waiting for someone to
come tell him what was going on in his city.

Perhaps the strangers, the new ones, had something to do with Matilla's death. They might be
blamed for it, in any case, if there was no other way.
But the news of a death in the city, from whatever
means but the ceremonial one of the Test, would
shake the city's very foundations.

Too bad it couldn't shake those foundations loose
from this mire at the end of time.

But it couldn't. Genos knew that like he'd known,
long ago, that terrible trials and evil were at hand.
Knowing a thing will happen does not prepare you to
fight it.

Sitting there, waiting for his daughter and his advisors to counsel him and the newest strangers to be
brought before him, Genos wondered if he hadn't
brought all of this upon himself by his very efforts to
prevent the worst.

Abdicating power, however tacitly, clearly had not
been the right thing to do.

What was right, in the face of sudden death where
death did not belong, eluded him.

It eluded Crevis, the seer, too, as was evident when the sturdy man arrived, shaken as if he'd already seen the corpse in the garden.

"Sire," said the seer with a hasty bow, "we've more strangers—interruptions. And it's raining outside as if it never wants to stop—our storms. And the strangers say they've come in search of Nikodemos, but the queen won't let them see the consort, who's meditating in preparation for his Test—"

"Didn't my runner find you?" demanded the king. "There'll be no Test today."

"Yes, I got your message. But the Test cannot be put off, not even for Queen Tabet's sake. I must counsel—"

"The Test can be put off," said Genos, crossing his arms and shifting on his throne. We've had one death today in the city. Take that heart and put it on your altar, if you must put a heart there before the sun sets. See if the Storm God will be satisfied by the unbeating heart of Matilla, our beloved serv—" The king broke off, his voice choked with unregnal emotion.

Crevis hardly noticed. "A death? Matilla? How? Where? What—"

"When the rest arrive, I'll show you. Now think, seer, about how to put the best face on this, before the people, before my daughter. We can't have an evil omen for her Queenship."

Crevis looked slowly up at King Genos. "You're positive that Matilla is dead?"

"Dead from a fall that crushed her bones. Dead as dead can be. Dead as a fish that falls from the sky. Why didn't you worry about the deaths of all those fish, seer? Why didn't the Storm God's priest put those fishy corpses upon his altar? Why?"

The question made no sense to Crevis, Genos realized, and bit his lip and looked away.

He must take hold of himself, of his feelings, of his temper, before his daughter and the rest got here.

He thought he'd done that, prepared a calm and reasonable way to tell his advisors and his co-regent what he must, until they came straggling in, the strangers bringing up the rear under guard.

And when he saw the strangers, who were like mythic statues come to life, like colossi and not like mortal men, so perfect were their forms and stern their visages and fierce their musculature and their armor and their ceremonial weapons, he was struck speechless.

Seth, of course, was not. The warlock, who seemed somewhat disheveled and out of breath, had been talking in muted tones with Tabet, whose face was set in an expression her father knew too well.

"King Genos," said Seth to him, "our revered queen does not accept my analysis that we should speak with you—the co-regent and myself, plus your other advisors, without these strangers—who claim to be friends of the Consort—present."

"Father," said Tabet, "I want you to meet the Lady Jihan and her travelling companion, Lord Tempus, from—"

"Later, daughter. Have them wait outside. Wait with their attendants, and not go anywhere. Whatever they need will be brought to them in the antechamber. Does that meet with your approval, Co-regent Tabet?"

Tabet looked at him and nodded primly. His daughter the queen was not simply his daughter anymore. He kept remembering the way the sorcerer had touched her at the feast. But that was ridiculous—she was betrothed, with all the fierceness her young heart could muster, to the first stranger, Nikodemos.

As the two sojourners were ushered out, unspeaking, unprotesting between the palace guards, Genos felt a modicum of relief. It was bad enough to have to tell his daughter of Matilla's death, and face the doomcrying of his advisors, and argue for prudent, nonhysterical readings. But it would have been impossible to exercise even a shadow of kingship with strangers who looked like angry gods staring him in the eye.

As he broached the subject of Matilla's death, he could still see the fiery-eyed goddess in her scale armor and the heroic form of her companion, whose helmet was studded with boar's teeth and whose mantle was of leopardskin.

There hadn't been people like that, in the city or outside it, for thousands of years.

And it occurred to Genos, in his desperation, that perhaps these were the gods themselves, come in person to exact their tribute, their retribution for all his failures these many years.

At that moment, he would have done anything to restore Matilla to life, even given his own life in her stead.

But once the arguing began, once Tabet commenced to wail and beat her breast, once the warlock had to be called upon to make a potion to calm his daughter and the priest began to babble about deific retribution, Genos no longer felt that way.

If he could, he would have strangled everyone in his chamber, including his beloved daughter, with his own hands and with those hands buried all of them in the garden, secretly, beside Matilla.

Even that horror he would have perpetrated, rather than let the city know that death and destruction were holding court inside her gates.

Chapter 14: Strangers at the End of Time

There had never been a funeral in the city that Tabet could remember.

There had never been strangers in the city such as Nikodemos, her consort, or his dark and terrible friends, either.

Now there were both. There was the loss of Matilla, like a hole in her heart through which the storm that lashed the city blew with keening force that shook her soul. There was the appearance of the formidable pair of close-mouthed sojourners who looked like animated gods and who looked upon her and her city as if upon something broken, waiting to be fixed.

Niko had said to her, just before the pair on the smokey horses arrived, while th wind was rising and the Test seemed mere hours away: "You're different, Tabet—more different than sudden queenship can account for. Why is that?" His hazel eyes had probed her until she could no longer meet them.

She'd seen the mercenary in Nikodemos then, the cautious soldier who'd roamed the wild world, trust-

ing to himself alone. Their former intimacy seemed a
sham or an illusion. His face was taut and hard in its
angles; his brows drew close as if shielding his eyes
from the sun. And all the muscles in his shoulders
were tense as if he were consciously mimicking the
Storm God's likeness, which he so resembled, in the
temple behind their backs.

There in the wind that whispered its promise of
rain, there in the faraway strobe of the storm's distant lightning, she saw the warrior she proposed to
marry. And she was afraid of Nikodemos for the first
time. The boy she'd seen in the man who fell from
the sky had vanished; a wary fighter had taken his
place.

When she hadn't answered for longer than he
liked, Niko had exhaled a deep breath like the storm's
song and said, "Ever since I left you with the warlock, you've been different. I saw him touch you in
the fete hall—he lay his hand on your spine three
times. And you allowed it. Why, I don't know. But it
can't happen again. His kind are too dangerous. Don't
let me catch him near you, or—"

"You are telling me whom I can speak to and
whom I can stand beside?" The words had come out
of her with all the incredulity of a queen, masking
the hurt she felt. "Do you dare instruct your monarch?" She caught herself, smothered the rest. He
was her consort. He was facing a test, for her sake—a
test he might not survive.

But he had responded, there in the open before
the temple of his god, with courtiers close by and
functionaries of the temple lurking near, "I dare to
tell my wife-to-be when I see danger. Three taps
from a sorcerer, on a woman's spine . . . who knows
what may come of it? I—"

"Hush," she demanded.

The storm wind lashed his face and blew ashen
hair in Niko's eyes. "I'm here to help you—on the

sword's point, for your sake and the city's. I'm not arguing the risk of having second thoughts. But you and I made a bargain. Don't play queen with me. I know the World and the magic in it. I agreed to marry a princess, not a witch or a warlock's pawn. Watch yourself with Seth, or I'll make sure he can't put another hand on you, once the Test is done."

"You're so sure you'll survive it?" Her voice quavered. Out of the corner of her eye she saw lurkers whispering together; people were assuredly beginning to talk.

He shook his head at her, a tiny movement, an eloquent dismissal, a devaluation made in disgust. And then he turned away from her, took a step toward the temple at her back.

When he did, Tabet saw the strangers with their horses and the gate guards. A horse they led behind trumpeted loudly, a sound caught up by the rising wind.

Had the wind lashed her to fury? She didn't know why she'd lost her temper then, and darted after her consort. "How dare you, stranger? A rain of fish is all we have to prove you're what you say, besides your word. What gives you the right to treat me like a wife? I'm queen in my own—"

As she grabbed him by the shoulder, he spun around. His hand caught her wrist in an eyeblink-fast move that twirled her and pinned her by a crushing grip against him, her own arm a lever he used to pinion her back against his front.

She was still and breathless, her words frozen in her mouth. His arm across her chest, his forearm under her chin, and his grip upon her wrist felt like iron. She could hardly think, for the fear. Who and what was this man she'd chosen, this first man in eternity she'd invited inside her?

He'd never denied he was a killer; it had been there in all he said, explicit by implication—he was a soldier, a mercenary fighter. Blood and conflict were his stock and trade.

She'd been about to break free, by the strength of her queenship and her dignity, find some way to force his grip from her and then tell him she'd reconsidered their betrothal. She was thinking that Seth was right, that what he'd said to her while they stood together watching Niko and her father was the real truth here: that the stranger was too different from the city folk, too much a creature of the World; that she must go carefully, take her time.

Yes, she thought, we'll put off this marriage—it was her choice to do so for seven days. And she was going to face him with her decision, so much more costly than a slap across the face, when she shrugged off his imprisoning limbs that were mere male force, a show of strength and temper.

But then he did let her go, suddenly, with a little push, the way you'd shove a kitten from your lap, and she realized from a quick glance that he'd forgotten all about her.

Then she'd heard the horse's trumpet again, and looked herself, following the gaze of the man called Stealth, and her breath was squeezed from her, seeing the strangers for the first time.

They'd come straight up to Nikodemos, as if they saw nothing else nor any reason to go carefully, ignoring her, the temple, the functionaries, even their own guards.

The sable colored horse reared and whickered and nickered and pranced, while the woman-thing held him fast on a tether and the man who was like a god said, "Life to you, Stepson, and everlasting glory."

And Tabet's consort replied, "And to you, Commander. And to all under your protection, by the aegis of the Storm God, our lord."

Ritual. Tabet had not grown up a princess for

nothing. She knew ritual when she heard it, and she knew royalty when she saw it.

"Stepson?" she piped up, insinuating herself into the conversation, moving so close to Nikodemos that her arm brushed his. "Consort, is this your father?"

Niko ignored her. "Riddler, we must talk. Soon. Jihan, can I have him?"

And the strange woman whose skin glowed and whose stature was so imposing brought up the wildly dancing horse, holding it with a strength in muscled arms that Tabet had never seen a woman display in all her life. And with a skill that made it seem perfectly reasonable that she should hold so wild a beast by the muzzle, as if he were a pet.

Tabet skittered out of the way of hooves and teeth. Dust blew up, swirled by the storm wind, and surrounded her consort and the plunging horse.

When the dust settled, the horse stood, his head pressed against the soldier's chest, snorting softly. Niko was scratching it behind its ears and its eyes were half closed. His were moist, from dust-brought tears or something stronger.

The remarkable pair had looked on in silence while man stroked horse, and checked tack, and touched in turn each piece of warrior's gear slung from the beast's saddle: fine sword in ornate scabbard, knife in sheath on a belt bristling with sentry's accouterments; enameled shield and cuirass, crossbow and quiver, helmet and spear.

Finally, Niko came around the horse's off side, his hand trailing from the sable's croup. "Commander, it's good to see you here. I've a Test to take, in the Storm God's temple. This place is—"

"Genos' city. I know, Niko," said the big man in a deep and gravelly voice. "What's this about a 'consort'?"

"Ah . . . Sir, I'd like to introduce the just-made Queen Tabet, Genos' new co-regent, my betrothed for the next seven days."

"For the next seven days?" the woman in scale armor had said, as if she too were used to demanding explanations from Tabet's consort.

"I *said* we should talk." Niko's head went down slightly. "This test of theirs is fabled to be deadly. If I survive it, the queen and I may marry." He shrugged and Tabet didn't like that shrug at all. It was defensive, it was sheepish, it was . . . embarrassed.

"Queen Tabet," said the man whom Niko called his commander. "If you need to test someone before the Storm God, test me. I am this man's commanding officer, and the Storm God has sent me here to intercede."

"I fail to recall a proper introduction," she'd said to cover her shock.

"Tabet," Niko said under his breath, a warning he had no right to issue to her, his queen. "May I introduce Queen Tabet, Ruling in Wisdom, daughter of Genos, daughter of Tebat, Queen of the City for Eternity. May she rule in Peace."

It wasn't quite the proper formula for address, but Tabet was mollified. She bowed her head primly.

"This is my leftside leader, Tempus the Black, the Riddler, ruling eternally by might and the Storm God's favor, creator of many armies and champion of Enlil."

A look passed between the two men that Tabet did not like, but did not understand.

"Your Highness," said Tempus gravely, with a little bow.

"And the Lady Jihan, Froth Daughter, Child of the Primal Storm, Regent of Water and the Eternal Sea at our backs," Niko continued in that same odd voice, as if he were speaking words from some play.

"Tabet," said Lady Jihan, clearly telegraphing her parity in a voice that was husky and so sure of itself that Tabet could not summon up queenly anger at being addressed so casually, no matter how she tried.

"May we see your father, straightaway, child? We have important matters to discuss."

Just as Tabet had been framing some sort of retort, a runner had come from the palace, saying that the Test must be delayed, and that Tabet and the newcomers were wanted by Genos in his throneroom immediately.

And so it had come to pass that Niko was left there, alone before the Storm God's temple with only his horse and a few functionaries of the temple for company, while Tabet and the two newcomers were hurried up Processional Way to see her father.

She tried not to think what it might mean that she trod the mirrored way with these specters from the World. But in father's presence, she heard of Matilla's death and thought, *That omen, at least, is fulfilled.*

For seeing the strangers with their warhorses and their armor and their weapons—which no one had succeeded in taking from them—was an unequivocal sign of Enlil's displeasure.

No matter how she tried, Tabet could not shake the presentiment that her fate, and her father's and her brother's and even the city's, was suddenly out of the ruling family's hands as it had never been in all these years, until the city had become mired at the end of time.

Not even Seth's comforting touch could give her solace, in the face of Matilla's death and what her people would make of it. The warlock's hand at the small of her back was warm and she answered his pressure by leaning back against his hand, but it did not buoy her as it had during the ceremony, when he'd whispered, "Let my art lend you strength," and she'd taken it.

This time, there was death all around. Death was the one thing that the city never had to fear. Now it was present in spirit and in flesh. She never remem-

bered going out into the garden, but she always
remembered looking down on Matilla's corpse.

And she always remembered that, when she'd first
come into her father's throneroom to hear the news
of Matilla's death, she'd had Niko's commander and
his traveling companion, Jihan, with her. And that
they seemed like Death incarnate—or at least like
Conflict in the shape of human beings.

So it was no wonder, and no failure of Seth's
magic, that his touch could not comfort her when she
stood over the corpse of her handmaid as Crevis
haltingly proposed readings of this awful omen meant
to convince the people that Matilla's death did not
mean that Queen Tabet had come to the throne as a
harbinger of destruction, bringing death and dissolution upon the city.

And Seth said then, in her ear, so softly only the
two of them could hear, "It's not you, Tabet, but
Nikodemos, who brings death to the city with his
awful mentors. Disallow him, my queen. Instruct us,
who give the Test, that it must be deadly to the
death-bringer. Marry me, my queen, and my magic,
all my art, will be forever at your disposal—the
fervid wedding gift of a suitor lost in your much
stronger spell."

Then she chanced to look up and see her brother.
She hadn't noticed Macon's entrance. But now he
was all she could see, and his eyes were red from
crying.

Her hands found their way to her ears and covered them. The low conferring of advisors around
her became like the buzzing of angry bees in her
ears. The room began to spin.

The last thing she remembered, before fainting
dead away to slump over Matilla's corpse on the
garden's ground, was Niko's commander saying, "If
you must test someone, test me."

And then she was lost in a dream, wherein Matilla

was alive and holding out broken arms to her, and Seth was by the handmaid's side, beckoning. But between her and the two stood Tempus and Nikodemos, shoulder to shoulder, their awful weapons drawn and slick with gore, while at their feet demons clawed their way out of the earth. And those demons all had their slitted yellow eyes fixed on Tabet and their hungry mouths open for Tabet, and their dank and gleaming claws outstretched to grab Tabet by the ankles and pull her down into the dark earth, where Matilla's grave was waiting, newly dug.

CHAPTER 15: REUNION

Niko's horse quivered with pleasure as he curried it in the alley beside the temple. He was absorbed in the task, so far as any could see.

And there were many to see: junior priests, acolytes who seemed young but were probably thrice his age; curious folk who had come to witness the test and had to content themselves with watching a man groom a horse; women who came in twos and threes and giggled together and minced away, the copper beads on their skirts' hems tinkling.

Niko knew how to wait, and what was worth paying attention to, in life. The stable stallion was so full of the World that every stroke of the finish brush on those high withers was as deep meditation to Nikodemos, who was not alone any longer, now that his horse and his commander were here.

The Test seemed far away, and receding. With it went his concerns for the rightness of his actions, if not for the fate of the city.

With Tempus here, the truth would out. The city's

battles would be fought truly and well, and if more was needed than Nikodemos had to give, then Tempus would surely give in.

He was still uneasy about Tabet, but that too would shake out, with the wisdom of the Riddler here to see whatever Niko might not.

And if he were to marry Tabet, then it would be with Tempus' blessings, not as some furtive ritual he'd undertaken to save his skin.

He was content to wait and let Tempus come back to him with word, with wise counsel, with orders on how to proceed for best result. The Riddler's presence was all the city needed, though it did not know it yet, to live or die in accordance with Enlil's will.

That the god had manifested Tempus and Jihan in this place eased Niko's conscience. The possibility of conflict, of failure, of loss to the World of this place, was not less, but all outcomes were different now: more meet, more proper in measure, more the sorts of things a man of the god could rest easily doing—or, having done, ride away from with heart and soul intact.

Or not. Niko feared death like a sane man, but he feared wrong action more. The Riddler was wiser than the city's wisest, the god's strong right arm in the world. Here it would be no different.

Except here, Niko had until recently been content to stay—to marry, to languish, to live eternally if the city could be saved.

Seeing Tempus and Jihan, the wild sprite crying freedom with every inch of her, he was no longer sure he wanted to spend eternity—or his life's poor span—within the city's walls with Tabet, even if she wasn't involved with the warlock.

Yet the city's fate must be settled. He'd given his word. The Test must be taken—and by him, for it was his word that was at stake.

When Tempus came back, Niko resolved as his

sable warhorse stretched out his neck and snorted in pleasure, he would make it clear to his commander what responsibilities were whose.

Only when he'd finished grooming every inch of his horse, from hooves' frogs to forelock and eartips, did Niko turn to his weapons, his panoply that was his by the grace of the lord of dreams.

He slipped his swordbelt over his hips and fastened it firmly; its weight buttressed his own strength. He checked his throwing stars and settled his dagger in its sheath. He brought his sword from its scabbard and examined the blade with care for dirt or knicks.

When he came to his cuirass, he paused. On it were mythical beasts from unknown ages, from the time when the city was young. Its workmanship was equalled only here; its scenes were scenes from a mythology that had its roots here, in the city—at the beginning of the world—as well as in the land of dreams.

The gear had come to him so long ago, under such difficult circumstance, that he never thought of it as a privilege to possess such armaments. They were marks of the dream lord's hold on him at one time; then, they'd become only the marks of a mercenary who'd lived long enough to acquire the best, and was strong enough to fend off any who tried to take it from him.

He'd never thought of his dream-forged sword or his cuirass with the elder gods enameled on it, as omens of anything, or passage to anywhere.

And yet it could be no coincidence that he, and he alone, who possessed these implements of ancient design and deadly purpose, had come here to take Enlil's test. It was Enlil who ranged with wild beasts upon his sword's scabbard; it was the Storm God's bulls and his lightings which decorated his cuirass.

Niko did not like fatedness; his life was dedicated to man's will in the World, to man's mind prevailing against forces of nature and against the supernatural enemies of humankind; to man's strength and determination being enough salvation for any purpose.

He was a soldier, before he was anything more. A soldier could not go into battle and strive until his blisters bled from foot and hand, and until his wounds bled upon the battlefield, if he believed the outcome of every battle was fixed and written in the gods' books already. He was a mercenary for the gods' will because his wisdom said that not even the gods were omnipotent, that all things came from struggle.

As Tempus put it, so Niko believed: that all things came into being out of strife. And strife's implement he was, honed and tempered. He'd fought under a warrior-priest of Enlil's before he'd come to Tempus's service. He'd fought himself before that, learning to master the mystery of his *maat*, which study had been known to kill unworthy students.

All of these years, Nikodemos had pitted his will against every enemy that came at him, always sure that his fate was his own to barter.

So his fingers trembled, on the cuirass for whose value a lesser fighter would long ago have died. And he did not put it on, here in the city where death did not belong, although he wore his sword and personal weapons.

The cuirass, he decided, he would wear only when he took Enlil's test, to show the god who and what he was, if the deity were forgetful.

To wear it here and now would have been a surrender of a sort—to the wisdom of the dream lord and a fixity of fate he could not admit. Should he die in the Test, then for him it must be a matter of triumph or failure in the moment, not a slow predestined closing of his fate.

He was just replacing the cuirass on his saddled horse when someone cleared a throat behind him.

He turned. "Commander, I—"

A hand forestalled him, Tempus' raised hand, as strong as the storm that broke at that moment, pelting men and horse with driving rain so fierce it grayed the air between them.

"Bring your horse out of the rain. We've a stall for it next to ours in the king's stables."

Whence Niko had first come. He shook his head and said, "but the Test—"

And Tempus had said, "The Test is officially postponed. Till the storm stops, at least." Tempus turned and Niko had no choice but to take his horse and follow.

"Commander, it's my duty to take this Test. The depiction of the Storm God in the temple, have you seen it?"

"No, not yet. Tell me." The Riddler's head was down against the storm, his helmet somewhere else than on his head. His hair was soaked in moments. Beads of water glittered on the lashes of his long eyes.

"The Storm God's face is mine," Niko blurted. "His form, his armaments—everything."

"Live long enough, and everything will happen to you, Stepson. Living is the point, not dying for someone else's cause."

"The Test can be surmounted—"

"You know nothing about this Test of which you speak." The rebuke slapped Niko, so abrupt it seemed laced with the thunder that cracked at the same time. Niko's horse started and whinnied. From the palace barn, the answering calls of Tempus and Jihan's horses could be heard above the rising gale. "There's been a death here today—an old woman in questionable circumstances. For these people, it's a bad omen, a unique occurrence—"

"It's sorcery, by my sword," Niko said.

"We'll look into it. As for the test and who takes it,

and the visage of the god in the temple—follow my lead, rightman."

"As ever," Niko said, glad the storm cooled the flush that flared on his face.

They led the horse down a storm-emptied street in silence and Niko searched in vain for something to say into Tempus's questioning quietude.

Finally he managed, "Tabet—she was just a princess when this started. They were going to force this Test on me, and the warlock was pushing me. They were talking as if death were certain, some ceremonial slaughter—"

"At least they didn't lie to you. These folk have forgotten half of what they should remember and misremember the rest."

"I'm trying to explain about the marriage . . ."

"Go ahead, Stepson. I'm listening. When you've done, we'll concoct something to tell Jihan, who's already dreaming of a double wedding."

Niko tried to smile, to catch Tempus' long eye. But he couldn't. This all must read awry to his commander. "I fell out of the cloud, in a rain of fish—carp, actually. Into their stable. The eldest prince and Tabet found me. She . . . you know how it is with me and women."

"Go on."

"She seemed my only hope—she crawled into my bed. I did what a man would do, to secure an ally against the warlock and a city seeking a stranger's blood to grease its mired wheels. But she announced her intention to wed me, and her father made her queen to gain control of things."

"And did he?"

"I don't know. If the Test is Enlil's test, what harm is there in it?"

"What harm is there in this place dying—it's older than I am. Its time may be at hand."

"I— I'd lost you, Jihan, my horse, my gear . . . I

didn't know what else to do but make the best of it. Life here seemed preferable to death here. Escape wasn't an option. Where could I have gone? I . . . thought you might come. Tabet dreamed it."

That stopped the Riddler in his tracks. Ancient eyes met Niko's with a shock like lightning running up his sword. "What else did she dream?"

"Fire and scourging, so she said. A waking dream, but she described you and Jihan as if she knew you. So I waited. My *maat* thinks it's the city's test, not mine. And then there's the god in the temple. Could I have been . . . destined for this place?"

"No such thing as destiny, not the way you mean."

"That's good," Niko sighed. "Then we can make what we will of our chances, like always."

"Like always," said the Riddler. "Nothing's fixed. You cannot step twice—"

"—in the same river," Niko finished for him. "Yes, I remember. But tell me the dream lord's not in this."

"The dream lord's not in this."

"Don't humor me, Riddler. My gear, it's from the time of this place's youth. So is the temple, the god's face."

"*I* am from the time of this place's youth. Does that mean I had to come here? I came here, as did you, Stepson, because of our crafty, ill-tempered god wants to teach this place a lesson. Humbling folk who think eternity's their birthright calls for a rain of fish here, a coincidence there, and the occasional bit of bloodshed."

"The god spoke to you."

"Would that He had not."

The sable horse shied at something in the mud, and Niko hung for a moment, feet off the ground, from the reins he'd wound around his hand.

When the horse was calmed, Tempus said, "Please the god, and let the city's fate be what Enlil decides.

Don't leave your heart here, Nikodemos, in any sense. There may be no more immortals when this Test is done—not them, nor me, not Jihan."

"Are you saying that our survival's in the god's hands?"

"Our survival is in our own hands, always. Not god or wizard owns a man's soul unless he gives it. When people who are immortal leave this place, they leave as mortals. Didn't your betrothed tell you that?"

For him, Tempus had come to a place which might strip him of his immortal gift and leave him naked before his supernatural enemies, who abounded in the World. Niko nearly dropped his horse's reins. He stopped and watched the man in front of him trudge on through the storm-washed streets of the strange and beleaguered city.

Then Tempus called back, "Niko, everything under heaven is not your fault. We'll put this matter to rights as the god demands, and be on our way."

"Yes sir," he said, hurrying to catch up with Tempus so that his horse broke into a trot, not realizing until he'd regained the Riddler's side that the matter of his possible marriage to Tabet had just been settled, so far as Tempus was concerned.

Niko reached out to touch the sodden leopardskin mantle, and pulled his hand back. He started to form a plea of personal moment, but the words wouldn't come.

He was a rightman, sworn to duty—half of a Sacred Band pair of which Tempus was the other half; an adept of the misty isles, of *maat* and the balance of right action in the world, of Ennina's shrouded coast, where he must eventually return. He was no prince of noble blood, no hunter of fortunes or kingships.

He was, most specifically, a hard-working soldier between battles who'd been caught up by a god's

maelstrom and plunked down where he was *in order
to do the god's bidding.*

Which, for Niko in the World, was whatever Tempus decided it was, and had been so for a very long time. What had come over him, that he'd thought things were any different here?

Was it the beauty of the city? Was it the lack of obvious foes? Was it the hidden nature of the city's evil—its greater goodness, its majesty, its legend?

Tempus was the only legend Niko could afford to believe in; Tempus and the prompting of their common bond, the oath he'd sworn.

For Tempus knew the god as fey and fickle. When Tempus was interpreting Enlil's will, there was never a doubt in Nikodemos of how to proceed, only of his ability to triumph or to survive a constant testing as arduous as any the city could devise.

And those thoughts lightened his steps as he followed the Riddler toward the palace stables, where the horses and Jihan waited.

He had his horse back. He had his gear back, with whatever sanctification or parallelism that implied. And he had Tempus here to counsel him. And Jihan, who'd been born out of this sea at the end of time.

Whatever the Test entailed, whether or not Tempus could interpose his eternal person between Niko and its exigencies, Nikodemos had no doubts now that he was in the right place, at the right time, for the right purpose.

It would be difficult to explain this to Tabet, though, who was a queen and had been a virgin princess when he took her.

Just as they neared the stableyard, Niko said, "About Tabet— "

"Explain nothing. It's too early. And there's the question of sorcery—she and the warlock are close allies. We'll see how close they are when the corpse's heart is on the altar and the dead buried in consecrated ground."

"Commander?"

"There'll be a funeral. They've never had one. They have a heart for the god's altar, at the least. And there's a wizard's heart in all of this. Niko, just soldier. You have a knack for witches; keep your belt buckled if you can. And leave the priest and the seer, the king and the queen, the sorcerer and the gods to me. As I said, Jihan can't be allowed to begin thinking about marriage. The results of that are worse than this whole place torched and razed until scorched earth is all that remains."

Grooms were running out to open the gates and greet them. Water was sluicing into the whitewashed stableyard as it had when Niko had been dropped there from the sky.

This was no time for further talk or for strategy, not in such mixed company: Macon, the prince, was there, talking with Jihan and admiring her warhorse who was crosstied in the barn.

And Tabet was there, crying softly in the clean hay of the stall readied for Niko's sable—weeping as though her young heart would break.

When Niko put his horse in for the night, closed the door with a rag in hand to wipe the rain from the sable's coat, he found the girl. And there was nothing for it but to take her in his arms, for she was a young woman who'd lost a nanny, and who'd lost her courage in the face of death, a young woman grieving who needed strong arms around her and a quiet voice to tell her that everything would be all right.

Only Niko wasn't sure that it would—not for Tabet, whom Tempus thought embroiled in sorcery; not for her city, either, which the very Storm God had set his mind to humble or destroy.

Her own dream of fire and destruction should have told him, Niko chided himself as he held the shivering queen and wished she were older, more devious, or in some way less than what she was.

But Tabet, shorn by tragedy of her gloss of queenship, was the same pliant girl who'd seduced him above this very stable, full of nothing but a hunger for life and needs his body, despite Tempus' words, wanted nothing more than to fulfill.

CHAPTER 16: FUNERARY GAMES

King Genos presided at a solemn dinner where the three strangers sat to table with king, queen, prince and all of Genos' principal advisors, as if deaths and funerals and tests of the god at the end of time were routine occurrences.

Macon was full of resentment and horror. Everyone here was his enemy: the newcomers, the stranger who'd become his sister's consort; his father and Crevis the seer; the priest of the Storm God, Jamad, who'd so clearly allied himself with Nikodemos, and—most especially—Seth, the warlock who'd sacrificed Matilla in some awful rite meant to make Tabet his love-slave.

Macon was miserably aware that Seth might have it in mind to make the entire city his. If Macon came to kingship under the aegis of such a power, who would be king? The sorcerer already had a secret to hold over Macon's head that stuffed the prince's mouth more completely than any gag, that wound around his chest more tightly than any ropes; which bound him hand and foot and kept him from jumping up and shouting that here, at this very table, was the culprit, the evildoer who'd murdered Matilla and thereby made Macon his thrall.

Were any of them safe? Macon couldn't be king while his father was. What did the warlock have in mind for Genos? And whatever it was, was there anything that Macon could do about it without making things worse?

Had Macon sold all their souls to Seth to keep his sister by his side? For dreams of forbidden love? Or for even less? Out of drunken jealousy and childish pique?

He regretted, oh how he regretted Matilla's death. He kept trying to tell himself that making an end to the strangers, and to his father's sad excuse for rulership, was worth any price.

He kept trying to tell himself that the city's survival was worth all costs, but he was no longer sure that it was true, even were it possible.

He'd witnessed dark magic such as no denizen of the city had ever seen, and he did not like it.

But he was trapped and he knew it. The small talk at the table seemed ludicrous and vain, even though he'd been trained well enough to know that the talk was neither small nor vainly entered upon—the city's very future was being discussed. And all of theirs.

"So tell me, Lord Tempus, about the world from which you come and what you did there," Genos said carefully over a winecup shaped like a gauntleted fist. His father was using the best tableware tonight, a sign that he wanted to impress his guests.

"Simply Tempus will do, King Genos," said the big man with the gravelly voice, the massive shoulders, and the long and hooded eyes.

"Tell us, then, Tempus," Tabet chimed in sweetly, "what you and Niko and the lovely lady, Jihan, did in the World."

Jihan was a vision of womanhood such as Macon had never imagined. She leaned forward like a soldier, both arms on the table, and pointed a finger at the king. "We're here to do what you could not, by the Storm God's will, in the very backyard of my youth. Don't play with us, Genos. If you have worries, now's the time to air them. If you have troubles, trot them out. If you have doubts and fears, enlist our aid. Else what we do here will come upon you hard and fast like the storm beats the sea against the shore."

In the face of such discourtesy, her companion Tempus wiped his mouth with a napkin; Nikodemos tilted back his chair to eye the man he called his commander; Tabet blanched openly; Seth sat up straight with hell in his eyes; Crevis examined his fingernails; Jamad, priest of the Storm God, winced and looked at Genos covertly.

Only Macon's father seemed undisturbed. He nodded with such equanimity as he might have displayed at a tally of the city's grain supplies that meant measures must be taken to replenish. He drank deep from his cup.

Then he said pleasantly to the newcomers, looking from one to the next as he did, "You know death is strange and unwelcome here, a thing of evil omen. The Test we have set for my daughter's consort does not necessarily lead to death; many strangers have taken it and walked out the city's gates—all, in truth."

He paused and no one said anything.

"But every stranger must take it," Macon said, crossing his arms. "Especially now."

"Especially now," echoed Jamad, an unexpected ally. "The god wants a heart upon his altar."

Then Tempus leaned forward, "Give Enlil Matilla's heart, and we'll solve the mystery of her death and perhaps satisfy the Storm God as well."

Jamad muttered to himself. Crevis scratched his

broad forehead. Seth said something to Tabet that Macon didn't catch.

Niko's chair legs hit the floor with an audible thump.

"If there is no objection," said Genos, "we will try this suggestion. We have no funerary rites as such, strangers. We will take your lead in how to proceed. And Nikodemos' test will be delayed until we have tried the heart of Matilla upon the god's altar and seen the results of that."

All three of the king's advisors spoke at once, then stopped, then resumed a long-winded discussion to which Macon paid no mind.

"What will happen," Macon asked as soon as there was a lull in the conversation, "when Matilla's heart is on the altar? She won't come back to life, will she?"

If she did, she'd incriminate him as well as Seth. His own heart refused to beat until someone answered his question.

That someone was the man whom Nikodemos called the Riddler, who said, "Only the god knows what He wants from the city, but want something He does. We must wait and see. In the mean time, I'd like to see the original prophecy, and have someone acquaint me with the circumstances that mired the city here. And also, Jihan would like to closet herself with your wizard and compare notes."

"We're not called wizards here," Seth said primly. "I am the city's chief warlock, Lord Tempus."

"Are you indeed?" said Tempus. "I'll remember that."

Nikodemos had reached out to touch Tabet's hand as Seth was speaking. She jerked her hand away.

Queen Tabet was watching the warlock with a lovesick look that made Macon even more unhappy, if that were possible, than he'd been until now. What had he done? How could he undo it? If he didn't know better, he'd think that the city's plight, too, was all his fault—everything else that was terrible and tragic had happened because of him.

But it was Genos, he told himself fiercely, who had gotten the city trapped here where the sea had no end and life had no hope.

If Genos had seen what Macon had seen, in the warlock's sanctum—demons from beyond and horrid snakes and sorcery on the loose—he would have done whatever was necessary to avoid this moment and all it threatened. But his father had not done anything, and the city languished, filled with her own evil and the worse evil of strangers.

Macon nearly wept in public, nearly rose to his feet and confessed all, nearly ripped open his shirt and pounded his breast and offered his heart to the hungry altar of the god.

But he was a prince of the city, eldest son of an ancient king, and he could not make a spectacle of himself in public—not without being drunker than he was.

Thus he set about getting drunk enough to do just that, paying no attention to the conversation around him, so that when Jihan left with Seth and Tempus with Jamad, he hardly noticed.

But when Tabet left with Nikodemos, he was suddenly and completely sobered. He sat at the nearly empty table, with his father and with the palace's chief seer, and looked from one to the other. Then he said, because no one was saying anything and the silence was pressing upon his ears, "How can you let her go off with that . . . that . . . guardsman . . . seeing the nature of his companions and our fate clear as can be?"

"How's that, son?" said the father, informal now that company had left.

"Well, she's going off with them, unless we stop her, like some common camp follower. Isn't she?

Unless we stop her? By omen or magic or something?" He glared at the seer, who was regarding him pensively.

Then he faced his father and said, "This is all your fault." His voice raised, words tumbled from his mouth, words he'd never meant to say: "You did this to us. It should be your heart on that altar, for letting mother go and grieving endlessly, without any joy in life or any thought for the future. Now we don't have any future but black magic and blacker death, and it's all your fault."

He was standing now, not knowing when he'd risen. He shut his mouth with an audible snap and saw servants peeking from behind columns. His voice had been so loud he could still hear its echoes in the rafters.

Then, just as suddenly as he'd shouted all of that, he backed from the table and ran from the room. He had to. Otherwise he was going to weep, to sob and groan and moan and pound his fists, where his father and Crevis could see.

And he couldn't do that. He was still too much of a prince for that. And he was still a prince who would be king.

As he fled the room, Macon heard King Genos ask the seer, "Well, Crevis, what does my son's behavior portend? You're the omen-reader. Read me that one, and those that issue from our unexpected guests."

But Macon didn't stop to hear the answer. He ran as fast a he could to his rooms, where he vomited up the wine he'd drunk and then buried his head under his pillows, sobbing all the while as childhood fled and the fear of a man faced with forces beyond his control took its place.

His father the king had enlisted the strangers' aid to find the culprits behind Matilla's death, and to make the right sacrifice to the god. In his guilt and misery, Macon couldn't imagine that the heart the god wanted was any other than his own.

Unless it was the warlock's. But the warlock was busy with the stranger woman, so he couldn't go to Seth for solace. There was nowhere he could go, in fact, to hide from his fear and his guilt and his horror.

Not until his tears stopped. Not until his heart ceased breaking. Not until he got control of himself. And not until the warrior-woman was gone from the warlock's sanctum.

Then he'd do something, he told himself. Then he'd try something, anything, to make things right.

But whatever he did, there was still tomorrow's funeral, and the rite that might find him out, and a dangerous ally in Seth, one whom he couldn't trust but couldn't do without. Not now.

CHAPTER 17: TILL THE STORM STOPS

In life, there are nights of pain and nights of change, nights of love and nights of loneliness, nights of rest and nights on which the best a soul can do is find shelter from the storm.

The storm raging over the city brought different things to different folk, but left no heart untouched by its passage. To the common folk of this uncommon place it brought a renewed reverence for the god who manifested weather as His nature. They listened to the whining wind and the howling wolves outside the gates and they shivered before their fires, humbled in the face of gale and rain. Their oxen lowed and their dogs bayed and their housecats slunk into corners. And everywhere people poured the first of their wine on the flames and threw the best piece of meat on the coals and gave the choicest jug of oil they had to the god's altars in unused corners of the houses, as if heaven could be bribed and fear could pass as worship.

The palace functionaries had a gilded chapel to

visit and this they did, dressed in their finest damask cloaks and floppy hats trimmed with ermine and pantaloons of shorn silk velvet. There they clustered around a laden table, eating cakes after a comforting sermon that reaffirmed their faith in the gods as champions of the city and themselves as the true servitors of heaven's will. They put their heads together and gossiped about the king and his new queen and the eldest of the princes, seeking to blame their ruler and the malfeasance of his household for the stormlashing the city was taking.

Someone close to the king had heard tell that Prince Macon had bargained with the warlock for the sake of his sister's soul, and this was how the prince became Seth's apprentice. This, so the taleteller opined, was clearly the reason that inclement weather had descended on the city like a shroud.

The person to whom that theory was confided retorted that it was the king, not the prince, who was to blame for the storm: that the king's knowledge of the prince's deeds, and his failure to act on that knowledge, was what had turned heaven's heart against the city.

A third palace-watcher, taking offense at this, interjected that the king *had* done something: he'd made Tabet queen, and now would marry her himself—make the ultimate sacrifice to save the city and the dynasty he represented.

A fourth pundit, overhearing, wanted to know how any marriage could save the city from the sea at the end of time. Anyone with a lick of sense, this wise man said, could see that the city and all within were doomed to decrepitude, dissolution, death and destruction. All that faith and right action had held in abeyance these untold years would come upon them now with a vengeance—the vengeance of thwarted gods.

"How could he know this?" the first taleteller demanded.

And the fourth sage rubbed his chin meditatively before he replied that everyone knew that the queen, when she was still a princess, had seen the strangers in a dream—that she'd predicted the arrival in storm and fire and destruction of the man called Tempus and his creature, Jihan. Since the sojourners had subsequently appeared, so must the rest of her dream prove true.

But this attempt to shunt blame for the city's ills upon the newcomers fell on deaf ears among the sophisticated congregation in the palace temple. These were the politically adroit, the insiders, those who had the most to gain and the most to lose, depending upon how King Genos fared in the coming days.

Here were men who shared the confidences of the warlocks. Here were moralists who listened to the sermons of the priesthood, nodding with satisfaction as the shepherds attempted to herd the flock back into line. Here were the seers of the city, who read the omens and the evil in men's hearts and who knew the power of a prophecy to shape the future it described, and used it. Here were the rich and the powerful, the husbands of the status quo, the midwives of the eternal city's fortune.

The question became, as the storm grew fierce and the roaring of it made power players dare to speak aloud, a question of fitness: was Genos fit to rule, who'd brought the city to this impasse? Was his daughter soon to be their ruler? If so, who would rule by her side: warlock, stranger, benighted prince . . . or no one?

Would there be a city, when the storm and its aftermath were done? Was this the prophesied destruction, final and complete? Was the death of Matilla, as old as any of them and arguably as wise, a sign for the sighted to heed?

Was their way of life doomed beyond salvage? Would death and oblivion become their lot? Would they sink down, like their city's watery wheel, into the mire of ignorance? Would their torches go out and their wisdom be lost forever?

And if so, was the fault in themselves somewhere? Had they failed to counsel the king wisely enough? Had they hoarded their wisdom too close to their collective chest?

Or, as some maintained, were they merely frightened of supernal might and overreacting?

Gods, the priests had just finished reminding them, could be placated; gods could be bought. If a heart upon the altar of the Storm God was the price for the city's salvation, then they must give it, even if it be Genos' own.

For none of the handsome nobles of the eternal city truly thought, even for one moment, that what they offered to the world—hope, held out by example; wisdom, closely guarded and often secret; perfection, embodied in their ageless glory and attested to by the favors of the gods—was not worth preserving at any cost.

When the fourth pundit wondered aloud if they might not have lost the grace they claimed, if they might not have failed in their task by setting themselves apart, if more was needed by the World than a legend and a glory seen from afar but unattainable by the masses, this man was shouted down with boos and hisses.

They were the elite of the city. Their very existence was a light unto the dark World beyond the city's gates. They were the symbol to the world of perfection, not the unattainable perfection of afterlife, but the pinnacle of life on earth as man could live it. The gods had decreed this so long ago. The fact that these graces were granted to so few was natural and right and not a selfishness of the city's folk at all.

But some wondered into their sleeves and each others' ears if perhaps the city might have worked harder to spread her light beyond the gates; if merely existing was enough to justify their favored status under heaven; if things would have come to this, had the city shared her wealth among the downtrodden, her knowledge among the ignorant, her spiritual light among those living in darkness in the world.

Whatever she once had been, the city was now afflicted, all agreed. Whatever mandate she'd once embodied—of freedom of thought and speech, of rightness of action, of individual responsibility and of the sanctity of every human life—the city had lost something crucial to her own survival. She had lost the magic that had made her free and kept her strong. She had lost the strength of purpose that had guided her travels throughout the world. She had lost her leadership among the cities of the earth.

The city had lost, most precisely, her clarity of purpose, her purity of goal, her courage and her willingness to face adversity for principle's sake. She had lost her reason for being, her special gifts that once resided within the hearts of each and every man and woman of her streets.

And when the city lost these things, she lost her immortality, her god-given lightness that let her roam on wheels of water throughout the world. She had become heavy; she had become forgetful. And now it seemed she had become no better than any other city of venal men whose sight extended no farther than their own coffers. Having lost these things, the city had sunk into the mire by the sea at the end of time.

No one argued that point. But everyone argued about what must be done to recapture fleeting glory, moral highground all but lost, and the mandate that made the city eternal.

No one in the chapel dared to propose that the fault was not in their leader, that no one man could have made the city fall from grace. No one straightened his shoulders and stepped forward to offer his heart, pure and true and full of god's grace, as a sacrifice upon the altar to save them all.

None of them wanted to die. None could go to his death with equanimity, though all had lived as long as the eldest of the sojourners who'd come through the gates with weapons on their hips.

And each one of the citydwellers was certain to his core that what resided in his particular heart was too precious to lose to death, too special to be wiped out by a mere precession of days and nights, too important to the universe to be forgotten.

And the god looked down at these self-important folk who clustered in a house of worship but worshipped only themselves, who huddled together looking for a scapegoat, someone who could be blamed for the failures of all, and the storm raged ever fiercer beyond the palace walls.

All through the city the storm scourged, searching for a quiet heart or a pure thought or a person who truly revered the gods and was humble in the face of rampant fate.

But Enlil found only His own strangers: his mortal weapon, Nikodemos; the sprite Jihan who was not and never had been human; and Tempus, who read ancient wisdom texts by candlelight while the Storm God's priest paced the room and worried over what the Riddler might find.

So Enlil quested further, nosing in upon the doings of the benighted citydwellers, cocking his great ear to what was said, putting his supernal eye to this keyhole and to that.

Thus it was that the god saw the city's warlock try

to cast a captivating spell upon the spite, Jihan. He saw the Froth Daughter rise up and swat that spell like a troublesome gnat, without even concern enough to kill the warlock for his scheming, and laugh and cock her head at him and say, "What else can you do, wizard, that might be of interest?"

And the god saw Macon, the besotted prince, creep into Seth's study and whisper to the warlock to come outside, into the antechamber, and talk with him. and He saw the warlock leave the sprite to send the prince upon an errand:

"Go get me the heart of a pig—take a hefty sow outside the gates and slay her. Put the heart in oilcloth and bring it back to me before the dawn breaks, so we'll have a heart to switch for Matilla's before hers ends up on Enlil's altar."

"Me?" The prince was bitter, frightened, and dullwitted because of that.

"Would you rather be implicated by a dead woman's heart?"

The prince made no answer, just slunk away, thinking that no one had heard him, praying that Jihan had not.

And that prayer was answered, but Enlil himself followed the son of Genos to the pigsty and stayed his hand. No sow would come to him. The more he tried, the more squealing rose to heaven. This commotion roused the stablehands, who came asking the prince what help he needed.

"No help, no help at all," said Prince Macon, and skulked away to to the warlock's, and then to his bed through the pelting rain and wind that ripped at his clothes as if to strip him naked in the street.

Then the god turned his eye upon the prince's father, and found the king repentent and weeping on his bed. But no cry the king uttered had the god's name in it: Genos was filled with the folly of man and thought only of the error of man and the power of man.

For as long as the god waited, King Genos never called upon Him for help.

So Enlil looked further, into the hearts of the seers of the city, and found there only prophecies of doom.

Tiring of this crowd of men who could envision only things and their losses, who cared only for what treasures they had around them, the god turned at last back to his human implement, the one mortal in the city, Nikodemos.

Niko was sitting in his horse's stall, lest the beast panic in the storm. With him was still the city's queen, and she was saying, "Niko, I must tell you this: the warlock has said to me that if I wish, he can guarantee your Test will kill you—that I have but to ask, and it will be fatal."

"And will you?"' said Niko softly, without a hint of guile or plea.

"You're the only mortal in the city," said the queen, whose lip quivered. "How can you be so fearless in the face of death?"

"Am I facing death? I see only a woman trying to test a man's love, one who's not sure what love is, or what it means, and has power and honor and loyalty all mixed up with ownership and vengeance."

Even the god blinked an eye at that, and looked closer at a woman half-ensorceled and a soldier who knew but didn't care.

"The Storm God brought me here," said Niko gently to the queen, calm and unresisting to his soul, ready to act in a moment if the need arose, but content to wait until the time was right. "Enlil works His Will and His Purpose. I'll do the best I can, with all my heart, when the time comes. My commander will want to talk with you about the warlock, if you'll let me tell him . . ."

"No." The queen crossed her arms.

"Then I'll do my best to bring you to your senses, Tabet, but you're caught in a web of witchcraft and young girl's longings that you can't understand, let alone control."

In Niko's voice was a weariness and a wisdom that came from experience, a gentleness edged with a cutting sharpness that gave the god pause.

The god had been looking for a heart in the city, a heart that was worthy, a heart that knew true worship. And the god had found such a heart, and a voice that called upon Him without greed or demand, without wheedling or whining.

The heart of the prophecy did Enlil find in the stable while the storm raged, upon the altar that was the shore at the end of time.

But though the prophecy was fulfilled upon that moment, the humbling of the city had just begun.

CHAPTER 18: MOURNING FOG

Tempus never slept. Once he'd thought it a curse. In Genos' city it was clearly a blessing. There was more to be done here than a snoring priest could accomplish, and time was short.

The candles had guttered while he'd read the temple's lore: secret lore on crackling sheaves of parchment; older works rolled on papyrus spindles; tablets of clay in wooden leaves with green bronze hinges in between.

And bitumen records older still, he'd held in hands that until today he'd regarded as old. Among all this antiquity, among the texts of legends he'd heard mistold in youth and king lists long forgot, he was feeling young and foolish.

This lightened his mood and made him smile. He'd misread this situation. Not entirely, but somewhat. And where the will of gods was concerned, somewhat was quite enough.

The heart that the city needed, he was nearly sure, was not a dead heart, a dying heart, or even a heart plucked, wildly beating, from a heaving human breast. And if the heart was the sort of heart he thought, then the god had given it to the city, by dropping Niko here.

But the city was failing the god's test in every way. . . . *death will fly over the city as She has not done in millennia. Pluck a heart from a stranger, if the king loses his, and give it to the god if it is not his already.*

If the king loses his . . .

This was the admonishment, and the prophecy, in the ancient text. There was nothing further to go on but an equation of time itself with an altar of the god.

This misreading and misinterpreting of holy will by mortal power players was not new to Tempus. Men will twist whatever they can to personal advantage—this was not something to decry as venal, but something to accept as a necessary to survival.

But the twisting of the prophecy by priests and warlocks had brought the city to the edge of a terrible error.

Death will fly over the city as She has not done in millennia . . .

The ancient crone who'd fallen to her death had flown, after a fashion. Perhaps she'd flown further than from Genos' tower to the garden below, but even for just that distance, fly she did.

And the king had surely lost heart.

Giving a heart to the god was the matter most in need of interpretation. King Genos had intimated that no strangers had been slain . . . yet.

If Niko's heart was the heart in question, then the gift of it to the god was one only Niko could make. In truth, may already have made. But slaughtering a man of the Storm God, a man bound by Sacred Band oaths, was the way to certain destruction. Tempus, who knew prophecy, who knew gods more intimately than most, and who knew his own strength, was adamant on that point.

If Niko was singled out as a sacrifice by the warlock, or the frightened locals, Tempus would raze the eternal city until stone toppled from off of stone and there was nothing left here either white or gleaming. The electrum-clad bastions and the proud silvery ramparts would melt under the heat of his fury at a city so blinded by its moral lassitude that it would spend the honest heart of a mortal stranger to save its immortal hide.

Tempus ran a finger along the lines of glyphs on the bitumen tablet before him in the priests' library. As old as time itself was the clay he held. The chicken-scratch letters were gibberish to the priests here. Just as well, from what he'd seen.

They'd misconstrued quite enough without these imperatives from heaven to add to their confusion.

Together with the seers and the warlocks, it was now obvious to Tempus, the priests had colluded to tell a failing king exactly what the king wanted to hear, no matter what the truth was. And when truth is bent, and twisted, and taken for worthless, then everything that keeps the soul in man alive begins to die, and man becomes no better than the beasts of the field.

And in the city, the beasts of the field had no special grace. Like the carp that fell from heaven, they could flop and gasp and die in a multitude for lack of water. Or for lack of grace. Or for lack of souls, more correctly.

Tempus' hand upon the bitumen tablet was supple and strong. His skin was tanned and had a patina to it that the weather had put there. It was not an old hand. It was not a wrinkled hand. It was a sinewy, strong hand with a dusting of hair upon its back.

A strong hand was needed here, Tempus now knew. Nothing in all he'd read had convinced him otherwise. Nothing in all he'd seen among the nobility and the priesthood had shown him anything worth preserving.

Yet he hesitated, before he woke the snoring priest and pulled back the curtains. Outside, his ears told him, the storm had abated during the night.

Somewhere beyond these walls, magnificent with painted exploits of the Storm God (who looked very much like Niko), Jihan was loose in the city, learning what she could. And Niko was making his peace with the city's queen. And the king was wondering what the new day would bring, when it held a funeral in a city that had never had one.

And, too, the warlock was working. Tempus could feel it, like a thousand ants crawling up his spine.

Almost, he asked the god if the god wanted the city to persevere—asked Him outright.

But there were other gods here, revered gods who'd helped make the city what it was. Tempus had lived too long in the Storm God's shadow not to know that when Enlil, called by that or any of His Thousand Names, was roused to action, lessons needed to be taught.

The lesson he was to teach was clear from the prophecy and from the expectation of the city. If he could teach it without losing Niko's life, he would be content.

But this time, the survival of his rightman lay not in the strength of Tempus' arm against a horde of demons, or Niko's loyalty when pitted against sorcerous love, or anything other than whether Niko was what he'd been trying so hard to become: a true man of the god, with a heart pleasing to Enlil, right where it was, beating in a human breast.

The rest—the sorcery, the politics, the miserable lot of human failings—was much easier to estimate than whether Niko was, finally, all that Niko could become.

Tempus put down the tablet he'd been holding with an audible thump that made the priest snort and twist in the chair where he slept.

The Riddler got up and went to the window, brushing aside the heavy hide curtain like a veil. And he looked out upon the city and saw nothing.

It wasn't there. It was obliterated by a fog so thick that Tempus might have stood at the end of creation. All beyond was featureless, a grayish white that glowed with an inner light like his horse's coat under a summer sun.

Tempus knew his omens and this one called him. He'd been intending to wake Jamad and warn him of the errors of thought and deed so clear to a man who could read the texts with an open mind.

The featureless expanse told him not to bother. The die was cast. After a night of seeking a supernal loophole, a way to placate a god whose anger was never unjustified, he'd convinced himself of that.

And he'd found a way, too, to separate his thoughts of the eternal city from his image of himself. They were both of another time, but one had forgotten its purpose.

Tempus knew his. His hand dropped from the curtain to his swordbelt, resting there upon his weapon's pommel with comfortable familiarity. He'd never really thought the god was joking. Enlil didn't. Nor testing him. The god's resolve was so much a part of him, he was its affect in the world.

If blood must be shed here and flame ignited, then it was a sad day, but not a catastrophic one, as long as the shedder of that blood and the lighter of that flame was a man the gods had sanctified for the task.

What he had not learned still troubled him, if only slightly, as he looked out upon the murk through which a man could see no farther than his hand could reach. When this was over, what would remain of the city? What would become of its wisdom, which was here yet, though lying fallow?

And what would the god ask from the heart of Nikodemos, an adept of the balance, a child of maat, to make this matter right?

Affronts against heaven were never cheaply paid. Leaving the library of the temple, stepping carefully over the outstretched legs of its sleeping priest, Tempus could feel the god rustle in him.

It was a sense of fullness in his head, as if his skull contained the world; it was a sense of power in his loins, as if the god were hungry for sensation; it was a sense of heat all up his spine in a fountain that crested somewhere between his eyes, and out of those eyes he could feel Enlil, looking about with all His fervor.

The world was empty without men and gods, and yet seldom could they share what both created. In those moments when the god inhabited Tempus, his wrath was boundless over every wrong he saw, yet his joy was neverending, over what god and man had made. The expanse of the world was phenomenal and full of death; eternity was like the fog before him, full of nothing, empty yet full, unformed but exact, unbounded and bounded with unyielding limitations.

For god and man, those limitations were lifted, each in his contact with the other. In Tempus, where man met god and the passions of both merged, the god's tempering force remade the disappointing evils of mankind.

Walking with the god fully resident inside him, down the temple's back stairs and out into the white fog, Tempus let the god guide his steps. He could not see a thing. The fog caressed his cheeks and arms and kissed his swordbelt and his sandals, and in it he felt as if he could walk this way to heaven. With the very Pillager inside him, god of war and strife and lust and striving, nonetheless, he thought he felt what peace might feel like—the featureless stretch of eternity before him and behind.

It occurred to the part of his mind that was always his own that some of these were the god's memories, superimposed over an evocative bit of weather, for Enlil was not talking today.

Tempus preferred it thus, so he did not goad the god to talk to him, to raise a voice and point out some path or other through the pearly air.

The ground beneath his feet was paved, this much he could attest to, as he let happenstance chart his course. And as he walked the city, a wordless debate went on inside him, between the man who thought the city was worth saving, and the god who wanted only catastrophe and change, His lesson taught, the fear of Him put into every denizen who lived here.

But it will be like this, Lord, if Thy wrath knows no bounds. And then there will be none to worship You, none to fall quaking at Your feet, none to praise Thy glories on a feast day. There will be no feast days, and no days of mourning, for nothing will be left. The city will be gone; only the fog will remain. What lesson is there in obliteration?

But the god did not answer him, only rustled slightly at the base of his spine, as if settling into the most comfortable seat in some amphitheater, waiting for the games to begin.

Did not answer, unless the lifting of the fog that commenced then was an answer. It swirled up from Tempus' sandals as if he could lift it by his steps. And in his heart there was no great unease, as there had been when he stepped out of the library, out of the temple, into the streets, worrying over Niko and the city and all their fates.

The fog was soft and moist and full of promises of eternal sleep that did not daunt him: what the god had showed him, if it was death's door, was not an end to thought, or knowledge, or even time, precisely. And through it, now, shapes of great buildings could be seen.

Tempus was not, like Niko, sure that he was earning a soldier's afterlife, a seat on the right hand of Enlil in some special heaven, but Tempus had seen ghosts, friends of his from the other side of life, who'd come, discrete, from somewhere.

And if Niko spent the rest of his life in this city, or walked through the fog to an afterlife rising out of mist like the buildings of Processional Way, then that was Niko's choice.

Tempus' was clear enough: do the bidding of Enlil's wrath here and now, protect those he loved, including Nikodemos, from the depredatious sorcerers who twisted everything, even the heavens, into mockery, and keep himself sacrosanct.

Tempus knew now that he mustn't identify with the city. He mustn't make assumptions as to its piety or its sanctity, since the gods were here to prove that myth outmoded. And he must remember the rain of carp, who flopped and died and ended it the cityfolk's stewpots, and in the pigs' slop, and in the gardens, planted under stalks of corn.

To the gods, nothing was wasted. To Tempus, it must be the same. Niko's face upon the god's shoulders in the temple was a message meant for Tempus that had been placed there before either Niko or Tempus was born.

If Niko-as-Enlil was difficult for Tempus to come to terms with, then how must it be for Niko himself, who'd resisted and rejected all offers by powers more than mortal to make of him an avatar?

The time was gone, however, for Tempus to shield Niko from his future, if such a time had ever been. Like the fog that broke into wisps and tendrils and floated in patches before him as he strode toward the palace compound, lives such as theirs in the world were governed by indiscernable rules—until they were governed by the iron Will of heaven.

Having come to this conclusion, Tempus was not surprised when Jihan loomed before him, out of a rip of the fog as if out of the primal egg.

"Riddler? The warlock tried to seduce me." She grinned and cocked a hip at him.

"Did he survive you?"

"He never laid a slimy hand upon me, you lout!" She pouted and straightened her shoulders, thrusting forth her chest. "You are not jealous? Angry at his temerity? Will you not come and hack him limb from limb in my honor?"

"In your honor? *For* your honor, you mean," he said, stifling a grin of his own as she fell in beside him.

"Why not?" she demanded.

"I will not. You could hack him limb from limb yourself if you wished. For *my* honor."

This confused her. "Your honor?"

"His attempt to discount me by suborning you, Froth Daughter." He couldn't resist teasing her.

"Should I have?" she wanted to know.

"Your choice, I'm sure. Just what did he do—anything I should know about?"

"He . . . tried to spell me into his bed."

"But he didn't touch you."

"You jest. Without my permission? I would have frozen him to ice and taken his most obvious icicle and crushed it under my—"

Tempus couldn't stifle the chuckle that came out of him. "Then, Jihan, you have humbled him without any help from me, isn't that so?"

"But you're not jealous that he tried? I think you should be."

"Or flattered, perhaps?"

That she didn't understand at all. She scowled at him. "I want you to be jealous. Men are."

"In the way that you mean, I'm not a man." The god in him was rustling, roused by Jihan's titillating talk of jealousy and icicles and person touching person. This put a different light on things, and Tempus strove to steer the discussion to less dangerous ground. If the god took it into his head to have Jihan, using Tempus' body, there'd be nothing for it but to satisfy the Pillager. And now was not the time.

"I'll be jealous if you ever go near him again, but now tell me what you learned from him that I should know. Surely you didn't spend a whole night with the city's most malevolent warlock without learning something that will help us."

Her brows knit. In the fog, she was veiled and unveiled by the wind like a maiden in a glen and the god was more and more interested, nearly aroused. Tempus began peering beyond Jihan, looking for a likely alley.

He didn't find one, for Jihan chose that moment to answer his question: "The prince came by, Prince Macon, you know. He and Seth went into the hall where they thought I couldn't hear." She tossed her head. "Seth sent him for a pig's heart to substitute for Matilla's by some slight of hand before the heart is placed on the altar."

"We'll have to prevent that."

"No need," she said. "Macon came back later with no pig's heart, saying he'd failed. Seth was angry. They plan a spell to disrupt the ceremony."

"Did you hear what kind?" He took her by the arm, stopping her in the fog-swathed street.

"Let go, Riddler. No, they're at it now. But what difference does that make? Remember, this is my father's ocean we have at our backs. I can bring a fog thrice as thick as this, or a torrent, or drown them in their beds or have an octopus rear up from the sea and ensnare them. . . ."

"And you need me to discipline the warlock for

you? None of that, Jihan, unless I ask you. You must promise. No matter how angry you get: this whole affair involves Niko too deeply."

"Niko," she sighed. "Sometimes, Riddler, I think you love him better than me."

"Sometimes, Jihan, I think I do too," he said under his breath.

"What?" she demanded.

"Sometimes I don't know what to do with you," he said.

"I know the answer to that," she said coquettishly, reaching for him in the street.

He told himself it was her doing. When her hand closed on him and the god reared up to take control of him, body and soul, all his plans had to wait while Jihan's needs and the god's were satisfied.

He didn't mind the act, or even Jihan's forwardness. But he did mind that it was not his choosing, nor the proper time or place. But the war-god had always been one to do it in the street.

And he minded the lost time. If the warlock was working spells to affect the outcome of the presentation of Matilla's heart to the god, then Tempus felt justified in doing whatever was necessary to incriminate Seth publicly, especially now that he was sure that Seth could and would be incriminated.

If the warlock hadn't had a hand in Matilla's death, he'd never have sent the prince to find a substitute heart. That Prince Macon was involved up to his royal nose wasn't welcome news, but not totally unexpected either, given the prince's behavior—and considering how much a crown prince had at stake during times like these.

As soon as Jihan and the god-given lust filling him were sated, he must propose funeral arrangements that would openly implicate both parties, without letting on to King Genos or the priest what he was about.

He wasn't worried about Seth, whom he knew was occupied trying to prevent just this result, objecting openly. Nor was he concerned that Crevis the seer or Jamad, high priest of the Storm God, would take offense at Tempus' meddling. The king had deputized Tempus in front of his advisors to make whatever funeral arrangements Tempus chose.

He'd spent the night in the temple library partly so that he could claim to have familiarized himself with the city's ancient lore and customs: neither priest nor seer would object to ritual purportedly gleaned from tablets which they themselves could not read.

And as for the warlock's fear of being unmasked by Matilla's heart, that was a stroke of luck for which Jihan deserved even the price she now demanded, no matter the fact that time was suddenly precious.

Without Jihan, he'd never have known that the heart of the handmaid might tell the true tale of what had happened to the chest in which it once had beaten.

And if he could get the god's attention, the heart might still have its chance. Pitting the might of the gods against the power of sorcery was, after all, one of the things Tempus did best.

CHAPTER 19: THE FUNERAL

Once the fog burned off, the sun beat down like a signal beacon on the funerary bier in the palace courtyard, baking away the dampness and making everyone sweat as they waited for the strangers to appear and the ceremony to begin.

Since all the gathered folk were pulling at the collars of their robes and wiping their upper lips and fanning perspiring cheeks, Seth's nervous perspiration went unremarked. For this he thanked the powers that he served, if briefly. The warlock was not feeling thankful today.

Not yet. Everything had gone awry with his plans so far, forcing him to more drastic measures. If only Macon could have got the pig's heart, then the warlock needn't have employed so wildly dangerous a spell as the one he'd prepared to evoke with a single whispered word when the time was right.

But Macon had not acquired the sow's heart, and Seth had been too busy with the weird woman from the World—if woman she was—to think of conjuring one from elsewhere—until it had been too late.

Once all his brethren were awake and bustling, once the sun had defeated the fog, there was no time, no privacy. Truth be known, there was no concentration in the warlock's heart, and concentration was the most primary element of successful sorcery.

First he couldn't think of anything but Matilla's heart and the moment it would be placed on Enlil's altar. Then he couldn't think of anything but the woman who called herself a Froth Daughter, and what it would be like to command such a one. Then he couldn't think of anything but how she'd shrugged off his potent lovemaking spell as if it were nothing.

And then Macon had come, and he couldn't think of anything but failure. When the Froth Daughter finally left him, he'd been obsessed by sudden fear, wracked by a terror that made his palms sweat, his face whiten, and his knees weaken.

And then, through the window of his tower, the sounds of construction had begun: hammers thumping, lumber clattering, horses neighing, men shouting. And from that moment to this, the consternated warlock had been locked in a fearful restlessness like a room with no exit, in which he distrusted everything and everyone and most of all, whatever sort of snare the strangers had contrived to entrap him.

For it was clear to him now that they knew. Else why would the man called the Riddler have sicked that soulless sprite on him, to distract him and make him impotent when he most needed to think his way clear of the very trap she represented.

He was lucky he hadn't said anything he shouldn't. Or done anything. He'd been almost relieved when Macon had come back whining about his failure, for the Froth Daughter had still been with him.

And when she was gone, there was the enveloping

fog, the mystifying fog, the enshrouding fog that cast a pall over the city and made it impossible for Seth to see what kind of observance the strangers were preparing, with the blessing of the king.

Only at the last possible moment, when Macon had come to find out why Seth hadn't appeared yet at the palace, had the warlock pulled himself together enough to contribute any spell whatsoever to save their skins.

Presentiments of doom were so strong in him, then and now, that he was a prisoner of panic. If not, he'd never have handed the tools of magic to Macon, and told the boy, "Place one of these at each corner of the bier or coffin or whatever it is on which they're going to lay Matilla's body."

"They're only incense," frowned the frightened royal pup. "What good's that going to do?"

"Just do as you're told, apprentice," ordered the warlock.

If his crime hadn't been so hideous, Seth might have enlisted the aid of his fellow warlocks. But it was and he couldn't. And there was the question of competence: he was the only warlock in the city who'd ever used the sort of spells he was now employing. His fellows cured boils and found water and helped lovers over quarrels.

So Seth was all alone with his fear and his failure, as the crowd thickened before the funerary bier of Matilla, waiting for the king to arrive.

The corpse wasn't laid out there. The bier, once he'd finally seen it, was nothing special. Wood had been pegged together to hold the corpse; kindling and firewood were under and around the plinth where she'd lie.

Statues of stone had been brought on rollers from the temples: the Storm God, the Earth God, the Gods of Life and Fertility, were at each corner of the bier. As were the four innocuous cones, like incense, that Seth had given Macon to place there.

At least something had gone right. But would it be enough? Seth peered around him through the white-hot day that hurt his eyes, eyes that hadn't closed all night and now were sticky and watering in the sun.

The folk of the city were crowding into the palace courtyard, buying cold drinks and apples baked with thyme and honey on sticks and little trinkets hawked by vendors who called out, "Throw a good-bye gift to Matilla when she rides on fire to heaven."

A carnival air was overtaking the funeral. People who'd never known death didn't know how to behave, and if not for the vendors, no one would have brought a gift for the departing soul at all.

But gifts were purchased by women in bright linen and by men in velvet cloaks; by everyone, in fact, but Seth.

He kept scanning the crowd for someone knowledgeable, someone who might know where the royal family was, or where the body was being prepared.

For Seth saw a chance, a chance his panic-stricken mind hadn't noticed until he'd gotten here and found nothing but a carnival of death and a picnicking crowd, all asking one another what the funeral would be like.

The corpse wasn't out here yet. It must be somewhere. If he could find it, perhaps he could steal the incriminating heart and feed it to a dog, a cat, or throw it in a well, a gutter . . .

The possibilities for salvation seemed endless. The only thing he wouldn't do was repeat the spell that had summoned the ectoplasmic vipers from the underworld. He wasn't sure how he'd sent them back—if he had.

As long as he lived, he'd never again ask for help from creatures not of this world. Doing it once had almost killed him as well as Matilla.

The warlocks of antiquity, who'd written that spell and used it, must have been made of sterner stuff than Seth. He was out of control, and this he vaguely knew; he was out of his depth, this he'd known since he'd performed the rite that killed Matilla; he was lacking in ruthlessness or some quality of discipline, this was proved by his failures.

But there was still time. He could still save himself. *Some* of his spells were working: he could feel the growing power of his love spell over Queen Tabet; he knew his power over her brother, the crown prince.

Seth stood on tiptoe, craning his neck to get a glimpse of where the corpse might be, and saw Crevis coming out of the palace.

He set out to intercept the seer, threading his way among women and children with real smiles on their faces and men with set grins like death's heads.

Just a few days ago, Seth would not have known what a face looked like, set in death. But now he did. And he knew more, and worse, from delving into the darker magics of his kind. If he was exposed as Matilla's murderer, what would happen to him? The city had no penalty for murder, for it had had no murderer in all its history.

Would they expel him into the dying World, where everything a man did came to naught, and all a man had to look forward to was a mulchy grave?

He shivered in the heat and bumped someone, and made a muttered apology, and bustled by.

But the offended party's hand came down upon his shoulder. He turned to placate whoever it was, and saw one of his own, a younger warlock, a canny man of good reputation.

"Master, can I help you? You look distraught. Is there anything—"

"Nothing," he cut off his acolyte brusquely, shook free of the hand on him, and blundered away blindly, into the crowd. There was nothing anyone could do but him. Especially nothing such a one could do.

He imagined that he'd seen a knowing look in the other warlock's eye, an eagerness to see him fail, a waiting look like that on a hungry dog, and a smile like a dog's smile when dinner's ready.

Well, the warlocks who were anxious to take his place, split up his goods and his hoarded books, and claim his power would have to wait. He looked back and saw three of them, huddled together, looking after him.

His back muscles knotted so that it seemed he was hung from a hook and all his skin was pulling away from his bones. He hunched his shoulders and pushed on, toward Crevis and the doorway into the palace from which the seer had come.

All the while he greeted this luminary and that noble and the other woman whose marriage he'd saved or whose child he'd disciplined, without hearing a word he said. All he could think about was the corpse and the heart within it.

If he could get to the corpse, he'd rip that heart from its chest with his bare hands. If there was no place to secret it, he told himself, he'd eat it on the spot. Whatever was necessary, he vowed, he'd do.

So singlemindedly did the warlock shoulder his way among the subdued people of the city, who feigned revelry and strove to imitate whatever conventions might be appropriate to this day, that he didn't see the prince until Macon was upon him.

"Well, Warlock, now what? I placed the cones, as you said." The prince's lips were blue; his teeth nearly chattered; sweat had stained his silken collar.

"Get hold of yourself, boy, is all," said Seth through teeth that would not come apart. "Where's the body being kept?"

"Right in there." Macon pointed. "You don't want to see it."

"I most especially do want to see it," Seth said, grabbing Macon like a striking snake and jerking the boy nearly off his feet.

"You don't," said the prince. "You should see my sister, though. She's asked about you twice. She says she has something to tell you that only she can say."

Seth was unresponsive, hardly listening. He propelled the prince toward the doorway where Macon had said the corpse lay, through which staples were usually brought to the palace kitchens.

"Did you hear me, Warlock?" the prince wanted to know.

"What? Yes, yes. But take me in there, I say. Quickly. I'll see your sister later."

"You should see her now. She's the queen, after all. I— Greetings Crevis, on this sad day."

"Nothing sad, say the strangers, about a funeral," said Crevis to the prince sternly. And to Seth: "Welcome to the first funeral, Lord Warlock."

The tone of voice that the seer used snapped Seth's head around. "The 'first?' You expect more deaths? Let us work together to make this a singular event in our city's history. Unless, of course, you have omens to the contrary?"

They were standing near the door that called to Seth with such compelling force. So near to it, he almost broke and ran, almost shoved Macon from him to use the boy to knock the seer from his path.

Crevis said, "The omens are no different than they were—you know that. The real omens have always predicted this."

"And more," Seth agreed, while the prince looked between the two palace advisors, squinting, his mouth drawn tight.

"The strangers say that death is a feast," said the seer. "That a city whose faith in the gods is strong must gather joyously to send a citizen up to heaven."

The seer made a face that said he believed such talk
to be less than truth.

"I want to see the corpse," Seth blurted, not knowing how else to get away.

"They'll be bringing it right out."

"Now, before they bring it out," Seth said, and
made to brush by the seer.

"You don't want to get too close," the omen-taker
called after him. "She's beginning to smell."

He paid no heed, but strode blindly up to the
arched doorway, which was open, and through it.

There his steps slowed and it was as if he trod
molasses, so precarious did his way become in the
dark that was green after the bright light.

He could see almost nothing. He could hear people talking quietly, like the buzzing of distant bees.
He flexed his hands, which were cold and numb. He
should have brought a knife. He should have brought
a saw, a bag, a potion carefully prepared to make the
corpse disappear.

But he had not. He'd never really thought he'd get
this far.

But he had and, as his eyes adjusted to the gloom,
he realized that there was no one clustered around
the corpse on its litter in the center of the hall.

This was his chance.

He nearly ran to Matilla's side.

His hands were reaching out for her before he
truly looked down at what lay there.

Then he stopped, frozen in horror. Matilla's face
was greenish white; her kohled eyes were open. Her
twisted mouth accused him silently.

And her heart was missing. She had not yet been
robed. She was naked and broken and slit from throat
to gullet. Inside she was all blue and green and he
thought it was maggoty. He thought he saw things
crawling there. He thought he was going to vomit
from the smell.

And he thought her right hand moved. It seemed to clench.

He stumbled backward, thinking she was reaching for him, that her clawed and dead hand with its purple-blue nails was striking for his throat.

His back hit a column in the hallway and there he stopped, panting. His lips were dry and his throat actually felt as though he'd swallowed a bowl of nails.

He slumped against the column and as he did he heard voices.

Then there were footsteps, and people separated themselves from shadows: the king, the queen, the two sojourners, and Nikodemos.

The queen was saying, "I really think this red robe is the best choice: it's so gay. And you said we wanted to show the people that death is nothing to fear. We must keep the mood festive."

"I agree," said the gravelly voice of the Riddler. "Too, if any blood happens to be wet enough still to stain, on red it won't show."

"Tempus," came the voice of Nikodemos, "gently with these folk."

"Gently? For a murdered soul's funeral, we're gentle enough."

"You're so sure," said the king in a reedy voice that seemed weak as the party came into a shaft of light and Seth's heart began to pound, realizing they could now see him, since he could see them.

Exposed, he waited for one of them to spy him, to accuse him, to point a finger at him. In his mind's eye, Matilla's corpse did just that: sat up, though it was just a hollowed shell of a person, and pointed at him, calling him her murderer with dead blue lips.

Queen Tabet was saying, "This embalming you performed, Lord Tempus, we thank you in the name of the city for guiding us through the preparations and—Seth!"

"Your . . . highness. Your—" Seth took three deep

and rasping breaths with all eyes on him, clutching the pillar against which he leaned as if it were a lover, for without it he might have fallen to the ground. "Your brother," he finished triumphantly, having thought of an explanation despite all odds, "said you wished to speak to me immediately, that you had something to say to me that couldn't wait and couldn't be carried by a messenger."

"Oh, you know Macon—always exaggerating," said Tabet with a wave of her hand and a gay lilt to her voice, which was too forced. Then her eyes slid to Nikodemos and Seth realized that her words were for the soldier.

A spark of hope flamed in his heaving breast: had the princess come to her senses? Was she going to take him up on his offer of insuring the fatality of Niko's test?

But hope fled in the face of the corpse and the three sojourners, who looked at him with eyes full of condemnation. Could he do what he'd bragged he could do in order to impress this woman who was half in love with him because of a spell he'd put upon her in the fete hall?

Could he do any of the things he'd planned, if he could not find the heart of Matilla in time?

And it was clear he could not. It was clearer when he met Tempus' eyes and saw the amused, triumphant look therein.

So he said, summoning his composure and his dignity: "Then we'll talk later, at your convenience, my queen," and slid around the column to take his leave.

It wasn't until he'd gotten away from the accusatory glances of the strangers and the dull anguished one of the king, who seemed a shadow of his former self, and the guarded one of Tabet, which told him nothing, that Seth remembered the cones he'd had Macon place around the bier.

Would he have done that, if he'd known that the statues of the gods would be at each compass point as well? What would happen, when the corpse lay upon the bier and the pyre was lit?

Did it matter that the gods' statues were there? Did it matter, after all, whether it mattered? Only time would tell, and time was running out.

But Tabet had looked at him without the horror in her eyes that would have been there if she'd learned what the sojourners so obviously knew.

If they hadn't known, the interloper Nikodemos and his allies who were so obviously more than human, then they'd never have scooped Matilla's heart from her body.

Would they?

What was embalming, anyway? He vaguely knew the word.

But funerals weren't something he'd had to know about, so he hadn't bothered to learn.

You gutted a fish or a bird or a cow before you ate it. Was Matilla being presented to the gods as food?

Would any god eat of such polluted flesh?

Seth wanted to vomit. He almost did, waiting for the corpse to be brought out.

And when the body was brought out on the shoulders of Tempus, Jihan, Nikodemos, and Genos the king, with Macon and Tabet mincing behind, throwing flowers and pouring oil and singing a hymn everyone in the city knew, it was too late to worry about what the warlock hadn't learned.

What he had done was about to become visible. His future, his fate, his very life rode on that litter with Matilla's corpse.

And when the four pallbearers put the corpse upon the bier and stepped back, all the people who'd bought flowers or oil or sweetmeats were encouraged to sing as they threw their tokens on the red-robed corpse.

Meanwhile, Tempus himself lit a torch from an oil lamp that was handed to him by Jamad, the Storm God's priest.

This torch he handed to Tabet, and in that instant, Seth regretted his plan and his spell and almost called out a warning.

But all the people were singing the foolish hymn to the Morning Sun and Tabet wouldn't have heard him anyway.

Please Tabet, please light that bier from the center, from the long side. Please, Seth begged in his mind.

He had no way of knowing how high the flames would rise, those flames which touched his cones at the corners of the pyre, flames he'd instructed to burn everything and anything until his guilt was burned away, to turn the corpse and its heart to ashes, and all who wished him evil to ashes as well.

Tabet walked forward with the torch and Seth nearly couldn't watch. He forced himself to see the fine fair maid, with her flower-braided hair and her dress of pristine yellow linen. Her young flesh was so ripe and so full of life. Life was putting the torch to death. He had brought death and death and now would bring more death to the city. . . .

She lit the bier in the center of the long side, away from the singing crowd, and smoke billowed white and pungent with herbs and flowers and the cedar of the bier.

The flames rose red and the people kept singing.

The body on the pyre seemed to be melting, from what he could see through the smoke.

He told himself he would not speak the word; that the spell would be no good without his command; that he could take his chances with the specter called the Riddler and his awful cohorts.

But as the flames licked toward the cones, it seemed to him through the smoke that the statues of the

gods began to move, to come alive, to rouse themselves off their plinths and flex mighty arms.

Out of his throat then came the single word that
ignited the everburning fire he'd called from Hell
itself and put into the cones.

This fire was not red and gold, but blue and white
and in it danced devils and demons. From it rose a
smoke that was black and ectoplasmic and which
formed itself into giant vipers, four of them, that rose
like dancing spirals, swaying to the music, from all
four compass points of the bier.

And these vipers of smoke, he was sure before the
flames grew too hot and the smoke too thick and
people started screaming instead of singing and the
whole crowd surged backward, dragging him with
it—these four hideous vipers of smoke seemed to
close themselves around each god's statue.

The vipers wound about the statues and the statues moved. Their arms of granite came to life and
wrestled with the ectoplasmic pythons threatening to
crush them, to coil around their throats of stone and
crumble that stone to sand.

All Seth could make out, as the crowd broke for
the palace gates in a rout and panic, was the battle
between the statues of the gods and the vipers from
hell, amidst the flames of unnatural heat, the hungry
flames he'd called upon to obliterate all his enemies.

Then the flames were a hungry wall that cut off
the place, and Seth's sight of the sojourners, of the
soldier Nikodemos, of the royal family and even of
the palace's high tower where the king had so long
sequestered himself.

All he could see was belching black smoke that
rose to heaven, until, through tearing eyes, he saw
the snakelike tendrils of that smoke curl around the
palace ramparts, slither up the tower, and wind there.

Before the gates were closed and guardsmen pushed
him to his knees, he thought he saw one single, giant

viper with a red and gleaming eye arch itself over the city, its trunk wound around the king's tower, hissing with a forked tongue as long as a man.

And he thought he saw Enlil—or Nikodemos, or a phantom of white smoke in the shape of a god or a man—rise up and plant its feet firmly upon the battlements, smoky sword in hand, to do battle with the viper from beyond the grave.

CHAPTER 20: THE TELLTALE HEART

Niko was running with Tabet in his arms, her skirt pulled up over her head. Her outraged screaming was muffled; her legs kicked slightly, a good sign.

He could barely see but he could hear his horse's screams and the stables were where he was making for in the melee.

He heard Tempus organizing a fire brigade, but he had the queen, and their horses, to think of.

Through the pall of smoke, coughing and running with the girl in his arms, bent as low as he could and still carry her, he fought blindly toward the horses' screams.

And when he found the stableyard door, it was open. He thanked Enlil for great favors and pushed his way within, already yelling to the grooms to get the animals out of their stalls by blindfolding them.

"Wet the blindfolds. Get them to the outer gates and set them free. All of them. We'll worry about catching them later."

It never occurred to him, or the stablehands who

ran to do his bidding, that he had no authority in this place. He was too busy trying to catch his breath and make his uncertain way to the watering trough with the struggling queen in his arms.

He dropped her uncermoniously into the trough and held her there a moment, his hand firm on her head, before he pulled her up and doused his own head.

Then he realized she was trapped in wet garments, and set about tearing them from her face.

He tore himself a piece of her gown and wrapped it around his own head and face.

Breathing through the wet fabric was easier. Seeing was another matter, but Niko had seen enough. He knew where his duty was.

"Tabet!" He had to shout over the animals' screams and the yelling grooms and the awful roar of flames. "Take my horse. Ride out the city's gates. Wait there."

She didn't move, though he'd turned and headed back to the palace compound. He had to find Tempus.

But when he looked around a second time and she hadn't stirred, he came back: "What's wrong with you, girl? Get up. Get out of here. The whole palace is going up."

"I can't leave."

"Can't you ride a horse? I'll get him for you." That must be it. The stable stallion was a handful, and if she weren't an experienced rider, in the confusion, with a blindfolded horse and smoke and flames all around, while everyone with a lick of sense was headed out that same gate, the one gate leading to the World . . .

"No, don't get him. I'm not leaving the city." She pawed soaked and tangled hair from her face, smearing soot over her cheeks.

"What? You can't stay here—"

"None of us will leave," she said with a sniffle and

a cough, struggling to her feet and stepping out of the trough.

Her skirts were impossibly heavy, even with half of them gone. He should have helped her. He should be with Tempus now, helping his commander. He hesitated, pulled in two opposite directions.

Then he jerked down his linen mask and said, "Tabet, I can't argue with you. What is it, you're afraid of the World? Then stay, but stay here, where there's water."

"If I go out there, I'll have deserted my people." Her lower lip was trembling. "And I'll die. I'll get old. I'll—"

"Not old all at once, at least I don't think so—" He couldn't argue with her. He didn't have time. She was a queen, after all. "Look, it's your city. I need my horse if you don't. I've got to find Tempus—"

"Go, Niko. Don't worry about me." She straightened her shoulders. "You'd leave me eventually, for him and your duty." The words were bitter. "Seth said you would."

All he could think of was that this was no time to argue sensibilities and loyalties with a foolish woman who didn't seem to realize that her city was burning to the ground. But her words echoed: *Seth said.* Not, "Crevis said." Crevis was the seer.

That damned sorcerer was up to his witchy ears in this.

"Fine, Your Highness," he said, and changed direction, pulling up his mask as he passed her, headed for the stable. He didn't like leaving his horse's welfare to someone else in any case.

When he rode out, hunched over his blindfolded horse's neck to get through the barn's low door, he had Tempus and Jihan's horses on leads, and the grays were more than enough for him to handle.

But she was still there, sitting on the trough in her

dripping skirts, holding a wet piece of linen to her nose.

He told himself it was shock. It must be. But he said, as he rode by, "Look up there, woman. Look at your palace's high tower. The god and the smoke-snakes fight there for your city. Shouldn't you do something more than sit here and hold your belly and worry whether my love is true? Or that you'll get old if you do the smart thing and run for safety? Don't you think this place is going to need a monarch when the smoke clears?"

She didn't respond. She didn't look up. He had two very strong, very spooky horses on tethers who wanted their masters, and he had work to do.

He called back one final time, "Look here, we'll be at the Storm God's temple, if it's still standing, seeing what Matilla's heart does to stop this blaze, and what it has to say about her murder. If you're determined to stay in the city, maybe you should be there."

But he wasn't going to take her. She could have ridden on one of the grays, but it was out of the question for some reason that was no reason, but a fact as immutable as birth and death and the laws of nature.

He didn't ask and she didn't answer.

One of these days, he told himself, if he survived this trial by fire, he'd learn to do as Tempus advised and keep his belt buckled.

But this day, he was going to find the Riddler and Jihan, deliver them their horses, and do his part before the altar of the Storm God, who had manifested, at least in Niko's eyes, upon the battlements.

When he found Tempus, black as his nickname and overseeing the fire brigade in the palace court-yard, he called out, "Riddler, did you see the Storm God on the high tower? Fighting the snakes?"

Jihan came up and took the tethers from him. Her hand rested on his leg. "We all saw, Niko," she said.

Tempus hadn't answered. He was telling the captain of the guard, "It's not possible to save the whole city. Find Genos and see if he agrees that we concentrate on the palace and the temples. Spread your men among the civilians, but don't ask for miracles: it's an unnatural fire. It's spreading too far, too fast."

The captain, covered in soot, straightened up from his bucket and his huddled officers, awaiting instructions. "Too far? Too fast? We can't let it burn."

"Then you'll lose it all, by trying to save too much. Your choice, and your leaders', not mine. I'm taking the servant woman's heart to the Storm God's temple—tell Genos if he wants to know."

And Tempus left the firefighters, striding out of the boiling smoke like the god himself. He held out his hand for his horse's reins and Jihan relinquished them.

Before he swung up on his blindfolded horse, he gave it his hand to smell. It whickered and its ears swivelled. He felt its blindfold, then called for a bucket.

With his big hands he moistened all three horses' blindfolds, and when he had done with Niko's he said as he passed by to mount, "Good job, Stepson. Let's see what a heart can do to halt this."

Then he reined his horse around and cantered into the thickest smoke, unconcerned whether some innocent might get run down by a horse who couldn't see and riders who could do little better.

It was like dusk when they got to the temple. Black ash was raining down like snow, big flakes of it that turned the horses' gray coats black and made Niko sneeze despite his linen mask.

The temple, too, was blackened. A sound was coming from it, distinct from the other sounds of roaring flames and cracking timbers and exploding

windows and screaming or sobbing folk—a sound
like the earth moving.

The Storm God's priest was at the front door,
watching and leaning there as if it were some festival
taking place outside, instead of a fire that seemed
bent on leveling the city to the ground.

"Jamad," said Tempus, "thanks for coming."

"What else could I do?" replied the priest. "We've
wet down the roof with water from the cistern, as
you asked. All is prepared. Crevis the seer is here to
bear witness. Beyond that—" Jamad shrugged. "The
Storm God's statue is . . . by the bier, or come to life
and fighting snakes on the battlements, depending
on what you think you've seen."

"I don't worry about what I think I see," Tempus
said as he slid down from his horse. "We're bringing
our mounts indoors. The god will forgive."

"If you say so," replied Jamad, and led the way
with only a suppressed wince as the first hoof rang
on sacrosanct marble tiles.

Inside the temple, the air was better. There were
no open windows; the doors had been closed; ash
hung here and there, floating like dark clouds in the
torchlight from sconces on the walls.

Walking his horse into the Storm God's temple
made Niko's hair stand on end. The hooves and
footsteps echoed. The place seemed cavernous.

And wet. Which it was. The floor, the walls, everything had been doused with water. He went carefully, mindful of his mount's purchase on the slick
marble tiles.

In the torchlight, the great depictions of the Storm
God fighting the spawn of hell seemed to move.
Worse, they seemed very much like what he'd seen
outside. And the god still had his face.

The altar of the god, however, seemed small and
bare without the statue that had guarded it.

Small and bare and very, very old.

Crevis's robe was gray with soot as he waved to them from behind the altar, but there was no one else inside but the priest and themselves and their horses.

Niko stroked his mount's neck and talked to the horse. He took a chance and pulled its blindfold down. It was not every day a horse stood in the temple of Enlil with the blessing of His priest.

Somehow, Niko wanted his horse to see.

Jihan saw what he'd done and did likewise. The air was so much better here, Niko could again make out the soft glow that came from the Froth Daughter's skin.

She held out her hand with a look that made him give her his horse's reins.

Tempus was already at the altar, pulling a pouch from his belt.

Niko met him there, and Jamad did also, and Crevis stepped close.

"Words, priest?" Tempus asked.

"Under these circumstances? Let's get this done, if it's what the god demands, and turn our energies to saving the temple."

"If anything saves the temple," Tempus said in a hard and unsympathetic voice, "it will be this, not man's effort against the flames of magic."

"What do you mean?" Crevis asked.

"Come, seer. Have you lived so long for nothing? Can you not see the nose on your face? The god fighting the snakes of evil on the tower, as he fights the dragons and the spawn of hell in this very place? That fire, out of control, is out of control because of sorcery—your warlock's trying desperate measures to save himself."

"Save himself from what? Seth's done nothi—"

"We'll see what Seth's done, soon enough." Tempus turned from Crevis to Jamad. "This placing of Death's heart upon your altar precedes Niko's test—

and if it satisfies the prophecy, precludes it—that's the bargain I struck with your monarch. Attest to it in the house of the god."

From above, the timbers creaked, as if the roof had caught fire somewhere.

The priest's eyes went to the shadowed vault. "I'll attest to anything you like, stranger. But I can't see how you think it matters now, when we may not have a city, or a monarch, or even an altar by tomorrow."

"It matters that the bargain be kept. Shall I do this, my way?"

"Please, by Enlil's will," said Jamad. "We've no protocol for testing a dead heart, only a live one in a human breast."

"Then step back. You too, Niko."

Nikodemos did what he was told.

Tempus pulled the heart from his pouch and laid the grisly thing upon the altar.

The severed tubes leading out of it gaped; it was blue and white and reddish brown and globs of fat clung to it. It looked too old to eat, Niko heard himself think.

Then he was glad he was standing back, as the heart on the altar began to steam.

Mist issued from it in profusion. It rocked where it was, and Tempus himself stepped back quickly, until he stood at Niko's side with his arms folded.

Niko stole a glance at his commander and Tempus, seeing him, lifted one eyebrow slightly and gave a little shrug.

Then Niko realized that not even Tempus knew what might happen now.

And as he turned back to the altar, to see what he might see, Nikodemos thought that the Storm God on the wall, the painted god who looked like him, who'd had his sword lifted in battle against an ophidian enemy for millennia, brought the sword down and smote the great coils of his adversary.

Niko blinked, and he realized that the paint of the temple frescoes was beginning to run, as if the walls were melting.

He looked at the far side of the room, where reliefs were chiseled, and there too, edges were beginning to dull and fold and sag.

Then a noise brought his attention back to the altar.

Again he blinked. Nowhere he'd been, never in all his travels, not in the bowels of witchery or even in the land of dreams, had he seen a sight like that before him.

The excised heart of Matilla the handmaid was no longer lying flat on the altar of the god. It was upright, as if there were a body forming from the mist streaming from it. It floated above the altar as high as it would have been if a human body were surrounding it, and it in its proper place inside a chest.

It shivered back and forth there; then it began to sprout veins and arteries. And more.

It exuded tissue; it exuded bone. It brought forth from inside it all the things that made a body human, and this it ordered into flesh and blood, and a person started taking form there.

This person was not palpable, its bone not white and red with marrow and blood in it, but semilucent, ectoplasmic like the snakes of the sorcerous flames. But a body it was, with arms and legs now, and a face forming.

Niko heard Jihan's sharp intake of breath, but dared not look around.

He'd never seen a thing like this in all his life and hoped he never would again. He was praying to the god fervently that his bowels would not betray him, as liver and spleen and blue sinew and cartilege and muscle and skin all overlayed each other, but no part of this person obscured the portion underneath or behind.

And when the person was as complete as a nightmare person could be, it began to have features upon its face. That face resembled Matilla's face as death resembles life.

There was a tongue in its jaws now. Niko could see it moving in a mouth with teeth whose nerves showed clearly.

And then Tempus said, "By our Lord Enlil, speak to us of prophecy and vengeance, of truth and culprits, of right and wrong and then begone to your eternal rest, spirit."

"*Spirit?*" The whisper came out of Crevis, horrified and unbidden, as if the thing had made him call its name.

It was opening those see-through lips and moving all the portions of its throat and larynx and diaphragm and more: "Seth and Macon killed me. Seth despoiled me, raped me and murdered me in his chamber. I am the Death of the prophecy. Avenge me. I floated over the city from the warlock's tower to the tower of the king. Avenge me. I cannot rest in peace without your help. The city suffers the snakes that killed me, by the warlock's bidding. Avenge me, or join me."

And in a hiss and a sputter and a bright blaze of light, the whole compilation of flesh and bone and organ and blood burst apart with a flap and a whap and a terrible thump.

Niko threw up his arm to shield his face. It was instinct.

When he brought it down, he wasn't soaked or covered with gore. There was only a heart, rocking slightly on the altar of the god, with a little mist and a bit of moisture lingering around it.

Niko's horse threw up its head and whinnied. The sound bounced off the rafters and he looked up.

There were sparks among those rafters now. He touched Tempus' arm and pointed.

"Look at the walls, Niko," Tempus suggested.

The melting was worse now; the magnificent paintings of the god were distorted, unrecognizable, changing as he stared.

And the room, he realized, was getting hot. No longer was the air so clear here; no longer was the ash eddying here and there.

Ash was everywhere, darkening the chamber. And from the marble tiles, the water was beginning to steam.

"Let's get out of here, Commander. We've got our proof, if there's any warlock or city to need it."

"The cellar," said the priest of the Storm God. "The fire's gotten in the cellar."

"And on the roof," Tempus said calmly, as if remarking on a throw of the dice.

"Niko, let's wet these horses down and get them out of here. Crevis, Jamad, you heard. Can we now agree that Niko needn't take any Test, should there be a city tomorrow and a king to demand one?"

"We . . . must confer," said Crevis, hands in his sleeves.

"Confer away, you and yours. Priest, if you want our help saving this temple, come along. First we'll need water for our horses. . . ."

The priest made his choice and went with Tempus. Jihan followed. That left Niko staring at the heart upon the altar and the seer beyond.

"You lied to the king about this prophecy, didn't you?" said Niko quietly.

"I . . . Soldier, this is no concern of yours."

"If you don't try to make it mine, I don't care what the ruling family knows. But we all heard what we heard. Make sure you tell it right, just like the specter said it," Niko warned, and let his hand fall to his sword to make the matter clear.

Then he had to wet down his horse and help Tempus teach the priest what to do to save something from the fire that raged citywide, in pockets fierce and pockets sly, still belching too much smoke for Niko to tell whether the god was yet on the ramparts, fighting demon snakes, or not.

CHAPTER 21: FIRE AND SNAKES

The city was ablaze with fire and nothing its folk could do would put that fire out. Macon knew this with glum and guilt-ridden certainty.

They were all going to die—every undying soul among them, in a conflagration wrought by sorcery, predicted by the gods, but brought into being by Macon's meddling and Macon's lust for power and Macon's own two hands.

He stumbled through the smoke-choked streets, coughing black gobbets from his straining lungs. His eyes teared freely. His skin was blackened as if the fire had already charred him to cinders.

What would be left of the beautiful white and gleaming city when the warlock's fire burned out?

Nothing, that was what. And it was all Macon's fault. He stopped in the street, panting, his way blocked by a family lugging its belongings from an ancestral home and piling the blankets filled with goods upon an already overburdened donkey cart.

It was all his fault. The screams he heard, the

weeping, the destruction all about. The fire seemed to lick toward him hungrily from every burning window. The roar it made had his name on its hot and angry tongue.

His fault. Oh, Seth's fault too, for bringing the awful spell into being. His father's fault, he told himself fiercely as he stood there, unable to decide if he should try to climb over the blankets and the people and the maddened, braying donkey and its soaking, ash-grimy cart.

His father's fault most of all. It was Genos' mismanagement that had brought the city to the end of time. Brought the city to this awful pass, to this hideous end. It was King Genos' fault, for turning the city over to inadequate advisors and letting power fall into the hands of a warlock.

But it was Macon's hands—his ash-muddy, scraped and shaking hands—that had placed the cones at the four compass points of Matilla's bier. Macon had done Seth's dirty bidding and brought destruction down upon them all.

A beam crashed inward and downward somewhere within the house behind him. Startled, he ran forward. Once he was running, he couldn't stop.

He leaped the pile of blanket-wrapped goods and when he landed on the other side, his feet slipped on the slick pavings.

He pinwheeled there, his arms making circles in the hot and filthy air, and for long instants he was sure that he would fall: fall into the horrid mud, fall into the fire reaching toward him, fall atop the donkey cart.

But he found his balance, righted himself, and sprinted on. He was running blindly now, toward the palace, out of habit. Toward Processional Way, the mirrored thoroughfare of mythic power. He knew he shouldn't set foot on Processional Way, guilty and maddened as he was.

But he couldn't stop himself. He ran on, took the turn, and stopped in his tracks.

The Way was a portrait of disaster. The mirrored walls magnified the fleeing refugees until they were uncountable.

Half the city was here, staggering in a long slow dance toward the Lion Gate, and safety.

Safety: was there safety in the World, that dark and ignorant place from which the Riddler, Nikodemos, and the creature named Jihan had come to witness the city's fall from grace? Was there safety anywhere?

There was no safety on the Way, and that was certain. Too many folk had caused a snarl of wagons; no one was going anywhere, except around in circles. And all this, the mirrors reflected, darkly, their bright faces smudged with greasy smoke and dirt, their mythic power to show the future showing only horror, and loss, and panic, and grief.

He backed away from Processional Way, his calf muscles trembling so that he thought he might fall to the ground and be trampled by the fleeing folk who came on and on, their belongings on their shoulders, their lives packed into ox carts and donkey carts, their children wailing like banshees.

Macon ran blindly from this proof of what destruction his own shaking hands had wrought. The city was blazing around him, down past the byway, where more modest houses once had shone in neat rows with their whitewashed walls and their garden trellises carefully tended.

He kept looking up to the sky, as if a reprieve might come from heaven. If only it would rain. If only the heavens would open up and quench this awful fire.

But the gods were angry with the city. The gods were angry with him, for falling into the clutches of the warlock. He should have acted sooner, and acted on his own, to supplant his father. He should have gone to Genos and faced the king and asked him to step aside in favor of his son.

He should have faced the truth. They all should have, when doing so might have saved the city and sent her on her roaming way among the plains and valleys of the World. But he hadn't. He'd been too afraid. He'd been, he realized bitterly, unwilling to grow up, to be a man, to shoulder a ruler's burdens when a strong pair of shoulders would have done some good.

And if he loved his sister, he should have owned to that, and married her. Or at least talked to her about it. Or studied long enough and hard enough to have found out that he could.

But he'd done none of that. He'd strutted around in princely ignorance, blaming everyone else for everything that was wrong, even though he saw what was wrong well before the rest.

Or so he told himself as the flaming city burned around him, and the smoke grew oily and as thick as soup, and the day grew dark as night. After a while, he didn't know where he was running, or why he was running. He simply ran, ran until his heaving lungs objected. Ran until stars twinkled before his eyes and he could no longer catch his breath.

In the murk and grimy smoke, he kept bumping into people, though now he walked, unable to run. He'd thud into this one and careen into that one. He staggered from one side of the street to the other as if he were drunk, hearing only the pounding of his pulse in his ears and the coughing of his labored breath in his lungs.

His nose whistled when he breathed. It ran and when he wiped it, his hand came away smeared with red and black—blood and smoke.

Blood and smoke. The image stuck with him, though all beyond his lids was grainy. Pinpricks of light centered his vision and danced lazily from top to bottom at its edges.

He wondered if he was dying, like his city must be dying. He walked into a wall and hurt his head. He leaned there, and then proceeded, like a blind man, guiding himself with one hand, palm to the wall, to keep him balanced and upright.

He dragged that hand along that gray wall without concern for where he was or where he was headed, until the wall fell away from under his hand altogether.

He stood at an intersection. Across the street was the warlocks' citadel. He could just make it out through the ruddy smoke.

And the warlocks' walls were not burning. Their towers were not aflame.

He ran toward the sanctuary, hot breath full of cedar and destruction in his nostrils, hot shame upon his neck. He'd be safe there. He was the chief warlock's apprentice. They'd let him in and succor him.

He'd earned it.

He didn't realize he was crying. He was sure it was just tears from cinders.

He was as much a wizard, he told the man who opened a peephole in the courtyard gate, as any of them, by now. "Maybe moreso. I know how the fire got started—I had as much a hand in it as your Lord Warlock, my mentor, Seth. Unless you want the whole city to know who started this fire and what kind of fire it is and why my father's guards can't put it out, you'll let me in, fool!"

And in he went, through a hastily opened gate. He was hustled by warlocks with downdrawn cowls, up the stairs of the sooty citadel, and into chambers that, in his memory, had never been less dark than they were today.

The fire had left its mark here: warlocks coughed as they went about their business, scurrying in the halls. Warlocks could be heard in meditation, chanting like ghouls amid the fire.

Yet no warlocks were packing up to leave. This must mean something, Macon told himself, desperate for a sign of hope.

He was escorted to Seth's sanctum, and there he was left alone. He went to the high window, out of which they'd thrown Matilla, and scraped at the gummy film on the glass.

He succeeded only in smearing the window, and so he opened it. Hot air blew in with a rush. On it, sparks rode. A spark caught the warlock's velvet curtains, a hungry spark like a tiny snake that wriggled its way up the fringe of the curtain too fast for Macon to have stopped it if he'd tried.

But he hadn't tried. It was somehow fitting that he'd let the infernal fire into the place from which it had issued. For once, Macon had changed the course of things, not been used by powers he didn't understand to further ends he'd never have sanctioned if he did.

He kept seeing the handmaid locked in horrible embrace with the sorcerer, right where the curtains were starting to blaze.

The curtains gave off an acrid smoke and as they burned the sound was like distant thunder.

So loud it was, that Macon didn't hear the door open behind him. He heard the shout, hoarse and furious, and the curse that came on its heels, as Seth saw his curtains ablaze and Macon standing there before the wide-open window.

"You idiot! You fool! What are you doing here?" Seth wanted to know, once he'd called for help. Then he must have realized who it was he was asking such leading questions, and shut the door, fire or no, help or no.

The warlock leaned on it and looked at Macon, whose eyes were smarting so Seth looked to him like a man seen through a glass of sloshing water, or in a mirror badly crafted—all wiggly and shivery and distorted.

Thus Macon couldn't judge the warlock's expression, which was so contorted that Seth didn't look like Seth at all, but like some stranger. He told himself the distortion was caused by the quickening blaze of the curtains behind him, but he did not believe it.

He wasn't sure what he believed anymore. No matter his confusion, some explanation was due the warlock who'd asked him such foolish questions, despite the fire in their midst. Macon chanced a glance around. The flames were climbing, spreading. Soon they'd reach the curtainrods, and then the scrolls and parchments of the warlock's wisdom would be in jeopardy.

Macon glared at the warlock who waited stoically for his answer, as if the two of them were standing by a fountain in his father's garden on a clear blue summer's day. Could it be that the warlock didn't care about his books, his scrolls, his wisdom? Here in the warlocks' citadel, of all the city, there seemed to be hope of salvaging something. At least there had been, until Macon opened the window.

The prince, who had nothing more to lose, palmed his smarting eyes and answered the warlock's insults, still hanging in the air between them: "You know who I am, posturing and fey magician. Let me tell you who I'm not: I'm not a man who looses powers I can't control. I'm not a warlock who reaches far beyond his station. I'm not a fool. It would take one to call me thus, in the fiery proof of his own inadequacy."

Macon had never uttered words of such quality before. He was stunned at the sound of them when they left his mouth. They sounded like words his father might have spoken, in his prime, not the words of a guilty prince who'd made so many terrible mistakes.

"Are you not a fool, Prince Macon?" The warlock pushed away from the door and came toward him. "You like what you see, don't you, Prince? You like the fire, all the power of its light." He gestured to the curtains at Macon's back, blazing bright now so that long and grotesque shadows of Macon himself danced over the floor, and over Seth's face, and over the closed door at the warlock's back. "You like the destruction of all you couldn't abide. You like seeing your father brought to his knees and your sister humbled—your whole city in an uproar."

"I don't."

"You do."

"You arrogant—" Macon bit off the words and looked around for something better than words to throw at the warlock. He was standing near Seth's desk. He saw something gleaming there and reached out to grab it.

Before he could think about the consequences of his actions, his fist closed on a chunk of crystal and he hurled it, with all his might, at the warlock.

Seth caught the missile in midair and hefted it in an open palm. "Get used to passion in yourself, apprentice. Get used to the violence in your soul. I didn't put it there—you did. Or it was there from time immemorial, waiting for this day." The warlock bore down on him, holding out the crystal in which growing firelight was reflected.

"You see this? You could have brained me. If I were weak and foolish, you would have. It doesn't take sorcery to kill, just the nature. *And you have that nature.* I didn't give it to you, or spell it on you—I recognized it in you."

"You lie." Behind the prince, the fire had reached the shelves of scrolls and parchments. They caught like tinder, sighing as they burned. Macon took a step toward the warlock, away from the heat at his back.

"Do I? What you are, you and your gods have made you. It's the god—the benighted Storm God and his fellows from heaven, who do this to your city, not my magic. You flatter me if you think otherwise."

"It's your fire." Macon gestured over his shoulder as he said those words. Didn't the warlock care that the place was going up in flames? Were they both going to roast here, arguing qualities of their respective souls and whose fault the fires were?

"The fires of hell aren't mine, fool. But they're fanned by the wrath of heaven, here. I asked only that my enemies be destroyed. And look out there— the whole city's going up in smoke. The god wrestles the snakes of the underworld upon the battlements. And you think *I* did all this? You overestimate magic, my boy—and underestimate the power of vengeance in the mind of god and man."

"I . . ." He didn't know what to say. He blurted: "Can't you stop it?"

"I'll try. We had stopped it here, but for your interference." Now Seth did pay attention to the fire at Macon's back. He raised his hands and seemed to stroke it. He spoke words to it that Macon's ears could not identify.

And behind the warlock, a pounding began on the shut door.

"Open it," Seth ordered Macon, as if Macon were a footman, a house servant, a child.

Macon realized, as he scuttled away from the burning wall of curtains and scrolls, Seth considered his concentration too important to be broken by something so trivial as letting firefighters in the door.

When Macon had opened the door and acolytes crowded in, bearing buckets of water and odd brooms and pails of flour, Macon turned back to the wall that had been ablaze.

It was not blazing any longer. The fire was separating into snaky lines of flame, as if vipers clung to the walls and ceiling. And these vipers of flame, Seth was coaxing down the wall with his hands, like a snake charmer putting his pets into a basket—never touching them, just directing.

All the acolytes swarmed round their master, and in the confusion, Macon was crowded out of the room, into the hall full of smoke.

There he stood for a moment, shivering despite the heat and the smoke. Then, breathing hard, he gathered his wits as best he could.

And ran. He had to find his sister. He had to find Tabet and explain. He had to make sure she was all right. And he had to stand before his father, while Genos was still king of something that could be called a city, and confront the king.

He would tell Genos what he'd done, and why. He would make clear all the reasons. He would demand that his father step aside, right now, while there was still time. Only Macon knew that the fires would die when Seth's enemies were dead, and not before.

To his frightened, addled, smoke-filled mind, it seemed clear that the death of some was preferable to the death of all. Seth might be a liar and a manipulator, but his power over the flames was very real.

Macon had seen it with his own eyes, and seen the city's last slim hope of salvation, he was sure. If the warlock's flames could be bedded, as he had just seen in Seth's sanctum, then the city could still be saved.

Under Macon's rule, it could be saved.

Under Genos', everything Macon loved was bound to perish.

Chapter 22: Vengeance of the Heart

Tempus called as loud as he could through the din, "Jihan, Jihan!"

He listened for an answer but heard no reply. He'd lost track of the Froth Daughter in the melee of firefighters and crashing timbers and crumbling roofs and fleeing folk.

Flight should be quick, not this slow stumble toward questionable salvation. None of these families could be convinced that the snarl at the Lion Gate was too great for them to get out any time soon, that they needn't hurry. In fact, that it would be just as wise not to try to flee at all.

They were frightened and, in a line that moved only ephemerally as people packed in closer, they prefered jostling each other to helping the firefighters.

Even here, people were all alike. If Tempus had had under his command every able hand that was turned to packing and pushing and shoving, they might have put out the fire by now.

But he didn't have them, and they were obstructing the guards' efforts and those of the populace who were trying to help. He'd done all he could here—more than he could. He knew it in his bones.

He knew it from the way the god rustled restlessly within him. He knew it from the obfuscation of smoke over everything. He knew it because he could no longer see the god's image fighting the vipers on the battlements.

And he knew it because of what the heart of Matilla had told him: avenge me, it had said.

There was no quenching this blaze until that vengeance was done, he'd convinced himself of that. He was ready to start hunting the warlock through the smoke-filled city streets. He needed only to find Niko, and give him command of the firefighters.

And to find Jihan, and try one last, desperate measure that would forestall total destruction here. He'd tried reasoning with the god in his head, but the god was obviously not listening.

The god was humbling the city. The god agreed with Matilla's heart that vengeance was theirs to take. The god liked vengeance even better than copulation. And the god had Tempus on site, to do the deed.

There was no way around an inevitable confrontation with sorcery, unless Tempus was willing to gather up Niko and Jihan and let the city burn to the ground.

Which he was not, quite. And if he had been, he couldn't find either of his cohorts in the confusion. He could see no farther than the end of his arm in the smoke. He could barely breathe. He spent half his time wetting down his horse and his gear and his mask and the horse's blindfold, so that the hair of man and beast and the linen on both did not spontaneously combust from the heat, or catch fire from an airborne spark.

"Jihan," he called again, and threw the sponge

he'd been using into a scummy bucket. He swung up on his gray and reined it around so abruptly that it reared. Jihan was the only hope he had of altering what seemed to him, despite what he'd told Niko, a fixed future—one he did not like.

He scolded the god remorselessly as he rode through the streets, uncaring of who got kicked and what property got crushed by iron-shod hooves as he went.

"Jihan! Niko! Jihan!"

There was no answer in the burning city, no sign of either one on the destruction-darkened thoroughfares. He kept riding. He kept coughing. He kept one ear attuned to his horse's breathing: this whole place wasn't worth the life of even one such horse, though it might be worth the life of all within it.

He wanted to save it, because now he knew that the god's wrath, which was boundless, was on the loose. He wanted to save it because ignorance is not evil. He wanted to save it because, for so long, he'd been destroying, not saving, cities.

He'd sacked a hundred cities as large as this in his extended lifetime. But he'd never sacked one with so much true wealth within it: the wealth of human thought and human history ought to be worth preserving, no matter what the god thought. The wealth of gold and wrought noble metal and precious stone— this he'd always thought debilitating to the mortal soul.

These were not mortal souls, he had to remind himself as he rode among the panicked and the suddenly homeless, the new refugees crowding toward the impassable Lion Gate. These were privileged souls who'd lived immortal lives here, ancient lives, lives much like his own.

But they were souls who had just learned their mortality—souls who could die, in frail flesh, as he could not. Souls who would die, like any other folk,

once the city was a pile of smoking rubble and they
were wandering in the world.

He tried again to speak to the god in him, saying
that he would deliver the promised vengeance, if
only the god would let him put out the fires. The god
need not put it out for him, Tempus offered, merely
let *him* put it out however he might—with whatever
help he could bring to bear.

One had to be tricky with the Trickster.

In his head, the god cocked an eye.

He could feel it. The god was finished battling the
snakes, this he knew because, when the god had
fought, he had felt the absence of Enlil from inside
him. In the temple, the god had not been within
him, but above, his mighty feet spread.

And Tempus' arm ached, his sword-arm, from the
god's battling.

Enlil was resting, and watching the fruits of his
labors through Tempus' eyes.

*"Bring Me the head of the evildoer, and the heart
of the evildoer, and the soul of the evildoer who does
not revere My name,"* said the god to him in an
earsplitting yet soundless voice, implacable and hungry for the vengeance Matilla's heart had decreed.

"I will. I promise. But let me do what I can for the
city."

*"The city is filled with sorcery, with hubris, with
men who think they can challenge the gods and call
upon all the hells to aid them!"*

"The city will give up witchcraft, if you but let it
save itself," he promised, though he couldn't make
good on such a promise.

There was a silence in his head that let him hear
his horse's snorts and the cries of the folk and the
crackle of the flames, and the crashes of collapsing
buildings.

Then the god said, *"My Mercy is yours to dis-
pense, if you can find it. But My Vengeance must be*

*sure and swift, and there must be no doubt of it in
any heart. And no end to the cleansing here—by
flame or sword. My Will be done."*

"Right," said Tempus. "I hear and obey." It was a
good thing the god couldn't see him smile, for it
wasn't a pretty smile, but a mere baring of teeth that
signified disgust and the fulfillment of his most un-
pleasant expectations.

At least now, if they could put the fires out, those
fires that the god had set, then that much of the
blaze would stay out. As for sorcerous fires in foolish
hearts, those were other matters.

He wished the god was more reasonable, but neither gods nor men were ever thus. The anger in
him, part god-given and partly a result of what he'd
heard when Matilla's heart spoke from the altar,
would do the rest.

If only he could find Jihan.

"Jihan," he called again in his battlefield voice that
cut like whetted iron through the din.

And this time, since the god had agreed not to
meddle, he heard a distant answer: not Jihan's voice,
but the sound of her mount, the mate of his, calling
to the stallion.

He slackened his horse's reins and told it, "Seek
Jihan. Seek."

The warhorse flicked its ears at him. That command often was followed by the command to kill.
The gray stallion liked Jihan. But it sought her through
the streets for him, raising its muzzle, distending its
nostrils until the red inside them glowed like Jihan's
skin.

It sought her through smoky byways and streets
full of overturned wagons and houses whose walls
had crumpled onto the pavings so that the gray had
to jump barriers which were hot and smoking and
nearly as high as his barrel.

But jump them he did, and when they found Jihan

and her horse, he almost forgot to tell the stallion, "Easy. Hold."

But he remembered in time, and her mare whickered and arched her neck and pranced where she was tied.

Jihan was not on the mare, but down on her knees, comforting three grubby children who'd lost their parents in the chaos.

"Leave them," he commanded.

"I will not!" She put her hands on her hips and glared at him through red-glowing eyes that were bloodshot from the smoke as though she were human.

"You will. I need you. I need your power, your father's grace, your control over water and storm. Unless, of course, you were merely boasting and you can't call a deluge to put these fires out?"

"I thought you'd never ask, Riddler," said Jihan as she got up from the huddled children and headed for her horse. "Stay right here, little ones," she called back with a tenderness that made Tempus uneasy. "I'll be back for you. Be brave. You are under my protection, my loves."

He had to choke back an admonition. She wasn't coming back for any clutch of soiled city brats, if he had anything to say about it. But this was no time to argue with the Froth Daughter. He had a city to save and a warlock to confront. And a royal family to chastise, at the very least, when that was done.

But now, there was reason to be concerned with all of that. There was a glimmer of hope, bright as Jihan's fierce and inhuman eye. If the Froth Daughter could and would do as she'd said she could, he could begin to sort this matter out.

When she was mounted, he bowed low in his saddle with a sweep of his arm: "After you, Savior of the City."

She liked the sound of that. She kicked the gray mare into the lead and he followed, not knowing where a proper place for Jihan's rite might be, or what the rite might entail.

When they'd gone but a little way, she pulled up her horse and turned in her saddle. "Where's Niko?" she wanted to know. "He should be here to witness my power on the wing."

Tempus squeezed his eyes shut, and behind his closed lids he saw the countenance of the god, which in this place Niko shared. And the god was chortling.

"Niko is . . . busy with the business of saving as many children as possible," he fabricated. "You wouldn't want to disturb him just to make an undo show of so gracious a deed."

"No," she agreed after three heartbeats worth of intense consideration that pleated her forehead. "You are right. Niko will see the sky split, and rain come from my father's sea, and then he will know that it was I who—"

"Could we hurry this up, Jihan? Do the deed while there's still something here worth saving?"

He saw her stiffen and wished he'd held his temper better. But then he apologized and she relented, at least enough to answer his question as to what a suitable site might be.

"The highest point we can reach, Riddler. When the skies open and the sea lifts up and comes down upon the city in a torrent, you wouldn't want to get your feet wet."

"Indeed," he said, and suggested a route, this street and then that, which would bring them to the palace compound's rear, where the ground was highest.

When they got there, she wanted to be cajoled, and he did his best at it. He showed her the city—what they could see of it through the smoke—and told her how grateful everyone would be. He put his hand out to her, and kissed the hand she put in his.

Finally she said, "And how grateful will *you* be, Riddler, to have the city saved at your behest?"

"Jihan, I will be eternally grateful."

"And you will show your gratitude in any way I choose?"

He was suspicious now, but he had no choice that he could see. "In any way."

"You will immediately give me a child, upon this spot, as soon as the fires go out."

"As soon as the fires go out," he said, having walked into her trap. And the god inside him was laughing so that he could hardly hear her words as she, still on horseback, raised her arms up to heaven and petitioned her Father for all the water she wished from the sea at the end of time.

Her fingers wiggled, pointing heavenward, and the sky grew darker even than it had been.

Her face turned upward and a drizzle began, dirty at first because of all the char in the air, but a drizzle nevertheless.

She moved her fingers faster, and the drizzle increased. She closed her fists and thunder sounded.

She opened them wide and lightning flashed.

She brought her open palms down to her sides and the rain began in earnest.

It was a salty rain. It was a torrential rain. It was a rain that washed the ash from the sky and spat as it struck the fire.

Soon it was more than rain: it was gale of overwhelming force which blew the fires out. It was a sheeting torrent of water which hit the ground and bounced knee-high.

And in it were fish. Big fish. Little fish. Seaweed-wrapped fish. Striped fish and spotted fish and lungfish and shellfish, as if Jihan's father had scooped up the very sea itself and now poured it over the city.

Tempus thought of Niko and his story of arriving here in a rain of carp, and wondered if he'd told the truth when he'd told the Stepson that there was no fate, in the way that Niko meant.

Then a fish hit him square on his head and he reached for his helmet. Hanging on his saddle, it was filled with water. He poured the water out, and poured out minnows upon the ground.

The rain went on and on, and the fires it soaked went out. All over the city, fires flickered, sputtered, and died.

Wild water raced, then raged, through the streets, fishy water, seaweedy water, water with such froth on it as only salt water has.

This water flooded the streets and carried off the char, the ash, and the mud, sweeping them into the grates of the sewers, and into the aquaducts, and into the great water canals that made the city's watery wheels.

And the sluicing of the water through the waterwheels loosed the city from the mire at the end of time.

Tempus felt it before he saw it: the ground beneath him rocked and quaked.

"Jihan! Stop the rain! Now!"

The soaked and bedraggled Froth Daughter looked at him through strands of sopping hair. Her face was puzzled.

"Stop it? But you wanted it to rain and rain and—"

"Enough, Jihan! It's rained enough!" Water sprayed from his lips as he yelled at her.

Her face seemed to contort. He thought he saw anger or disappointment, perhaps frustration there. Then he didn't see anything like those emotions, but he saw concentration and determination. And a wily, canny look that made him remember what he'd promised.

He realized then—or realized again—that Jihan had no sense of proportion. She'd gotten caught up in her rain-making, in the manifestation of the principle that had spawned her. If he hadn't stopped her, she'd have rained the city out of existence.

But now she knew it was time to stop the rain. Almost regretfully, she raised up her hands again and opened her mouth to the sky from which rain was yet pouring. "Father, stop! Bring a clear sky. Return the fish to their ocean and the shellfish to their mire!"

She closed her fists abruptly and brought them down.

There was a single burst of blinding lightning, unaccompanied by thunder, that shook the ground and made both horses rear.

Was her father annoyed, or just saying farewell?

Tempus couldn't fathom it, for then the thunder came rolling across the heavens and boxed his ears.

When they'd calmed the horses once again, Jihan was dismounting, looking for a suitable spot, and saying, "Come, Riddler, remember your promise."

He wanted to say that he wasn't certain all the fires had been extinguished. He wanted to tell her that he wasn't sure his mere willingness to get her with child would do the deed, in any case.

But he'd given his word. And mud or no mud, he had to make good.

"Look here, Jihan," he said, "climb up on this horse with me and I'll show you a trick that beats the mud, hands down."

The vengeance of the Storm God would just have to wait until Jihan was satisfied. Under the circumstances, he was sure the god would understand.

CHAPTER 23: THE WARLOCK TAKES A QUEEN

Tabet was up to her knees in mud and destruction, trying to calm the mob at the Lion Gate. She realized she looked less than regal, in her torn skirts with her filthy skin and matted hair, but she was queen and her presence ought to do some good.

The people should listen to her. The guards at their posts should take heart from her presence here. They *should*. She'd given up her own chance of escape to be here.

She yelled herself hoarse to no avail. She thrust herself upon the captain of the gateguard, demanding that he help her to the top of the guardtower, where the people could see her.

The soldier was beleaguered beyond politeness. If truth be known, he failed to recognize his queen at first, having his hands full with overturned wagons and mired donkeys and injured folk all sluiced together by the mud into one horrible mess of limbs and broken traces and confusion that had washed downhill with the pouring rain to pile up as high as his head at the Lion Gate.

There was no getting out of here now, even if the logjam of folk and wagons could be cleared away. It would take days, his sappers estimated, to clear the mud by hand, even if you had the shovels.

And he didn't have the shovels. But he had nobles aplenty on his tail, demanding this special consideration or that courtesy due them by their rank or their power or their tenuous connection to the royal family.

The captain of the guard wasn't so sure there was a royal family any longer. He wasn't sure there was enough of a city to sustain a king. But he was an officer in a hierarchal command. So when he realized that the bossy, impertinent girl before him, whose dirty knees were skinned and bare for all to see, was actually his queen, he looked up from the scene he'd been staring down upon and tried to make amends.

He brushed at his ruined uniform. He executed a tired, desultory salute. He squeezed the mud and blear out of his eyes and tried to focus on the face spouting orders at him—commands not even the gods of the city could have obeyed.

When Tabet was finished, the captain said, "Madam Queen, I'm sure you can see that nothing short of a miracle's going to clear the gate. Nothing short of an appearance by the king himself's going to calm these people or convince them to go back to their homes—those that still have homes to go to—until we get this mess sorted out. So if you'd go get your father—"

Tabet struck the captain of the gatehouse guard across the face, backhanded.

He caught her wrist without thought. Then, very slowly, he let it go.

Tabet rubbed her wrist with her other hand and said, "I will forgive your impudence, given the circumstances. We are all tired, under terrible strain.

Now, if you'll escort me to the top of the guardtower, soldier, I will address the people. I will send them back to their homes. I will require the able-bodied to become your deputies, and aid you in the clearing of the gate. But I ask you to get hold of yourself, and maintain discipline and order among your ranks. The city needs you, soldier, as never before."

The captain blinked again at Genos' daughter, so recently become queen. She could see him assessing her and a flush began crawling up toward her face. Was discipline totally gone here? Was order a figment, a half-remembered dream? Did no one care about more than his own skin in this city? "*Now*, Captain, or face disciplinary action when order is restored!"

That worked better than had her slap. The guard captain wiped sweat and dirt from his forehead with the back of his hand and muttered, "Yes, my lady," before he started yelling commands to his lieutenants.

The way to the top of the guardtower was treacherous with rain, mud and the sooty remnants of the fire that still smoldered here and there among the wreckage of the city's streets.

It took her breath away to see the devastation. Where all had been white and gleaming, char and ash had come to rest. The silver and electrum towers of the palace were oxidized, streaked dark as if the very sky had cried sooty tears upon them. As she climbed, looking out the arrowloops, the true breadth of the havoc that god and sorcery had wrought upon the city became clear to her.

Her eyes misted. Her knees grew weak. And the captain she'd treated so brutally, who climbed the steps beside her, began to seem formidable, to grow larger, to turn from a minion she could command without thought into a man at wits' end who might no longer be a loyal servant of the royal family who'd brought such evil upon the city.

Suddenly she was cautious of him. She was frightened of him, of what it might be like to be the guilty party in his eyes.

He was large and strong and harried. He was armed and dangerous, gruff and stubbled about the chin. He was like a hunting dog who hadn't been fed or bathed in far too long.

She wanted only to tell him to leave her. She said, "Go back to your duties, Captain. I can find my way to the top without you, now."

"You're sure of that, Queen Tabet?"

Was that a taunt in his voice? Was that glance of his resting too long on her naked legs, on her clammy clothing, which stuck to her revealingly, soiled and damp in too many of the wrong places? She hugged herself before she replied, in a voice too high and too sharp, "Certainly I'm sure, Guardsman. Go back to your gate-clearing, I say."

"Yes, My Lady," he said. Not "Yes, Your Highness" or "Yes, My Queen."

But he went. Or at least he turned on the shadowy stairs and she heard footsteps descending.

As she climbed alone in the gatepost tower, up stone stairs, one hand on the dressed blocks of the walls, she kept listening for his footsteps.

In the dark, she couldn't tell if those footsteps were going down, or had turned and were coming back up.

She tried to smother the sudden fear that soured her mouth. She was a queen, not a powerless woman who must fear the senseless violence of a chance-met man. She was *his* queen and he was her captain of the guard. Surely, the danger she sensed was the danger they'd just weathered.

When one has been the object of nature's senseless violence and the caprice of fate, one loses sight of one's own strengths, she told herself. The fabric of the city's society might be strained by what had happened, but surely not ripped enough to cause order to break down altogether.

Yet she paused at every arrowloop she passed, on the landings where defenders of the city would have stood had there been a horde of barbarians trying to storm the gates from without. There she would peer down at the crowd milling before the impassable Lion Gate, jammed with wreckage and mud, and witness such acts of petty viciousness as might suit a crowd in the World, not a crowd born of the city and bred to its graces.

They were trying to get out. They wanted only to escape. They could think of nothing else. In fact, she soon realized, they couldn't think at all, for the danger they fled was all but over. They were the danger now, themselves.

They'd forgotten that the World was death, because suddenly death had roamed the city's streets. They kept fighting with one another, and with the guardsmen who sought to pull them back and send them to their homes.

They wouldn't leave their wagons. They wouldn't leave their goods. They wouldn't leave the mud and the confusion. They were like animals stampeded into a pen.

And she must somehow find the words to say to return them to sanity, to remind them of who and what they were. Remind them so that, with the return of order, they could become thinking persons once again, not volitionless parts of a mindless mob.

She climbed farther, envisioning herself on the flat top of the gatehouse, each hand on one of the toothed crenellations of the tower, leaning over and speaking words of such brilliance that everyone stopped and looked up, then smiled and cheered.

Then the imaginary crowd in her mind's eye dispersed to homes or to the work brigades she'd ordered. But it was not her imagination that only thus would the city be put to rights.

She understood their fear; she'd fought it herself, in the stables when the fire began. But even then she'd known she couldn't leave . . .

She was still hearing footsteps, she realized as she reached the stairs' top and her own were stilled. A chill ran over her. If that captain was coming back up here, she'd have his name this time, and when her father found out he hadn't taken her orders seriously, the soldier would be ousted from the city as quick as you could say—

"Niko!"

"Tabet, I've been looking all over for you," said the man who was her betrothed.

"Look no further." She crossed her arms, leaning back against a crenellation. Finding she could rest her rump there, she sat in the opening, back to the light of the sky, clear after the storm, and the milling folk below.

"What are you doing up here?" her consort wanted to know.

"Now that the danger is past, someone must reassure the people. I—"

"The danger isn't past, woman. The sorcerer's still loose. The murderers aren't caught. The gods are still angry."

"Murderers? Angry gods? What are you talking about, Nikodemos?"

Niko mounted the last stair then and squinted at her, saying ruminatively, "That's right, you don't know."

"Don't know *what*? And don't call me 'woman,' *man*. I'm your queen, and I expect some form of polite address."

"You're not my queen; you may be theirs," his

chin jutted to the crowd below, beyond the crenellation, "when this is over at last. Or not. But as to what you don't know, let me tell you what happened when we put Matilla's heart upon the altar."

She heard Niko's account of the telltale heart, which had incriminated Seth and her brother, with only half an ear and told herself it was all lies—or at least a twisting of truth engineered by the horrid sojourners to discredit the warlock and her brother. It couldn't be true, any more than Nikodemos' love for her had been true.

Had he not just said to her, *You're not my queen?*

When he paused, she said into the silence, "Then we shall consider the betrothal formally at an end, our vows to each other broken, all things as they were before we met." Her hands on her arms were digging into her flesh. It was all she could do to keep her voice steady. Consequently, her words sounded harsh and soulless, even to her own ears.

And Nikodemos, the handsome stranger who'd seduced her, the first man ever to make love to her, replied, "Tabet, haven't you heard a single word I said? You're in danger here. The warlock is still loose. Come back with me to palace where we can protect you better."

"Protect me? From Seth? You? *Ha!*"

"Tabet . . ." He reached for her.

She lurched backward to avoid his hand, his grip, his overweening and proprietary demands. Her buttocks on the crenellation slipped too far.

Overbalanced, she fell over the edge.

She heard herself scream. She saw Niko's lunge, his outstretched hands trying to grab her, hands that caught only a shred of her skirt.

The shred ripped without even slowing her fall. She was hurtling through the air, tumbling.

Her heartbeats were hours apart. As she spun,

she'd see Niko, leaning over the crenellation, his arms still extended to her. Then she'd see the blue and cloud-strewn sky. Then she'd see the crowd below, all unawares, and the mud, the street, the wreckage of wagon and dray beast, and soldiers milling among the confused folk. Then she'd see the dressed stone blocks of the guard tower. And finally, Niko again.

She heard the screaming stop, although she couldn't imagine why it stopped, or even be sure it was she who'd screamed and then ceased to scream.

Next, she realized she wasn't tumbling. She was floating. She was floating face up, as if lying in her bath.

And floating toward her, from the direction of the warlocks' tower, was Seth himself, striding on the air, a smile upon his face.

A wind seemed to blow her toward him. His arms, not Niko's, were outstretched to catch her.

I've died, she told herself. *I'm dead, my heart's stopped from the fear and the fall. At least I won't feel the pain when I strike the earth.*

But she wasn't dead. She was sure she wasn't, when the wind that carried her blew her straight into the warlock's arms: he was warm and smelled like smoke and man.

He clasped her to him. She could not be imagining his hot embrace, the velvet and leather of his garments, the jab of his belt buckle against her belly.

Into her ear Seth said, "Fear nothing, my love, when you are with me. Your life is too precious to lose. Will you come with me, Tabet, to a safer place than this?"

She knew the sound of ritual when she heard it. She knew she was making a choice. But Niko didn't love her and the ground was hard and waiting below.

The warlock's hand pressed against her spine and

from that hand came a sense of peace and purpose. To be the willing wife of such a man was to be a queen of more than just the city.

"Oh yes, Seth. Yes," she said. And in an eyeblink, tower and crenellations, Lion Gate and frightened folk, Nikodemos and everything else below and around disappeared.

All but for the warlock, who held her in her arms and now released her on a velvet-covered bed in a place she'd never been before.

CHAPTER 24: FATHER AND SON

The fires in the city were all but out, yet in the palace the pall of smoke lingered, making it difficult to breathe.

Or perhaps the words of his son were what made Genos labor for breath.

Stiff and white-faced before his father on the grimy throne, Macon was saying, "I tell you, Father, we must kill the warlock's enemies. That's the city's only chance."

"But Son," said the ancient king, "the city is all but saved, thanks to our friends from the World and the grace of the gods."

Genos stole a glance at the Froth Daughter and the man called the Riddler. Just before Macon had burst in here, the sojourners had come, with the Storm God's priest by their sides, to consult with the king on the matter of what Matilla's heart had said from beyond the grave.

"The city is *not* saved. I tell you Father, you don't know what I've seen. The warlock can call the fires of hell. He's done it once—made the flames do his bidding. He can do it again. We must round up his enemies, including these foreigners—" Macon pointed at the two sojourners with a trembling hand, "—take them outside the gates and slay them."

No one else in the throne room said a word when the prince stopped and glared about him. Genos saw the two sojourners exchange knowing looks, then turn their inhuman stares upon the king who still sat the city's throne, waiting to hear his answer to his son, who'd just demanded their lives to placate a warlock.

"You're saying, Macon, that we should give the rule of the city over to the warlock—to rampant evil. You're talking of murder and nothing less. Should we do as you suggest, we might save the city from more fire, but then it will be the warlock's city. We can't allow such a thing. We live by the gods' graces. I—"

"Maybe you do, Father. I don't. You're old. It's time for you to step down and give me my chance at rulership. You've botched yours, or none of this evil would have befallen us."

"Your sister. . .," the king began.

"My sister," his eldest son interrupted, "is a slut. A woman. And a bewitched woman to boot. Seth will marry her still, I think, if we ask him politely enough. If not," Macon puffed out his chest, "I will."

This brought a murmur from Jamad, and when Genos snuck a peek, the two sojourners and the priest had their heads together.

"Macon, what's gotten into you? You're a prince of the realm—"

"I'm not. I mean, I am, but I'm an adept of sorcery, too. As Seth's apprentice, I've learned wisdom of which you've never dreamed. Father, I'm telling you, these strangers must be slain. Listen to nothing that they tell you. They lie. They're liars from the dark World, here to destroy the city. All the evil that's befallen us came with their advance man, Nikodemos. All the horror and the flame came from their hideous god—"

Genos saw the two sojourners move quietly up on either side of his son, who didn't notice. The king tensed on his throne. There were still guards in the throneroom. He'd managed to keep the palace, at least, orderly. If worse came to worse, he'd signal his own men at arms.

But not yet. There was something deeper here than a childish tantrum born of fear and sorrow in the face of the city's loss.

Genos could see that in Jamad's face. The priest of the Storm God had never looked so solemn, or so sad, in all the time Genos had known him, not even in the midst of the fiery holocaust.

When Macon realized that the strangers flanked him, he stopped ranting. He took a backward step, then turned to bolt, but the big man and the woman of immortal strength were quicker.

So fast all motion was blurred, they restrained the youth and held him, hands to his side, facing his father.

Then Tempus said, "Jamad, Crevis—perhaps you'd better explain to the king what's going on."

Jihan's hand was firmly clamped over Macon's mouth. His son's eyes were wide above the woman's fingers.

From the far end of the hall, Crevis appeared, striding up toward the throne as fast as he could, his cheeks flushed and his chest heaving from his haste.

"What's going on here?" Genos thundered, his temper and his patience lost now. His son stood before him in the hostile grip of two strangers; his advisors were obviously in collusion with the sojourners; his city lay in ruin about him, and his son wanted to be king, right now.

He couldn't remember a worse day, except the

day his wife had left him, without so much as a note
or an explanation, and run off with a stranger into
the dark and deathly World.

Jamad said, as Crevis hastened to his side, "We
witnessed the speaking of Matilla's heart when it was
placed upon the altar of Enlil. It rose up and spoke
to us, spoke to all in attendance—to Crevis, to myself, to these two and to the stranger Nikodemos.
We wish to tell you, my lord King, what the heart
said and what remedy for the city's ills it advised."

"Yes, go on." Genos had not been king for so long
without learning when he was walking into a verbal
trap. He sensed the danger in permitting the priest
to speak, but he did not understand it. And in his
judgment, looking at his transformed son and the
two sojourners and the grave faces of his advisors,
more information was what he needed. No matter
what sort of information it turned out to be.

Crevis had regained his breath. He said, "My lord
King, permit me." He bowed slightly, smiled weakly,
and took Genos' nod as permission to continue.

"When the heart had manifested," Crevis said carefully, "on the altar, it singled out the warlock Seth as
Matilla's murderer, and your son, Macon, as a willing accomplice and a murderer by association."

Macon started struggling wildly between the two
strangers, who held the boy firm, silent but for muffled screams which Genos couldn't decipher.

"This can't be so," Genos said because he wished
that it were not.

"I'm afraid it is," said the Storm God's priest. "The
heart further demanded vengeance upon those who
murdered Matilla, for the breast in which it once had
beat. If the Storm God, my lord, is ever to turn his
face back to the city, if the city is ever again to flower
under heaven, the heart of Matilla must be avenged."

"But we're talking about my son!" roared the king.

"I'm not going to harm my own begotten son! And I'm not going to take a life in the city, ever!"

Then the big stranger said, "So Niko is free from your Test, by your own spoken word, since the Test may be fatal and you will not take a life in the city. There is no need for it, in any case, now that Matilla's heart has done that work and the god's will is known."

"But the city is still in danger," the king said uncertainly, looking from his seer to his priest and back to the seer again.

"The city is in danger only from sorcery," said the priest. "We—ah—misread the prophecies slightly, partly out of our desire to please you, my lord King."

Crevis added, "Once the vengeance of the heart is accomplished, King Genos, all will be well again. Thus do the omens proclaim." And he looked at his feet and said, "Although I must add that the entire prophecy *does* allude to a change of rulers, since you have lost heart, and a heart was given on the altar . . ." He shrugged. "I hasten to remind the king, my lord, that the will of heaven is heaven's, and not any man's fault."

"I will not execute my son."

"That will not be necessary, if you will allow us to lend a hand," said Tempus in a low voice.

All eyes turned to the big sojourner.

"Continue," bade the king.

"Give me your leave to punish the sorcerer as the god within me sees fit," proposed the stranger. "I will not defile the city with his blood unless it is absolutely necessary. The boy is a pawn of witch-craft, and can be saved by the priest and your own wisdom."

"Go on," Genos urged when Tempus subsided. "Tell me what punishment you and your god decree for my eldest son."

"Whatever the city decides, whatever the omens demand—but not murder," said Tempus. "Then the sorcerer wins, taking a once-innocent soul to hell to buy himself a better place there. Keep the boy alive, under discipline, teach him kingship as you have not done."

Genos winced at the rebuke, but said nothing more than, "Is that it, Sojourner?"

"I must point out, King Genos, that your city is no longer entrapped here. Did you not feel the tremor as she raised up from the mire? This is thanks not to me, but to the Storm God and to Jihan, beside me, Froth Daughter, whose father rules the sea at the edge of time."

Jihan smiled at the king and batted her eyes demurely, all the while keeping her palm stuffed firmly against young Macon's mouth.

"Is this so?" Genos asked his advisors.

"Indubitably," said the seer.

"By Enlil's Truth, it is so," said Jamad.

"Then set my son free, strangers," said the king, "and you may do as you will with the warlock, in my name and for Matilla's soul's rest."

"As soon as you have guards handy to take him," Tempus said implacably.

Genos stifled a retort, a rebuke aimed at the sojourner who ignored a king's command and told a king how to behave. Then he motioned forth his guards. When four of them were stationed around the crown prince, the strangers let the boy go.

Macon yelled, "Father, don't listen to them! Father, are you going to take the word of strangers over your own flesh and—"

"*Silence!*" shouted King Genos in a louder voice than Macon's. In the back of his mind, he was still hearing Crevis' words. His kingship was drawing to a close. It was one thing to delegate authority tacitly. It was quite another to be told to one's face that one was too old to rule effectively. Too old to rule much longer.

The king looked at his crown prince, his eldest son, his favorite son, and nearly wept. Was there any chance that the boy could be purified enough to eventually assume Genos' mantle? He didn't dare ask this convocation. He knew their answer, from what he'd heard and what he'd seen.

Or he thought he did. He hardly listened to anything else the strangers and his advisors said until his son was hustled away by the palace guards, to be kept under lock and key in the suite next to Genos' own, which had once been the rooms of the boy's mother.

Then, without the helpless, addled boy and his accusing, frightened eyes before him, Genos found the strength to discuss the future. He must discuss it. But as he was about to broach the matter of Macon's purification, there was a commotion at the far end of the hall.

Someone had come in, this the king noted with one part of his mind. The balance of his attention was still fixed on what he'd learned: Now that the city was freed, her grace all but restored, surely Genos could find a way to force the issue and cause Macon to be officially and ceremonially purified, restored in the eyes of the cityfolk and the palace hierarchy, if not in the eyes of all the gods. And that would be enough, with Tabet reigning in the interim, and Genos as her closest confidant. . . .

The man running up the long hall toward the throne was calling, "Tempus! Tempus!"

Genos looked around for a guard to restore order, but he'd sent them all to see to the confinement of his son. And then he looked again at the man calling the stranger's name, and realized that it was his daughter's consort.

Nikodemos was hoarse and dirty and wild-eyed. "It's Seth. He's got Tabet. Snatched her out of the gatehouse guardpost, right out of the air."

Tempus and Jihan wheeled and ran toward Niko, the king and his court and all else forgotten, checking their weapons as they went.

"Stay out of this, King Genos," the Riddler called back. "Remember, you gave me your word: the warlock is mine to deal with."

And then the strangers were gone, leaving Genos and his two closest advisors staring wordlessly at each other in the great, empty, smoke-smudged throneroom.

CHAPTER 25: THE WARLOCK CORNERED

"Well Niko, look on the bright side: Tempus has saved you from having to take the city's silly test," Jihan said as they searched the warlocks' tower, room by room, with angry wizards looking over their shoulders all the while.

Niko merely grunted. He kept watch on the sorcerers behind them around them with a suspicious, unblinking eye.

"Who knows," Jihan continued, "you might have failed the Test in order to stay alive, and then you would have gone through life thinking the god didn't love you." She chuckled throatily and poked Niko in the ribs when he didn't laugh.

"What's got Jihan in such a rare mood?" Niko whispered to Tempus as soon as he could, when the Froth Daughter found a witchy closet to crawl into, sword first, and there was a wall at his back and at Tempus', so he didn't have to watch the gathered wizards so closely.

"She wanted a price for her rain: she thinks I got her with child."

"*Did* you, Riddler?" Niko's right eyebrow arched in surprise; he knew how Tempus felt about Jihan's manic urge to motherhood.

"Only the gods know, Niko. Put out one fire, start another." Tempus' lips quirked. "She's not expecting me to wipe its cheeks, so I'll let nature—or whatever passes for nature in her—take its course."

A flippant answer was the best he could do, under the circumstances. "We've got a warlock to trap. Let's keep our minds on the task at hand," he admonished as he saw Jihan coming back out of the closet, crestfallen.

"No sign of him in there," reported the Froth Daughter. "It's like he dropped through the floor, right into some hell we can't see."

"We've got to find Tabet. None of this is her doing. She's a good girl, for a royal brat. I feel like I should have seen it coming . . ." Niko sighed and shook his head.

"That's it," Tempus said and stood up abruptly.

"What's 'it'?" Jihan brushed back matted hair from her eyes impatiently.

Tempus was already headed for the outer door, where suspicious magicians crowded, watching them closely lest they should steal some trinket of infernal power.

"What's *it*?" Jihan repeated, after she knocked a warlock from her path to get close to Tempus.

When Niko came out of the room they'd searched, slowly, his back to where he'd been and his sword drawn, Tempus finally explained: " 'Dropped through the floor,' you said, Jihan. 'Into some hell we can't see,' you said."

And he waited for light to dawn in two pairs of uncomprehending eyes.

Niko nodded first. "The cellars." There was little

enthusiasm in his voice. "Not my idea of a pleasant evening, Commander."

None of his fighters liked close quarters, house to house searches, or urban actions. Niko was no exception.

"You!" Tempus called toward the foremost of the mass of magicians in the doorway. "Warlock! Detail someone to guide us through your cellars—however many you've got."

The warlock who'd barred their passage at the outer gate and proclaimed himself acting master here now looked around him and chose the youngest face he saw. "You, boy. Take these strangers where they want to go. Mind they don't swipe so much as a candle down there, or it'll be your backside that smarts for it."

With their guide, they began descending stairs. First to the ground floor, where the crowd of sorcerers thinned and vanished. Then to the kitchens, where a stew was simmering.

Then their young, pale guide handed them each torches and Niko ducked his head.

"I don't like this, Commander."

"You don't have to come with us, Nikodemos," said Jihan sweetly. "We'll rescue the lady Tabet for you. You can stay here and have a nice hot bowl of stew and wait."

"Tempus!" Niko stopped in his tracks. "Would you ask Jihan when it was that she became your task force leader?"

"We're a bit short-handed for a task force, Niko," said Tempus. And, to Jihan: "Quiet, now. We need to listen for sounds that might give away a magician in hiding."

"Tabet will call out to us if she hears us," Niko said positively.

"Only if she wants to be rescued," said Jihan as

they ducked under a low beam and the guide before them thrust his torch down toward the floor.

The flame blew rightward. The guide said, "The undercellars. I've never been down there, so I don't know how much help I'll be. I'll take you, though—"

"No," Tempus said. "You don't know any more than we. Stay here. Wait for us. Don't move from this spot. I want your torchlight here as a beacon."

Jihan pulled on his arm, and then his ear when Tempus wouldn't bend down for her to whisper into it. "Do you not want the mageling as a hostage?"

"I doubt they value him, to have given him to us so easily." He watched his steps as he descended; the stairs were worn from millenial footsteps; the passage was close, barely wide enough for two to pass abreast.

Niko lagged behind, speaking quietly with the apprentice at the stairs' head. When Tempus was ten steps down, he called back, over Jihan's head, "Coming, Stepson?"

"Wouldn't miss it for the world, Commander," said Niko and began descending the stairs. Down a handful, he said in a low voice, "The junior thinks there are at least six caverns down here. There are definitely meditation cells for the adepts. He says Seth's been known to disappear down here for days at a time."

"So that means he has food and drink and—"

"Jihan, don't belabor the obvious," Tempus said. "And please be quiet. I'm trying to hear."

They descended in silence, their footsteps loud, down and down and down some more, and they heard nothing beyond the sound of their own descent until they heard a sound like a woman's sob.

"Did you hear that?" Niko demanded.

When his voice stopped echoing, the other sound had stopped.

Tempus reined his temper tight and said, "Why

don't you lead the way, Niko, since it's your betrothed we're rescuing and you're so anxious?"

That was when Niko announced, as he sidled past
Tempus to take point down the stairs, "We're not
betrothed any more, at least so she said before Seth
got to her."

And Jihan said, "Are you sure she said that *before*
Seth got to her?"

And Tempus said, "If the two of you can't keep
quiet, we might as well start singing a marching song
and calling ahead to the warlock to make sure he's
got dinner ready."

But it was too late. Tempus could feel a change in
the air about them, an electricity that made his gut
cold and skin crawl.

Seth knew they were here.

The warlock was ready for them; ready and waiting.

CHAPTER 26: WARLOCK AT BAY

Seth waited for his pursuers with a cold rage come from failure after failure. He was close to the end of his strength. Close to the end of his skill. Close to the end of his wits.

He was, in fact, in sight of hell itself. How had he come so far? How had he fallen so fast? Here in the deep bowels of the citadel it would end: all he'd reached for was either within his grasp or slipping from it. He wasn't sure which.

There was nothing left now but the final trial: the might of his spells against the god's men and the woman from the sea at the end of time.

He told himself that there was no shame in being beaten by superhuman adversaries, though his heart knew that he too was no longer simply human.

He'd lost that grace somewhere along the way, perhaps when he'd used Matilla for a ritual no warlock had dared employ for ages. Perhaps before that, when he'd been given all but total control of the city by its failing king and power leeched into him, replacing the healthy marrow of his bones with something malignant and foul.

He was playing for stakes higher than mere control of the city, now. Though he had the Queen beside him, bewitched and tractable except for occasional fits of terror, he no longer cared if he ruled the city or not.

Compared to death at the hands of the creature called the Riddler, his former aspirations seemed like childish goals. Compared to an accursed death that would deliver him to the demons of hell and to the vipers of the underworld and to the dragons of unending torment, whether Tabet loved him was as significant as whether he had a piece of meat stuck between his teeth.

But he'd come too far to stop now. There was no alternative but to continue the way he'd begun: to fight to the end, where death was certain. Someone's death.

He'd made his bargains with entities of power whom he'd known to be soulless and hungry, when this day seemed far away and only power over his enemies and the fools of the city mattered. In his terms then, he had been right.

Now, with mortality and accursed eternal torment close at hand, he'd have given anything, spoken any spell, risked all power and all love and all temporal glory, to have his soul back, free and clear, with no lien upon it.

It was too late to make a deal with Genos, except through his daughter. If it had been Genos, coming down here after him with torches and swords as if he were a maddened dog, he might still prevail. But the Storm God's avatar, who men called the Riddler, had no leniency in him. He was the god on the battlements, vanquishing the ectoplasmic vipers who had been the greatest powers Seth could summon.

How else could things go, but to the death?

He reached out a hand in the dark and felt for the queen he'd snatched from under the very nose of her consort. She might be worth something, yet. If nothing else, she'd be his company on the road to hell, the soul he traded at the underworld's dark gates for whatever comfort she was worth.

You didn't make the sort of deals with deviltry that Seth had made and go to your accounting empty-handed. You brought something, someone, with you.

As he had when he'd fled here. He'd doused every torch, but he knew this meditation chamber like he knew his own body's ins and outs. The queen's young hip was under his hand now; her pallet was just to his right. Beside that was a water barrel; beyond the barrel lay oil lamps and flint and a stack of torches.

If no better could be done this day than vengeance, Seth had a vengeance of his own to match the Riddler's.

He would douse the girl, and himself, with oil. He would set them afire himself, saying the proper words to consign her soul to him and his to the powers who had claim to it.

And when he spoke those words, he would be holding the piece of clay his fingers were busy modelling as he sat, cross-legged, beside his hostage: a model of the city would burn with them.

If his spell were rightly done, the city would begin to burn again as his flesh caught fire. The embers, still strewn throughout the streets, would glow, and fan, and catch—and blaze.

If he could cheat the Storm God and his avatar, and Matilla's greedy heart, of their vengeance, then he and his spells would win after all, though not in the way he'd first envisioned it.

He'd never meant to die to triumph, to burn the city to the ground to salvage something. He'd meant only to supplant the king, the prince, and rule beside Queen Tabet in eternal glory. It had been the god who started this, who upped the stakes and forced him to pact with powers he'd never dared to call upon before.

When life is not possible and death is sure, last statements and what marks one can make upon the world one leaves become the only things that matter.

Seth was going to his punishment and eternal unrest not with a whimper, but with a bang that would seal the city's fate as it had sealed his.

He hated life now that he must leave it. He hated all the venal power games he'd once played, and every other player. He hated the demons he'd served and the bargains he'd made. But he hated his adversaries most of all: the gods, the ignoble king, the city in its eternal smugness.

Once the clay model of the city was complete, once the fire consumed his flesh and it and Tabet's beauty, he would have won out against the god and all his enemies.

It was not much solace, but it was enough.

It would have to be enough.

The woman under his right hand stirred, and he chanted a few words softly, gently, to put her back to sleep. She thought she loved him, did Tabet. Love was not worth dying for, and this her flesh knew—at least, not the sort of love he'd instilled in her, a love born of incantation and machination, a love of obsession, a love foreign to her heart.

So whenever she woke from trance, she was frightened. He could tell her not to fear, and his voice would calm her, for he'd done his work well. She listened to his voice and heard truth there, no matter what he said.

But her body and her soul were listening to a different truth, and they knew they were in the dark recesses of the meditation caves for good reason. They knew their fate. They knew enough to fear.

He'd nearly finished with his model. Seth knew

his city so well he didn't need light to guide his hands. The outer walls were there, and beyond them the water wheels which carried the city throughout the world forever. Within the outer walls, the citadel of magic and the king's palace were fully fashioned, accurate and complete. He'd added the businesses and residential districts, and the granaries and storehouses carefully, for there the fires of hell would be renewed.

He wanted, for personal reasons, the blaze to start up in the stables. He wanted to roast the horses of his enemies. Like the consort, these sojourners loved their mounts above all else.

Above all else but their meddling, petty gods. Why was magic worse? Was there a difference between the hell he was bound for and the heaven the consort strove so hard to earn, a warrior's heaven? Must not an afterlife of murderers be full of strife? Didn't they want peace, these killers in the names of gods? Or only infinite conflict?

Was there anything in man but the urge to supplant and the need to command—anything but the drive to survive and to reproduce?

Seth once had thought he knew the answers to such questions. When he could look out his tower window, sure he'd live forever, learning more and better spells and ascending the hierarchy of his kind with sure, bold steps, he'd thought that life was the canvas on which the Will of individuality and personality created art from time.

History had been his to mold, and legend his to fashion out of whole cloth. Now he saw the trick of it, the joke of it, the uselessness of human endeavor in a universe that promised only death, eventually.

If he had known then what he knew now, he told himself, he'd have poisoned Genos in his sleep longsince, rid the city of the entire royal family and done whatever was necessary to protect it for eternity.

But eternity was denied the warlock now, and only history was his to command.

He could hear them coming down the stairs in the dark, his executioners. He could hear them whispering to one another. He could hear them argue among themselves.

The consort wanted to save the Queen—this was predictable. He smiled in the dark, with none to see.

His plan would work. When there was nothing left but history, there was honor and the survival of one's name. It was not a wise stance Seth took, or one a man who thought to go to heaven might choose, but he was bound for hell in any case.

And Seth wasn't at all sure that, if he cheated Tempus and his hungry god of their revenge, he wouldn't have won enough, in history's terms and afterlife's terms, to bargain himself into a place of power beyond the grave, with Tabet's soul to sweeten the deal.

So he got up slowly, carefully, so as not to rouse the entranced queen who slept beside him. Over her he stepped, hiking his robe high, and over to the oil lamps he went.

He took his tinder box and lit a lamp, then another. From them he lit three torches, which he slowly and methodically fixed in their sconces.

Then by their light he got out a baker's dozen of beeswax candles, and these he placed upon the stone floor at intervals around the sleeping queen.

When that was done, he stepped between the candles, a torch in one hand, an oil lamp in the other. The lamp he put by Tabet's head, in case his adversaries managed to wrest his torch from him, the lamp would do the trick.

From his robe he took black powder made from urine and other things found in barnyards, and this he sprinkled in lines between each candle, and in lines radiating from Tabet's pallet, and in lines com-

ing out from the place where he sat beside the
queen.

When he and Tabet were at the center of a glyph
of lines that radiated everywhere around them, he
sat back down to await the Riddler and the Froth
Daughter and the Consort.

Either they would be surmounted by his spells
and by their own hesitancy to slay the queen, and
leave Seth unharmed, or all of them would die there.
After all, was that not what life was about?

He carefully placed his clay city in his lap. It too
must die. If he were to give up everlasting life, then
it must too—he was a child of the city, a pawn it had
used to free itself from the mire at the end of time.

Everyone must believe he is put upon this earth
for some purpose. Otherwise, the joke of life's suffering with death at the end of it was just too foul.

For Seth, who faced an eternity of ectoplasmic
vipers and their masters, snake charmers from deep-
est hells, only revenge could heal his fury enough to
let him go to his just reward with a quiet heart—and
Tabet by his side.

Composing himself, Seth began to chant spells and
incantations meant to summon whatever help he could
from demonic realms.

CHAPTER 27: HOSTAGE IN THE FLAMES

All around them, Niko could smell the oil burning, and candle wax, and sorcery oozing up from the solid rock under his feet.

He knew the Riddler was beside him. He knew Jihan had mighty powers here, where her father's ocean rolled. But he'd been in tight quarters fighting wizards—and losing to wizards—more often than the pair beside him. And they weren't human in the way that he was.

Tempus, if he were crushed and mutilated, would heal. His bones would knit. Lopped-off limbs would regrow upon his heroic form; he'd live to fight another day.

In all the battling of all the years she'd been Tempus' bedmate, Niko had never seen Jihan bleed. He didn't know if she could.

Niko could bleed and Niko could die. But Niko had also been in the clutches of covetous witchy lovers, and he couldn't leave Tabet in such a state. He recalled the confusion, the deep and mind-killing passion, the fog of sensuality a mage or a witch could cast over a hapless soul.

The close passage of the stairwell had wound down and down and with every deeper twist into the bowels of the warlocks' citadel, Niko's chest had tightened. Here there was no room to swing a sword properly. Here there was no use for the crossbow he'd slung over his shoulder, just in case. Here there were shadows that could come to life and rocky outcroppings that could try to seize him.

Mist might come out of any crevice. The floor could open underneath him, demons could reach up out of the earth to take him, grabbing his ankles, pulling him down.

And then what help could Tempus be?

He loved his commander as he loved no other. Tempus had never disappointed him. Tempus had never failed to guard his back, to take his part, to rescue him or protect him, when need be, even when Niko didn't remember whom he loved, or his oath of honor, or anything.

Even when Nikodemos hadn't known who his friends were, the Riddler had still loved him, brought him to his senses countless times, and never once betrayed him.

Therefore, Niko pressed on. He was the rightside partner of the man called the Riddler, sworn to fight to the death, shoulder to shoulder, back to back. Never would he despoil that oath. Never would he hesitate to put himself between even the taint of evil and his commander. No sacrifice was too great between men who shared such a bond, for every sacrifice strengthened it. In a world where nothing, not even the gods could be trusted, a man could trust his partner.

They shared more than agendas; they shared a special world of understanding in which help needn't be asked for and honor was more solid than rock.

In this horrid, endless cavern, now that they'd gone past turning back, Niko had to remind himself of all of this. In spite of it, he was afraid.

Fear was creeping into his bones like the chill of the tundra. His hands were getting numb. His fingers were becoming clumsy. Sleep was stealing inside him, as if the cold were leeching the marrow from his bones.

His eyelids were getting heavy. When they closed, they seemed to want to stick together, as if ice crystals were forming on their lashes.

He knew that wasn't so. He kept shaking his head and repositioning his fingers on his sword and staggering forward.

Jihan and Tempus, just ahead, were talking but their words were funny-sounding, loud but distant, clear in tone but bereft of meaning.

How long had they been trekking here? Didn't the Riddler want to rest?

That brought a shaft of clarity into Niko's sleepy brain. Had he thought that thought? He knew his commander: Tempus never slept.

"Riddler! Riddler! Wait!" He was sure he yelled it loud, but the words sounded weak and fuzzy to his ears.

He could see Jihan's scale-armored back, a shadow with its own nimbus of light ahead of him, a darker darkness with glowing edges. And Tempus' aura was shot with red flares and danced around him, gold and blue.

Without his maat, Niko might have sat down then and there, might have thought he called to his companions that he was going to rest now, just a little.

But maat would not let Niko sit. It would not let him stop. It would not let him believe that he was cold, or that he was tired, or that he'd called a halt so he could rest.

It shook his soul. It sent bright spears of fear into

his brain. It fought the spell that Seth had cast over him so long and so hard that Niko stumbled as he staggered behind the Riddler and Jihan.

The sound of his sword striking the rocks pierced the argument between the other two.

Jihan was saying, "But we've been this way once already, I tell you, Riddler. Can't you accept that here I know a little more than you? My father's water courses beneath this place and I know what water I've walked over and what I've not—"

"Hush. Niko?" Tempus turned in his tracks.

"What's the matter, Niko?" Jihan took a step toward the fighter on his knees in the tunnel, who was shaking his head.

"Tired, cold—the warlock," Niko managed to whisper.

Then they were beside him, lifting him up.

"Why didn't you warn us? Call out? Before it got this far along?" Jihan wanted to know.

"I did," said Niko.

"He did," said Tempus simultaneously.

"What now?" Jihan wanted to know. "The tunnels go on forever, or we've been going in circles. Niko's spellstruck, and you won't let me guide you."

Nikodemos saw Jihan glare at Tempus and her eyes begin to glow like a wolf's in the dark.

"The smell," Niko said as loudly and distinctly as he could. "Can't you smell the tallow? Wax burning? Smoke?"

"Smoke?" Tempus paused. And sniffed. And sniffed again, holding up his hand to stave off any word or movement from Jihan.

"Smoke," he agreed, satisfied. "Jihan, use your 'superior' tracking ability to find us the place where the smoke is, since you know this land so much better than we."

"What about Niko?"

"We'll do what we can about the spell," Tempus was reaching into a pocket of his belt.

"What . . .?" Niko wanted to know.

"Can you walk?" Jihan was asking the fighter.

"Wait a moment, Jihan. Just wait." Tempus got a pouch from his belt and poured something into his palm. "Here, take this. It should make you stronger."

Niko opened his hand and Tempus poured some white powder into it.

"What is it?"

"A potion from the god to fight sorcery," said Tempus in an odd voice. "Swallow it."

The drug was salty on his tongue. Tempus was telling Jihan, "Be ready to move as soon as Niko can stand. And find this wizard fast, Jihan, before he tries some other spell on us, one that's harder to subvert."

The salty stuff was bitter. It made Niko's tongue curl. And somehow he could hear better, and see better now. Strength came back into his limbs. He flexed his hand on his sword and his fingers obeyed him.

He got to his feet and saw the two of them watching him. On Jihan's face was a suspicion obvious even in the dark tunnel; maat gave Niko a special sight.

"I'm all right. There's no spell on me that's going to make me hurt you, or forget who I am." He straightened his shoulders. "Lead on, commander. Trust me at your back."

It was a plea that made Jihan look away. Tempus regarded him in silence. Niko didn't know how much Tempus could see in this dark; whatever the god wanted him to see, no doubt. But maat and Niko's training made his commander's face a kaleidoscope of moving, colored planes that told Niko more about Tempus' heart than sunlight would have.

Tempus was deciding, here in the midst of everything, whether Niko could be trusted after sorcery had touched him. He was the weak link here. Or he was so, once again.

But Tempus nodded as if to himself, and said, "Lead on, Jihan. Find us the smoke that Niko smelled."

And his commander turned his back and followed the Froth Daughter as she led them deeper into the tunnels.

Nikodemos, checking his throwing stars in hopes that any adversary who came at him could be hurt by whetted iron, followed after, determined that, whatever happened, Tempus' faith in him would not prove to be misplaced.

CHAPTER 28: FIRES OF VENGEANCE

Jihan stepped aside and let Tempus enter the cavern first. The place was ablaze with light: three torches burned in sconces; there was an oil lamp by the head of the prostrate queen; Seth held another in his lap.

The sorcerer held something else there, too. A clay model, the length of Tempus' hand. And he held a torch, while around him burned thirteen candles. Radiating outward from the warlock and his hostage at the center were smudgy trails of black that Tempus recognized.

"Seth," said Tempus, "Give yourself over to the Storm God's justice. If the queen lives, free her into our care and it will go easier with you."

One had to say these things. It was a matter of protocol, of formality. Tempus no more expected the warlock to hand over the queen than he expected that the black lines on the floor were merely dirt.

"Jihan, don't let him light those trails of powder," Tempus whispered under his breath.

"What am I supposed to do about it if he tries?" she whispered back.

"You're the water-wielder. Think of something," advised the Riddler. Niko had just come up from behind him. The fighter paused at his side, and Tempus could feel a shiver go through his rightman, faced with the sight of Tabet ensorceled in a warlock's ring of power.

"Easy, Stepson," warned Tempus. The salt he'd given Niko had done the trick; the boy had more strength in him than he knew, to rouse from a spell's effect with the help of only a placebo. But here they faced a sorcerer in his lair, with a hostage beside him. Niko had too many memories of sorcery not to be shaken by the sight.

Just as Tempus was beginning to think that the warlock hadn't heard his offer, that Seth was entranced himself, the man in the circle began to speak.

The words the warlock spoke are not words to be repeated. Words of power belonging to the lost city's magic filled the room. And the walls of rock began to bulge and to shiver, to slither and to move.

"Snakes!" yelped Jihan unnecessarily, as the wall of vipers behind the sorcerer began to come apart.

As the snakes from the stone, some as wide around as Tempus' waist, reared their ophidian heads and came toward him, Tempus saw Seth reach toward the powder with the oil lamp he held.

Niko, beside him, burst into motion: a throwing star from his belt whizzed through the air, toward the warlock's gut. And Seth shivered at the impact.

His hand dropped the lamp, which shattered, spreading hot oil on the stone. Some caught the powder, which flared in a racing diagram of flame.

"Jihan, water!" Tempus called and jumped the flames, into the circle where the wounded warlock and the unmoving queen waited.

As he did, Tempus caught a glimpse of Jihan, her

arms raised to heaven. And of Niko, who was casting glances behind him as he hacked at a man-wide, ectoplasmic snake.

Then the flames flared higher and Tempus couldn't see beyond the circle. Smoke from the fires seemed to want to choke him, black and inky smoke like ropes that wound around his neck and his arms and tried to trip his feet.

Amid the smoke, the warlock sat, holding his belly and grinning like a madman.

"She's lost to you, avatar of a hideous god," the warlock called. "You'll never save her now. I've won!"

And with those words, the stone that flamed to Tempus' right and to his left cracked apart.

Through it, clawed hands and scaly arms and slimy heads poked up, reaching blindly for him. He severed the closest hand from the arm it searched on, using the sword the god had given him. And that sword glowed pink, sensing sorcery, and hacked around him with a mind of its own so that his arms and shoulders were jerked hither and thither, wherever the sword sensed demons.

These demons had no eyes. They had gaping mouths full of primordial teeth, though, and they were hungry. Around they felt, and out of the rock they levered themselves, uncaring that their sparse fur caught fire as they climbed onto solid rock.

So busy with the demons was Tempus and the sword of Enlil, that he'd forgotten all else. Niko's battlecry as the soldier charged through the flaming perimeter into the circle brought Tempus back to his purpose.

And then he saw the wounded warlock, no longer clutching the place where the poisoned throwing star had wounded him, but fighting off demons just as Tempus was.

But the warlock had no sword. And Niko's sword was busy defending Tabet, whom he caught up and slung, unresisting, over his shoulder as if the queen were a sack of rice.

She was unconscious, or dead, or entranced forever, and Tempus would have shouted to Niko to find out which and not burden himself, if anything could have been heard over the demons' howls. Or over the sorcerer's screams as the demons tugged upon his limbs, and the roaring of the fire that separated each combatant from the other, burning higher than any natural fire could.

Something grabbed his ankle, piercing his greave. Tempus looked down and smote the hand that held him, and when he looked up, he saw the warlock, being dragged down into a crevice by three demons.

But four more pounced upon Seth, even as the three were stuffing him into the crack in the earth, and these four each grabbed a limb.

Tempus actually lowered his sword as the demons fought over their prize, tearing Seth's arms from their sockets and his legs from his hips with a horrible cracking sound that echoed even over the blaze and the sound of wounded demons wailing.

The sorcerer's screams were the loudest of all. They were screams of renunciation, screams of incantation, screams of abomination, screams of rage, and screams of pain.

Tempus had never heard such sounds in all his life. He was glad his name was not mentioned, as he watched transfixed and, from above, Jihan's rain began to pour from solid rock.

The sorcerer was half into the rock now—at least, his trunk was. The legs and arms had disappeared with the demons who'd claimed them as hard-won prizes.

But the trunk still thought like a man, and hurt like a man, and talked like a man.

Niko, who had Tabet over his shoulder, and was separated from Tempus by a line of fire sputtering in Jihan's rain as it went out, called, "Commander, we're supposed to kill him!"

The two exchanged glances. Tempus saw the sick look in Niko's eye, the compassion there, and the plea.

"Give me the queen and do as your conscience dictates," Tempus called back.

Niko looked puzzled for a moment. "But you're the god's—"

Tempus' headshake stopped the question of propriety. It had been Niko's face on Enlil's shoulders, here in the temple above.

Nikodemos hefted the unconscious body of the queen across the thin and guttering line of fire to Tempus, and stepped in close, occluding all sight of the warlock's trunk and its screaming head.

Then Niko's swordarm rose and fell in a quick and final stroke and the screaming stopped.

The fighter jumped back as if the ground had opened under his feet. As he did, Tempus saw a hand, long-clawed and grasping, reach up from a newly opened furrow in the rock and grab Seth's decapitated head by the hair.

The warlock's eyes were rapidly glazing. Tempus thought he saw the mouth form a word, but he looked away. Heads, severed, could be made to act as though alive, by the proper manipulation of the neck stump.

Whether the warlock had been mouthing thanks or a curse was immaterial to Tempus. He had to get his people out of here, through the remains of the fire, past the snakes on the walls, and out of the citadel of magic under which they'd found the queen.

The warlocks above weren't going to be pleased that they'd succeeded, let alone killed their master in a battle that split the earth apart, or come out with a queen who they'd said had never come within their haunt at all.

Jihan's rain was making a smoky mess of the fire. Through it, Tempus could barely see Niko, outside the guttering ring of sorcery, come up close. Without a word, Tempus handed the queen to him, over the low-burning fire, and Niko lay Tabet on the ground.

He heard the Stepson's hoarse, "She lives. She knows me," as he searched the murk for Jihan, and the walls for ectoplasmic snakes.

The Froth Daughter's voice came from behind him, so close he jumped, and wheeled, and had his sword out to skewer her before he thought better of it. "Looking for someone, husband? I'm right here, my love. I'd never leave you. And don't worry about the snakes. They don't like my father's water, any more than witchy fire does. Just see you don't turn your ankle in those fissures as you go, or lose a foot in them as they close up."

He looked at his feet. Jihan was right. The openings in the rock floor were closing. Between two of them, a clay model of the city lay in a puddle of water, safe and sound; harmless now that its modeller had gone to hell.

He nearly jumped the black and steaming ring that marked the warlock's circle of power. Outside it, he knelt by Niko, trying not to think what Jihan's use of the term "husband" could purport.

Could she be pregnant? If so, could she know so soon? And surely, were she or not, she couldn't expect him to stay here with her. . . .

Niko was methodically rubbing the wrists of Queen Tabet, who was coughing as she struggled to sit up and Niko pushed her back: "The air's better, lower. Stay there until we're ready to leave. Then I'll carry you."

"I can walk, stranger," said the queen in a tone that told Tempus this was a matter for the two of them, and not him.

"You'll need my help," Nikodemos was telling her as Tempus started cleaning the gore from his sword and Jihan crowed about how completely her father's water was purifying this hideous cavern of sorcery, "so that no evil will ever be here again, or rain will come from out of these stones to wash it away."

When he had his sword clean and shining, using Jihan's water which rained the smoke and smudge out of the air, he stamped the model of the city flat, then gathered his companions.

Niko held the queen around her waist; his arm was supporting her. Tabet's face was pinched and drawn. She would not meet their eyes, but looked at her feet as she proclaimed that she could walk up and out of this place upon her own.

"Let her walk with me, Tempus, Niko," said Jihan, and brushed Niko's hand from the queen's waist. "This is a matter for women to discuss, a thing of propriety and deeper significance that men just can't understand.

So it was that Niko and Tempus led the way, and Jihan and Tabet followed. They couldn't hear the words the women spoke, but Tempus allowed to Nikodemos that, "It might be true that Jihan could help, if only she were a woman."

And Niko said to Tempus, in a voice meant to carry, "Whatever they decide, it's a decision that will last only until the next whim takes their fancies. If I were still the Consort of such a fickle female, I'd worry. But as it is, I'm ready to quit this place as soon as you are, Commander."

That started the two behind them whispering in earnest, and caused Tempus to look hard at Niko, wondering what it was that his rightman really did want: what he said, or the opposite.

And that thought made the Riddler remember Jihan calling him "husband," a memory that put him in so foul a mood that, when they came up out of the stairwell to the astonishment of the mageling, Tempus nearly lopped the boy's head off for sleeping on the job.

CHAPTER 29: THE TEST

The city was shimmering in sunlight that had broken through after a rain that washed its towers clean and left two rainbows arching over the palace, one inside the other.

Everyone agreed that this was the finest of omens for Nikodemos' Test.

Crevis the seer was on hand, and Jamad in his finest priestly robes, and Tabet's father, Genos, was wearing his crown as the royal family and its advisors made their way through the newly washed city streets toward the temple of the Storm God.

Only Macon was absent, and the strangers and the man who'd been Tabet's consort.

Her brother was under lock and key. A guard had been posted at his door. He hadn't eaten for the three days since Tabet's rescue. He wouldn't speak even to her. There was much discussion about what would happen to her brother, but their father had not announced his decision as yet.

Tabet had announced hers, though. She'd gone

straight to her father's throneroom after Niko and his sojourner friends had rescued her, and declared she wished to be wed to her consort there and then.

Niko had ducked his head in that way he had, and said nothing. It was Tempus, the inscrutable Riddler, who'd brought up the matter of Tabet having dissolved the betrothal.

"So it's not a matter of simply the queen's desire," the big man with the gravelly voice had said. "She's grateful, we all understand that. Marriage is another thing, one to be entered upon only after grave consideration. Nikodemos is and always will be a stranger here."

And as Tabet had stared, dumbstruck, unable to open her mouth to object, the mighty Jihan had crossed her arms and said, "Why don't we ask Niko what he wants, Riddler? It's his future here, not yours."

Niko had said, "The god brought me here to take a test. Perhaps I should take it—maybe it will tell me whether I should stay or leave."

Tabet had seen the fire in Niko's eyes as they swept over his companions and rested upon her.

Then a discussion had ensued, between her father and the Riddler and Enlil's priest, about the proper nature of the Test and how it could be taken without peril if it were given the way the god had meant, and not the way men had twisted its ritual to their purpose.

Without peril? Tabet's mouth had dried up and her tongue grown unwieldy. She hadn't known what to say or what to do. Her marriage hung in the balance. The god, not she, was going to decide if Niko was to be her husband.

First she'd been angry, then she'd been hurt. Just because, in a moment of rage, she'd pushed Nikodemos from her didn't mean she had to live by that decision.

She was sure they'd all worked together to concoct this scene just to embarrass her. Then, as the morning of the test drew near, she'd not been sure of anything at all.

Before they'd left for the temple, she'd found a moment to ask Nikodemos, "But do you still love me?"

And he'd said, "What's that got to do with anything? We'll see what the god has to say. If I stay, I'll stay as your true husband, with equal power and equal respect, and the god must sanction that. Otherwise, you'll decide in the morning that you've changed your mind. Or the morning after that . . ."

The god was deciding her fate. She was furious. She was frightened. She wasn't sure she wanted to marry Nikodemos after all. She wasn't sure he wanted her anymore at all. Perhaps he wanted only the power of the co-regency. Perhaps he wanted an easy out, a way to ride off with his friends without losing face.

What could the god say that would matter? What could the god decree that the human heart would heed? What could this foreign fighter whose eyes laughed at her bring to their marriage bed but trouble?

Tabet wished she'd kept her mouth shut. But she hadn't.

At the temple's door, Tempus and Jihan awaited, the Riddler in his leopardskin and the Froth Daughter gleaming in her scale armor that caught the sunlight.

They acted as if they owned the temple. They acted as if they owned the city. They acted as if they were the rulers here, and the royal family under their command.

"Come, Tabet, don't lag behind," said her father gently.

Inside the temple, all was dark at first and full of shadows. The damage from the fire showed here and there upon the walls and the floors and the roof was still smoke-stained.

Along the walls, sconces burned. By their light she saw the murals and what the fire had done to them.

The portraits of Enlil fighting the dragons were different: the faces had melted, elongated, dripped into new furrows and new expressions. Tabet glanced from the portrait of the god, to the Riddler, then back again.

Once the Storm God here had looked so much like Niko that it had seemed a message from heaven. Now the faces of the god all looked like Tempus: yarrow-honey hair, a high brow free from lines, fierce eyebrows and a jaw deeply shadowed.

She hugged her arms. Then someone touched her. Jihan said, "Don't worry, Tabet. This will come out aright."

What could Jihan know of such things? What could anyone know of the future in this uncertain world? The city was free to roam again, this was the only truth that mattered, Tabet told herself. It didn't matter whose face was on the Storm God's shoulders, here in the temple of Enlil.

If Niko thought she'd marry him after he'd embarrassed her this way—Test or no Test—he was dreaming. She would spurn him loudly and officially, as soon as the Test was done.

And this was not the Test as it had ever been performed in the city before. This was a Test from antiquity, involving a platter of herbs and the thighbone of an ox and a charcoal and a goblet of clear water on a silver platter, and invocations to the god.

There was a heart of a lamb on the altar, she realized as Jamad began the invocations: the heart of a lamb that the priest called "the heart of a lion, the heart of Enlil, the heart of the city."

"Do you take these herbs and this bone and this fire and this water, Nikodemos?" said the priest while Tempus stood behind the altar in his leopardskin looking like Enlil himself, come to life.

"I do," said Niko, and took the silver tray in both his hands.

"Then go before the god, kneel before the god, and offer your heart in exchange for the lion's heart."

Niko took the tray and walked with measured steps up to the ancient altar of Enlil. There he knelt, and bowed his ashen head.

Suddenly Tabet could *feel* the god in the temple, as she'd never felt the presence of a god before. Enlil was fire and sparks in the air; he was the warm breath of the sun upon the land; he was the devastation that had touched the city, sanctified it, and then withdrawn, leaving the populace chastened and wiser.

Enlil was not Tempus, she realized. He was a greater force, taller than the murals in the temple, wiser than the wind that scoured the mountains. And yet when she stared at Tempus, she saw the god as well: a great ethereal figure, bearing arms, as if Tempus cast a huge shadow and that shadow had its own face.

She looked up, into the space behind and above Tempus where the Storm God seemed to stand, and Enlil seemed to notice her.

For a moment, the eyes of the queen met the eyes of the Storm God and her heart ceased to beat. A thrill and then a chill went through her, and an apprehension of the power of heaven such as she'd never encountered filled her.

In the warlock's meditation chamber, she'd been a prisoner of the power of evil. The power of Enlil was greater, and as wild. She found herself sweating, breathing fast, and knew that she'd closed her eyes, trying to hide from the sight of heaven.

When she opened them, she saw Tempus staring at her, a meditative look upon his awful face.

And she heard Niko saying, as he cut into the heart of the lamb which he'd rolled in herbs and struck with a bone and dipped in water, "With this heart, my heart is Thine. With this knife, the hand wielding it is Thine. With this ceremony, the supplicant is Thine."

And Tempus nodded as if he were the very Storm God Himself.

When Niko put the heart of the lamb first against the charcoal and then into his mouth, the temple's torches flickered wildly. A vast shadow blocked out the altar.

Or perhaps Tabet only imagined it. She stifled the scream in her throat with her hand and looked again at Nikodemos and the altar before which he knelt.

Everything on the altar was gone: the lamb's heart, but for the single bite Niko had taken from it, was gone. The bowl of herbs was gone. The charcoal was gone. The bone of an ox was gone. The knife Niko had used to cut the lamb's heart was gone. The water was gone.

In their place was a glint of gold, a solitary item.

Niko said, "By the god's will, I take this token." He reached out and as he lifted up the glinting thing and looped it over his head, she realized it was an amulet on a chain.

Jamad was intoning words of ritual benediction. Even Tempus closed his eyes. Tabet had to close hers, and bow her head in this temple where at least one god truly lived.

And when Jamad fell silent, Jihan and Tempus began to laugh and to clap Niko on the shoulder and to make much of the amulet that must, Tabet told herself, have been put there by some slight of hand.

But now it hung around Niko's neck, over his heart. When she finally realized he would not come to her, she went to him.

She strode right up to the man who'd been her consort and interrupted her father, who was congratulating him on "having proved to us all that the heart Enlil wanted was one beating in a living breast."

She reached out and grabbed the amulet swinging from its chain around his neck.

Everyone fell silent. She'd meant to jerk it from his neck. She could not. It was warm in her hand, and she opened her fingers to look at it.

It was a model of the Storm God himself, his swordarm raised, his legs widespread as if he strode over mountains. On his head was the conical crown of kingship in heaven.

Her hand fell away from the amulet and Niko caught it. "Now, Queen Tabet, if your love is true, I'll wed you. In this temple, at this moment, with the blessing of Enlil and my commander. Or ride out, with no regrets. But if I stay, it will be to guide this city. Genos needs a rest."

"You're proclaiming yourself king?" She couldn't believe her ears.

"Only if you marry me to make it so."

Over his shoulder, Tempus was watching closely. Beside him was the Froth Daughter, her face expressionless.

King Genos, too, watched his daughter without a hint of what he'd want her to say.

They must have devised all this. Of course they had. To save face, as she'd suspected. To find a way out for everyone.

"And if I do, what of my brother and his purification?"

"Tabet," said her father. "We've arrived at a solution for Macon's sins: he'll be banished from the city. We'll thrust him from the gates, into the World, tonight. It has nothing to do with your marriage, and it's a better solution than endless punishment here."

"You can't decide his fate without consulting me!" Her poor brother. Her poor, demented, sin-ridden brother—out in the World, alone. Alone but alive, she amended.

And her father said, "Surely you'll concur—this fate is just. And so's yours: make your decision,

Tabet. This man's no longer your consort. Will you wed him, or not?"

Tabet looked at the stranger, who could be king. And at her father, who was trying not to influence her decision, but who seemed so tired and so old.

And at the amulet of Enlil around Niko's neck. Her eyes swept past the fighter, to the temple paintings. At least she wouldn't be marrying the god.

She said, "Only if Tempus and Jamad will jointly perform the ceremony, so it will be as binding to the god as the marriage Niko just made."

She was no fool. She knew what had happened here. Nikodemos had become god-bound, like the man he called his commander. How long could such a marriage last, with all of eternity to look forward to?

Her mind was full of objections. She could rule as Sole Queen, she knew she could. But the city needed a pragmatic hand right now; its people were shaken. The royal family had lost the trust of common folk.

Nikodemos could restore that trust. He'd taken the Test and passed it, in Enlil's eyes and the eyes of His priest.

She turned around, "Crevis, what omens are there for this marriage?"

"Travel, my Queen," said the seer who stood against a pylon. She thought he was smiling. "Travel will the city, and travel will its rulers. Throughout all time and the worlds of mankind. No evil do I see or I would surely tell you, Queen Tabet, Daughter of Tebat. . . ."

She ceased listening to the string of ceremonial titles. She looked at the man who'd so attracted her when he'd fallen from the sky in a rain of fish.

She walked right up to him, until their chests touched. She raised her hands and tilted his face so that she could look into his eyes.

And she said, "Tell me you love me, Niko, that

you do this for us and not for your commander or your god."

Niko's head came down and he brushed her lips with his. He said "I'll stay with you as long as you want, Tabet."

It wasn't the answer she'd asked for, but she knew, in front of all these witnesses, it would have to do.

She nodded and turned to her father: "With your blessings? You're not being coerced in any way?"

"With my joyous blessings; I'll advise your court the best I can."

"And you, Tempus," she said to the man who looked just like the god. "Have you any objections to voice?"

"No," said the Riddler in a strange tone, as if the single word were difficult. "The time's right."

Jihan was beaming at her. Tabet smiled back uncertainly. "Then let the wedding ceremony begin."

When it was over, she walked with her new husband upon the battlements and asked the obvious questions: "What of your friends? Won't it hurt to part from them? And your wandering ways? I want a king in residence, not the memory of a king who wanders where he will."

Niko said, "I married you. I took the vows. Nothing worth having in life comes without sacrifice, or without cost. You've got to trust me, Tabet. We've much to do, including cleaning out that nest of warlocks you've got here, so we don't wake up to find another Seth upon our hands or some other wizard under our bed."

She asked him, as the sun was setting over the city and the sea and plain beyond, "And my brother? Will you not commute his sentence? You can do it, now, with my concurrance."

"No," said Niko, and leaned over the wall, looking down on the lamps being lit and torches kindling in the streets.

"Just that? Just 'no'?"

"Tabet, let your brother go into the World and learn what he must. He'll find the city again, no matter how far it roams, whent he time is right. Anything else will go harder on him. The heart of Matilla must be appeased."

"You mean, your horrid god must have his revenge."

"Don't talk like that." He didn't turn to her, didn't take her by the shoulders and shake her, didn't display a single sign of anger. His voice was weary. "I've got to go now. I must see my friends before they take their leave."

"They're leaving?" She'd never been so glad to hear a thing, and wasn't sure just why. "Jihan too?"

"I'll be back by the time you've come down to dinner," he told her. "Wear something simple. I'm not feeling like celebrating."

"But our wedding feast . . ."

Niko was already headed down the stairs.

CHAPTER 30: SETTLEMENT

Niko caught Tempus in the stable, saddling up.

"Can't you stay, Commander? There's much to do here."

"I've got to take Jihan to the seashore," said the Riddler's scratchy voice, coming from a face turned away from him.

"I don't want you to go."

"You've made your choices, Niko. You've come to terms with the god. You've a city to husband—a special place to keep safe, wherever it roams." Then Tempus did turn, and leaned against the gray stallion, who arched his neck and nuzzled in Tempus' pockets, looking for treats.

"It's your city as much as mine. You saw what happened to the god's face in the temple."

"I saw you choose the god, unequivocally, at last. I'm not sure I'm pleased to see you follow in my footsteps, Stepson. But you have my blessing. That much was no lie."

Niko knew that Tempus meant that he'd followed

in his footsteps by taking on the mantle of the Storm God in the world, by becoming what he'd fought so long, an avatar of power.

He shrugged. "The time was right. The circumstances . . . it felt—"

"I know," Tempus said. "We'll meet again. Jihan's leaving you her horse for safekeeping. . . ."

"Leaving the mare? But why? Isn't she going with you to—"

"She's going to see her father. That's his sea at your back, remember."

"Riddler, I didn't know. You'll be alone. I never meant—"

"We're all alone, Niko. We have the god in common. If you need me, I'll know it. The city roams. So do I. We'll cross paths from time to time."

"You must think of this place as your home," Niko said desperately, trying to choke down the quaver in his voice. Leaving their last billet with Tempus hadn't been this hard, though he'd left his comrades and so much more behind. "Whenever you want, I'll go with you. Now, if you just say the word. I'll tell Tabet—"

"You have work to do here, Niko. Work for the god. Work for the people of the city. The wisdom here needs to be remembered, relearned, and shared. Remember, it was your face Enlil had, when we first came here. Do the work in front of you, Stepson, as you've always done."

"But we've been together so long, I don't know how to—"

"You'll live a long time here, Niko. You'll learn. The god has much to teach you." Suddenly Tempus turned away, swatting the gray's questing muzzle. Gathering the reins under his horse's bit, he started leading the big horse out of the stable.

Niko hurried to keep up. "I learned more from you, Commander, than I could ever learn from any god," he called softly as Tempus put the horse between them and mounted up.

"Niko, nothing's over. You have your own life now. Live it. Don't fear autonomy. Lead, rather than follow. You're ready. Risk is what life is all about."

And he reined the horse around, trotting toward the stableyard gate where Jihan waited.

Niko waved at the Froth Daughter, calling loudly, "Thank you for the mare, Jihan. I'll keep her ready for you." It was the best he could manage. He couldn't go over there to thank her properly. If he did, he was going to shame himself before the Riddler, begging like a boy whose father was going off to war, pleading with Tempus to stay.

Now that the trap had closed upon him, it was too late to wonder whether Tempus had had this end in mind from the first moment he'd set eyes on the face of the Storm God in the city's temple. Or before. Like god, like avatar—they were both tricksters.

He watched the Riddler hold out a hand to Jihan, and the Froth Daughter swing up behind him, her scale armor glowing in the dusk. He bit his lip, holding back further words.

His eyes blurred as the big gray switched its tail and trotted through the gate, beyond which lay the World. The horse let out a great neigh of farewell that Niko's sable and Jihan's mare answered as loudly as they could.

Niko heard his stallion kicking the stallboards and went inside to calm the horse. They had a home now, and responsibilities. He must find some way to make the horses understand that.

Around his neck, as he stroked his stallion, the little amulet of Enlil swung. The horse noticed it, and took it between his velvety lips and tugged upon it playfully as a stableboy came looking for Niko with a message from his wife that dinner was served.

CHAPTER 31: THE EDGE OF TIME

"So, Riddler," said Jihan, up to her knees in luminous surf. The moon was rising and it poured light over her magnificent form. In the moonlight, she was smiling. She rubbed her belly. "Thank you for your gift of life. My father will be pleased. The whole of heaven commends thee."

"Crap," he growled at her. "Are you sure, Jihan, that this is what you want?"

"Until my child is born, I must be among my kind."

Her kind weren't even vaguely human. "And after that? Will your father give you back human form again? And what of my son?"

"You're so sure it will be a male child?"

"Well . . ."

"Arrogant, Riddler. Unlike Niko, you learn nothing, just grow more stubborn with the passing ages. What of all the other get you've put upon human women, for this ritual or that? Is my child so special?"

He knew that tone. She was teasing him.

So he said back, settling himself in his saddle
better, "No, I was just curious, hoping I could get
you to promise that some half-fish, half-man wouldn't
come seeking me in a few years claiming all the
rights paternity makes children think they have."

But he was curious about the child. And, though
he didn't want to admit it, he would miss Jihan. He'd
grown fond of her.

"I'll make you a bargain, Riddler," said Jihan. By
some trick of moonlight, the froth of the waves seemed
to be crawling up her legs and spreading, making her
a gorgeous gown of brilliant lace that undulated with
the tide. "Once a year, I'll bring my child to this
place, for one day only—this day's counterpart. Any-
time you wish to see him, or me, just come here."

"To the sea at the edge of time? Why don't you
make it hard, Jihan?" He wasn't sure he could find
this place again without the god's help, and bargain-
ing with Enlil for personal favors wasn't ever worth
the price.

"Then come with me, Riddler, to my father's domain. Dismount your horse and free him. Shed your
mortal skin and let me take you beneath the waves."

"No thanks. I'll see you next year, or the next.
Thank your father for his aid and comfort, if you
think of it. . . ."

She was already fading, swathed in that lacy water
that crawled up her and obscured the human form
he knew. Her face seemed to float on a crest of a
wave. From those lips he'd loved so well, her voice
came once more: "Don't forget, Riddler, how I love
thee. Or all we shared together. Or that this sea and
all other seas can lead you back to me. Just enter the
water and call . . ."

A wave crested over her head, and she was gone.

He sat there a long time, on the beach at the edge
of time, his elbow resting on the pommel of his
saddle, his chin on his fist.

The night came down and covered him like a blanket. The moon above lit the city's spires and the waves' whitecaps.

And the gray horse under him pawed the surf breaking on the sand, anxious to be away.

He looked up the beach, and he looked down it. Ride north, so legends said, and he'd ride into the future.

Ride south, and he'd ride into the past. He almost did that, rode south where everything would be familiar, where time was fixed and nothing would seem strange.

Then he looked inland, toward the city on its hilltop, and saw a solitary rider come out the Lion Gate.

He clapped his knees against his horse's belly and the gray leaped forward, inland, up the beach and toward the rider headed for unknown realms.

West was the afterlife, the rest of the legend said— where Jihan had gone, where human time stood still. East was unknown, unknowable, places and peoples he'd never seen, adventures he'd never had.

And the rider he chased, and caught, and hailed so casually, was going to need a helping hand, headed east without so much as a glimmer of hope, with no fixed destination.

"Well, Macon," said the Riddler to the banished prince when the gray caught the other horse, "what say we ride together for a while?"

The prince wiped the back of his hand across his face, sniffled, and said, "I don't know where I'm going, Riddler."

"You're going somewhere, boy. So am I. Let that be enough."

Then the gray reached out with his muzzle and snuffled the prince's gelding, who lowered his head in submission and trotted meekly along beside, down the long hill from the city toward the distant copse.

When Tempus looked back at the hilltop, toward the city, there was no city there. It had gone on its way, forever.

And so had he.